Refusing to Bow

Published in the
United Kingdom by Bruce & Holly

ISBN 978-1-54838-389-3

The subject matter of this book was first
published (with photographs) in 2016 under the title
'Memory of Beheram' and that edition is still
available as a Kindle ebook

ISBN 978-1-84396-432-2

Catalogue records for this book are
available from the British Library and the
American Library of Congress

Pre-press production
eBook Versions
27 Old Gloucester Street
London WC1N 3AX
www.ebookversions.com

Refusing to Bow

Farida J. Manekshah

BRUCE & HOLLY

.

Contents

Foreword

Farida J. Manekshah was born 4th February 1945 in Andheri, India as the tenth of twelve siblings. Her father, Jehangir, was the son of a railway engineer who became rich through his skill as a portrait photographer.

In the years following Indian independence, Jehangir used his wealth to buy a palace in Karachi in the new state of Pakistan. The movement of populations which followed British withdrawal meant that there were many cheap properties coming on the market north of the border as wealthy Hindus sold up so that they and their families could move south to the safety of India. But the move to Karachi did not bring the family happiness.

Within two years of buying the palace, Jehangir was locked in a court battle with the Pakistan Government, which had requisitioned the whole of the ground floor to house foreign diplomats. Whilst this was going on, tragedy struck with the homicide of Farida's elder brother Beheram at Hawkesbay Beach.

It was then that Jehangir decided to move the whole family to England, where he had been stationed during the War. But before that move could take place he first had to win his fight with the Pakistan Government. It was won at the eleventh hour as the last of the colonial judges was about to transfer back to England.

Farida found settling into England difficult because she was denied the liberties which her English classmates took for granted. In desperation she entered into an abusive marriage in the mistaken belief that this would give her the freedoms she craved.

The marriage was problematic from the start because of her husband's excessive drinking. With the alcohol came the violence – and eventually to her husband's impotence.

Instead of enjoying freedom, Farida became trapped in a marriage which was as sexually unfulfilling as it was violent. It was then the same family from which Farida had earlier sought escape, which now rallied round to give her the courage she needed to break free. Then followed a seven year divorce battle before Farida was finally able to move on with her life.

It was during the years of her divorce that Farida sought solace in two extra-marital relationships. The first of these ended in further violence from her husband when she was found out. The other ended because Farida could not provide the commitment which her lover demanded.

Having shed her lovers, Farida has now devoted the rest of her life to her love of animals. It was in the months following the destruction of her dog Bootsie as an act of revenge, that she became an RSPCA volunteer to numb the pain of her grief. In fact it is fair to say that Farida cannot pass an animal in the street without the urge to take responsibility for its welfare.

As well as providing a record of events which actually took place, the book also provides rare insight the culture and beliefs of an ancient religion. The book also paints a picture of Pakistan as a young country, full of optimism and at peace with itself – so different from the war zone it is today. From Karachi, it transports the reader to the sights and sounds of 1950's London..

Although Farida retains a vivid memory of events and conversations which occurred many years ago, this book also includes reconstructions of other events and conversations which are within her knowledge but where she could not have actually been present or would have been too young to understand. Those particular events and conversations have been re-told from accounts given to Farida by her mother and elder siblings as she was growing up. I have no reason to doubt their authenticity.

Vivian C Ward
Friend and co-writer

In loving memory
of Beheram, my brother.

1 The News

It could have been an English stately home.

I sat at the side of the long oak table with my brothers Dara, Keki, Adil and my younger sister Dilnawaz. Papa and Mama faced each other at the ends.

Papa was in charge as he was in charge of everything. As always his thin waxed handlebar moustache was immaculate. He had the 'Omar Sharif' looks which the officers' wives loved.

Two man-servants stood behind, ready to do our bidding.

'Could we have some more alloo ghobi?' said Papa.

Within seconds a fresh supply of curried potato and cauliflower appeared.

From the teak radiogram, and in the background, came the shrill voice of Lata Mangeshka.

'Where's Rusi?' asked Mama.

'He's still at Elphinstone Street,' said Dara. 'He's waiting for the telex to come through.'

'Well, let me know as soon as it does,' said Papa. 'I need to know the prices for the new jewellery range. Then we can start importing.'

'I mentioned it to Dinshaw Avari when I went to Beach Luxury,' said Dara. 'He is very interested. The last lot sold out.

The guests loved it.'

'That's good. What about the other hotels?'

'Tomorrow I'm going with Keki to Metropole. We'll see Cyrus Minwalla. Perhaps he'll want to put some on display.

I looked at Dilnawaz and pretended to yawn, flapping a hand across my gaping mouth. Dilnawaz giggled.

I kicked her under the table.

'Ow!'

Mama glared at me, 'Have some manners Farida.'

'Maluck and Mahue are downstairs with their tennis racquets. We've got a game to finish. I don't want to be sitting here all afternoon listening to Papa and my brothers talking business. It's so boring.'

'Then go to the prayer room and thank God for this palace. But pray also for the Government tenants to be gone. Then we can all move back downstairs.'

'But I don't want Maluck and Mahue to be gone.'

'We can let them stay if you want to. And if we move downstairs you will be nearer your madajee.'

They were my four geese who lived on the front lawn of our palace. Even at eight years old I was obsessive about animals. When I grew up I wanted to be a Vet but was frightened of birds flying towards me. I'd flinch away. Papa said he'd take me to a psychiatrist to get rid of the fear.

Lata Mangeshka's voice fell silent. All that was left was the 'click, click, click' of the stylus on the spinning seventy-eight. Adil reached across and lifted it off the turntable.

'What time is Beheram coming?' said Dilnawaz. 'He's going to take us to The Regal to watch Snow White.'

'He might not be coming,' said Mama.

'But he promised.'

'Yes he promised,' I added.

'I'm sorry I should have told you. He's gone hunting with Douglas'.

'I might have guessed.' said Papa. 'Whenever Beheram goes hunting you have a face like an owl.'

'That's only because I worry about him.'

'When did he go?'

'Yesterday morning. He was very excited. They're staying over in one of the hunting lodges. I packed him some extra sandwiches. '

'Chutney sandwiches?' said Keki.

'Yes.'

The brothers laughed.

'You know what he does with your chutney sandwiches?' said Keki. 'He gives them to the sadhu he passes on his way to school. The one with the chalky face who sits on the ground. The old man tells his fortune.'

'So what fortune did he tell him?' asked Dara.

'Today, I don't know. But I know what the sadhu told him last week on his birthday. He told him not to go near water or he'd die.'

'Wow!'

'You remember Mama? He told you when he came home from school. You got angry and slapped his head.'

'Yes. I remember. I keep asking why he has to keep talking rubbish with that evil man.'

'It's a bit rainy for hunting,' said Papa. 'I hope he doesn't take any chances. After what happened to Farooq. Injured animals can be very dangerous'

'I know' said Mama. 'Rusi still hasn't got over it. Farooq was very dear to him.

'Anyway,' said Papa.

'As soon as we can start importing the new jewellery range,

I want to make another trip to Kabul.'

My ears pricked up. So did Dilnawaz's. Our friends downstairs could wait.

'Can I come too?' I shouted.

'And me?' screamed Dilnawaz.

Papa smiled.

'Why do you want to go to Afghanistan, Farida? Is it to bump along dusty roads in the jeep? Or do you want be frightened by lots of fierce tribesmen? Or is it because you've heard about Yasmin's ice cold kulfi.'

'The kulfi. The kulfi.'

'I don't know,' said Papa. 'I'll need to think about it. I don't want either of you to miss school. What do you think Mama?'

She looked at our pleading faces. Then at Papa. Then back at us. After a pause.

'Yes. I think we can allow Farida and Dilnawaz to go with you. But it'll have to be during the school holidays. And if they go, I'll have to come along too. We don't want either of them getting lost in Kabul Market. Or worse, getting kidnapped.'

'I won't be kidnapped.'

'Yes you will Farida,' said Dara.

'Someone will offer you sweets. And you're so stupid you'll take them.

'Then they'll put a hand over your mouth and wrap you up in their big clothes. And they'll take you up into the mountains and make you beg.'

'I'll run away.'

'Not if they blind or cripple you.'

'Watch what you're saying,' said Mama.

'Do you still want to go to Afghanistan, Farida?' said Papa.

'Yes.'

Keki walked over to the radiogram and rummaged through

Gustad's record collection. He pulled out a 12 inch and put it on the turntable. After the 78 had begun to spin, Keki lifted the arm and positioned the stylus. A second later came the deep slow soulful voice of Mohammed Rafiq singing 'Na Thamte Hain Aansoo'. Keki turned up the volume. But we did not get to hear any more of Rafi's lovely voice.

There was a 'bang bang bang' on the door.

Four young policemen entered the room without waiting to be asked. We called them 'red caps' because of the regulation red caps which they wore with their khaki uniforms and brown belts. Each sported a bushy black moustache of the type later made famous by a brutal Iraqi dictator. One of them was carrying a wooden box with a rope wound round the middle.

They had entered the first floor via the outside stairway of The Gift, which was an extension to our palace, and come in through the back door. Though to call The Gift an extension was an understatement as The Gift was a mansion in its own right.

It was where Dara lived with his wife Freyni, their children Helen, John and baby Christine. Keki switched off the radiogram. Adil got out of his seat to confront the red caps.

'Why are you disturbing our lunch? Has one of the dogs escaped?'

Dara exchanged glances with one of the red caps. It was his friend Omer. But this afternoon he was not smiling. It was another red cap who spoke first. Turning towards Papa he spoke quickly

'Mr Manekshah. I have terrible news for you. We believe your son has been drowned in an accident at Hawkesbay Beach.'

Mama shrieked, 'Son? Which son?'

'Beheram.'

Adil punched the policeman hard in the chest.

'You are making a joke,' he screamed. 'Beheram was a champion swimmer. How could he drown?'

'Carry on like that son and we'll have to arrest you,' said another of the red caps

Omer waived at the red cap to keep quiet.

Papa gently held Adil's shoulder and guided him back to his seat.

'Tell me what happened.'

The red cap turned to his notes.

'Yesterday afternoon we received a call from some people at Hawkesbay Beach who said they had seen in the distance a man and a woman carrying somebody on a stretcher. They were seen taking the stretcher to the water's edge and pushing it into the sea.

'We sent police officers to Hawkesbay Beach. We could not find any stretcher. But we arrested a young couple who were acting very suspiciously. The girl was very distressed and wanted to say something. But the boy would not let her talk.'

Omer chipped in,

'The boy is Douglas Jaimeson and the girl is Conchita Fernandez. We have them at the police station. Jaimeson has made a report saying that your son Beheram has gone missing.'

'How?'

'Jaimeson said they'd been swimming with him at Hawkesbay. He became worried after they had lost sight of Beheram and asked the skipper of a launch to go out to sea with them to help look for him. After searching for 20 minutes they saw Beheram's head come to the surface. But before they could reach him, Beheram had sunk beneath the waves.'

At that point Mama became hysterical. She got out of her chair and screamed and cried saying,

'It's not true. It's not true. It is a mistake. It is someone else.

Please God that it's not true.'

Keki held Mama in his arms as she was about to collapse and sat her down on the sofa. 'We all pray that it's not true,' he told her

'I'm sorry,' said Omer, as he handed Papa the box.

With trembling hands, Papa removed the rope surrounding the box and opened it up. Inside was a pair of shoes. Stuck to them and inside the shoes were grains of sand. There were also trousers and a jacket, still damp with seawater. Papa shook his head.

'I don't understand. He said he was going hunting.'

'It was raining. So the animals wouldn't come out. That's why they went swimming instead.'

Papa beckoned towards Omer and whispered, 'Did you believe Douglas?'

'No,' said Omer. 'It doesn't explain the business with the stretcher. And the girl still isn't saying anything. It's as if she's covering up.'

Omer whispered to his colleagues. They left, leaving Omer alone with us.

My parents and brothers could only stare at each other. There was nothing to say. Then Papa broke down in tears. Mama wailed into a handkerchief. One by one my brothers joined the chorus of grief, huddling together as they wept.

Whilst this was happening I had crawled under the table. Dilnawaz followed, holding my hand. The truth was that neither of us could understand what was happening. We had never before experienced death. We hugged each other crying, 'Beheram has gone. Beheram has gone. Now we'll never go to the matinee.'

It was as if we were watching the tragedy through cinemascope. That we were not really part of it.

Perhaps Adil had been right when he punched the policeman. Perhaps it was all a joke. Even Mama was saying, though her tears, that it was all a mistake. That it had happened to someone else. Not our dear Beheram.

Hawkesbay was not a place for inexperienced swimmers. A line of signs stretching out to sea and mounted by red and white flags shouted out warnings. 'Beware of Sharks'. 'Strong Currents. Do Not Swim'. They were written in English and in the native Urdu.

But Beheram was a champion swimmer. He'd already won four medals at his school. And he'd swam many times at Hawkesbay, sometimes taking us with him. He liked nothing better than diving off the sea-wall.

The 'wall' itself was a natural feature: a line of boulders of various heights arranged in a semi-circle ten yards out to sea. The highest was about shoulder height. Just right for sitting. Or perhaps for using as a diving platform. But only if you were strong and experienced enough to clear the stones beneath.

I was sure that any minute Beheram and Douglas would burst into the room. Then the wailing would stop. Everyone would start laughing. From beneath the table we stared at the door, willing it to open. But the door stayed shut.

Every twenty minutes Omer phoned back to the police station to see if there was any more news. But there was nothing.

When there were no more tears left to shed, it was left to my brothers Dara, Adil and Keki to fight back their emotions and do what had to be done.

'I think we need to find a dastur,' said Dara. 'We must start the prayers immediately.'

A sobbing Adil left Faridabad House and returned forty five minutes later with a white robed dastur and a mobed The priests brought with them sandlewood which they placed in a small silver container and lit from the flame which they carried with them. Each then put on a white face-mask to stop any of their spit spraying onto the sacred flames. The masks hung like beards from beneath their noses. Then they adjusted their black velvet caps.

Meanwhile Keki found Mama's blue linen scarf and wrapped it gently round her head.Papa and my brothers covered their heads with handkerchiefs. Omer did likewise. Then at a signal from the dastur, the men stood to attention with hands held out: palms upwards towards Heaven. Only Mama and us children stayed sitting. The priests understood. Only when everything was perfectly as it should be could the prayers begin.

The dastur and mobed then raised the palms of their own hands and, in unison, chanted the ancient prayers which they had memorised over a lifetime. The only other sounds were Mama's cries and the groans of Papa and my brothers. The prayers lasted about 45 minutes and ended abruptly. The priests left in silence. They would return tomorrow afternoon to repeat the prayers. By that time word had already got around about our tragedy.

The next day, as our priests prayed, we heard other sounds intermingling with their chants. It was rich accordion like music, throbbing to the beat of tablas and coming from the homes of our rich Muslim neighbours as qawwali minstrels sang out our grief.

Having spent most of my childhood in Pakistan, I had grown up with qawwali. It is highly charged religious music which is sung only at weddings and any other emotional time. The music starts softly and becomes louder and evermore hearty as, with one hand on their ears and the other raised towards heaven, qawaali minstrels sing out their prayers. As they immerse themselves in the music, Allah's spirit goes into them and sends them into a trance. The words, the sounds and their movements then come straight from their hearts. The music has the power and the prayer to heal the sadness of a broken family, which had lost a young life barely 24 hours earlier.

As we listened, the qawwali became more intense and we let its soothing energy flow into every pore of our bodies.

My brothers phoned the police every couple of hours, day and night. But there was no more news. Other then the fact that Douglas and Conchita had now been released.

Taking it in turns to make those disheartening calls. Taking it in turns to close their eyes in the search for blessed sleep. But there was no rest. After four days there was still no more news of Beheram. But there was a knock at the door. Papa rushed to open it

Standing outside was a short man, about 5' 7', with fair wavy hair. He also had a pink nose, pink cheeks and a white complexion. In fact his skin appeared to have no pigment at all. It was Cyrus Minwalla, the owner of Karachi's prestigious Metropole Hotel. Like the late Humphrey Bogart, Minwalla was always seen wearing a light coloured suit. Papa beckoned him inside. He embraced Papa.

'Jehangir. You are a brother to me. And Beheram is like my son. We are all praying for you and your family. Have you heard anything?'

Papa gently shook his head.

'Then I will send out a search party. We will keep searching – and searching – until Beheram is found. And he will be found. But in the meantime you need to rest.'

Papa looked at him,

'How can we rest?

'At least try to rest.'

Minwalla shook Papa's hand and turned to go. Papa touched his arm.

'Please stay. Take tea with me.'

Minwalla was as good as his word. At 8am the next day six speed-launches set off from Hawkesbay beach crewed by his own men. Some were his own boats. He borrowed other boats from Dinshaw Avari, owner of Karachi's Beach Luxury Hotel. Papa, He and my brothers went with the crews.

I and Dilnawaz stayed at home with Mama. She kept us off school during those dreadful days. I tried to cheer her up saying,

'Stop crying Mama. He's going to come back. He's going to come back.'

I really believed it.

There was no news at the end of the first day when Papa and my brothers came home. There was no news at the end of the second day. But it was during the evening of the third day that the awful truth was brought home to me.

In the intervening days there had been more qawwali music. More prayers from our own dasturs. But it was during the afternoon of the third day that I noticed a stream of people visiting Faridabad House to speak to my parents. Some were sobbing. Others walked stony faced.That stream of people included a coach load of students from Beheram's school who had come to pay their respects. Wasn't that Douglas standing amongst them? It all seemed very strange..

Whilst this was happening, I, Dilnawaz and other children were playing on the front lawn. We were running. Chasing each other. Giggling. Mama came over and shook me,

'Why are you playing Farida? Have some respect. I have to tell you that they found Beheram's body today.'

I froze as I took in the news.

So it was true. Beheram was not going to come walking back through the gates of Faridabad House. In that moment my childhood was snatched away. Beheram had been my favourite brother.

It had been Beheram who had taken Dilnawaz and me to the Regal and Paradise cinemas every afternoon, Friday, Saturday and Sunday. It was he who bought us ice creams from the Parsee usherettes. Though, as children in Pakistan, the only films were allowed to see were cartoons. Films like Popeye or Snow White.

It was he who was our companion when we went on vacation to Papa's other house in the hills of Shimla.

As Mama walked off to speak to Dilnawaz, I abandoned my friends and, ignoring the guests who were still milling around, ran straight up to my room. Once inside I broke down and screamed my heart out. Like my parents and brothers I couldn't sleep and I couldn't eat. I didn't want to speak to anybody. I just wanted to shut myself away.

Over the course of the next few days that I overheard Papa and my brothers talking about the discovery of Beheram's body. It had been around 9.30 on the morning of third day that the crew of one of the boats had made a discovery.

Three miles away at nearby Sandspit they saw what looked like a shirt washed against the rocks. The boats had closed in.

They said there was a body washed against the rocks. But it was half-eaten by sharks and already decomposed.

Minwalla's men had not wanted to touch it even after he had offered them double money to pick it up.

'Then none of you or your families will ever work for me again,' was his final word.

'Sir. We will do it,' replied one of the men.

Minwalla, Papa and several men had then clambered onto

the rocks and pulled the body down. Papa examined it. The features were unrecognisable. A leg was missing below the knee. The nose was eaten. The head had been chewed to the bone. The torso had become dark. It stunk. It was also wearing a black leather belt.

Papa had examined the belt-buckle. It was moulded in the shape of the letters 'BJM'. He wiped it with the sleeve of his tunic and pointed it out Minwalla.

'It is Beheram. This is the belt I had specially made for his nineteenth birthday in the initials of his name Beheram Jehangir Manekshah'.

Minwalla's men took the body back to Metropole Hotel and placed it in a cold store. It had to be done discreetly as I'm sure the hotel guests would not have been pleased if they had known. The only witnesses were the two dwarves dressed in the national green and white colours of Pakistan who were on permanent guard at the front of the hotel. But they were not going to say anything. The body remained at Metropole whilst funeral arrangements were hastily put in place.

2 The Tower of Silence

Two days after its discovery, Beheram's remains were taken to our Tower of Silence. It is the last resting place for Karachi's dead Zoroastrians. It is a large white circular structure situated within open scrub land at Karachi's Parsee Colony. Perched around the rim and on permanent guard are vultures. Sometimes the silence is interrupted by a fluttering as a vulture flies into the structure to search for a morsel.

It is after final prayers that a body is laid out within the open circular structure, to be picked clean by those vultures until the remaining bones are dropped into a pit. The dasturs knew each vulture by name. They had traditional Persian names like 'Sohrab' or 'Dinshaw'. Each of the vultures knew their name and their job: having done it a thousand times before.

When Beheram's body was brought into the Tower it would be wrapped in a white sudreh, or religious cloth. Pressed on what remained of his head would be a black velvet cap. Once inside, the dasturs would take charge. They'd lay Beheram's remains out in the centre of the open tower. More prayers would be chanted. Then in accordance with Parsee tradition, one of the dasturs would bring out a small dog on a lead. Its purpose was to sniff the body and make sure that it was dead.

According to superstition the dog would howl out its grief if the dead person had lived a good life. If not it would turn its head away.

According to Rusi the dog took one look at the stinking, half-eaten remains of my brother and pulled-away. The crowd gasped as the dastur hurried the dog away.

Dilnawaz and I didn't go inside. We stayed outside the Tower with Papa as the funeral rites took place. He couldn't bring himself to go inside. Jaap was with us holding Papa's arm. He was one of the unwanted guests on the ground floor of our Faridabad House after it had been requisitioned by the Pakistan Government to house foreign diplomats.

Mama couldn't bring herself to attend the funeral at all. She stayed at home. A dastur stayed with her giving her comfort. Only my brothers had the strength to go inside the Tower.

As soon as the prayers had finished and everyone had left the Tower, a dastur would lift off the sudreh and the black religious cap from Beheram's remains. Then looking upwards and around the waiting vultures, he clapped his hands twice.

From our viewpoint outside the Tower we saw the vultures fly upwards from the wall of the Tower, hover for an instant, and then descend towards the body. But on this occasion their descent was not complete. Like the dog, they turned away at the sight of the decayed remains and flew out of the Tower and away.

When Mama heard what had happened she put her head in her hands and turned towards the dastur,

'Why aren't they eating? If they don't eat, Beheram's soul won't be released.'

He rested his arm on Mama's shoulder.

'Don't worry. They are not hungry. We will starve them for a few days and then try again.'

Four days later we returned to the Tower and waited anxiously outside, in the spot we had waited before. The birds also waited along the perimeter of the Tower.

At the dastur's signal the birds took off, hovered and descended towards Beheram's remains. Only this time the descent was complete.

We waited as the birds gorged. Then, one by one, we saw them fly up carrying the rotting flesh, before returning minutes later to continue their feast, Until all that remained of my nineteen year old brother was a handful of bones. Again Mama had stayed at home.

When we returned back to Faridabad House we noticed Mama was quiet. She refused to speak to Papa.

'Why are you not speaking to me?' he said. 'Am I not also grieving for my son?' Mama broke her silence only to say.

'You killed Beheram. Not just Beheram. You killed two people when you broke the Murti.'

The stone Murti, of which Mama spoke, had been near the entrance to our property in an alcove. It had been in the shape of Lakshmi, the goddess of wealth, who was always seen carrying a pitcher of water. At night it was floodlit. And there was the continual sprinkling of water from the two fountains on either side. Like Da Vinci's Mona Lisa, its eyes seemed to follow you wherever you went. Mama put flowers round it for good luck. Papa hated it.

Three weeks previously, as Dilnawaz and I were getting ready to go to school, we had seen Papa with two middle-aged workmen. The men hammered away at the stone statue trying to dislodge it, whilst Papa supervised. Mama was alarmed.

'What are you doing Jehangir?'

'I'm getting rid of it. We don't want it here.'

'It's been here since the property was built more than 50

years ago. It's never done us any harm. It looks after us.'

'Mehera. We're not Hindus. We are Parsees. And we're living in a Muslim country. Which is why it's not good to have these things on our property. So go away and let us finish the job.'

Work resumed. This time with sledgehammers. After 20 minutes the men put their hammers down. They panted and mopped their brows.

'Sahib. We're hitting it but it's not moving.'

'Then hit it harder.'

The men hit it harder, taking deep swings. After five minutes the work stopped again.

'What is it this time?'

'I don't feel well,' said one of the men. 'I've got pains in my chest. I need to rest.' Papa was unsympathetic.

'I'm not paying you to rest. I want this thing moved. And if you don't get it out I'll be putting in a complaint to the company.'

The man picked up the sledgehammer again. He swung it once. Then he collapsed onto the ground.

'Damn!' said Papa.

Mama called an ambulance and the man was taken away to Jinnah Hospital. The other man went with him. We heard later that he had never reached the hospital. He had died in the ambulance

At first Mama didn't want to tell me and Dilnawaz. She didn't want us telling our classmates what had happened. But I had seen Papa whispering to Mama about the workman. And I saw the tear in her eye. So I kept asking her about it.

'God has called him,' was her reply. 'He had a weak heart.'

Meanwhile Papa phoned the company.

'Can you get someone else to finish the job?'

Next morning the company sent two men. They were

younger and leaner than the men they replaced. Alternately swinging their sledgehammers they maintained a rhythmic barrage against the base of the Murti until it became dislodged.

They were still banging away when Dilnawaz and I left for school. By the time we returned home the Murti had gone. The alcove had been bricked up. It was as if it had never existed

It was late afternoon in the day following our return from the Tower of Silence that we had surprise visitors. Four qawwali musicians arrived with a harmonium, sitar and tabla drum. They set up on our front lawn and began to play.

They were joined by our neighbour Alim Chan, who had organised the event, and his family. Later other neighbours came along to give their commiserations. The music and the singing continued throughout the night.

Over the following days, Mama made Beheram's bedroom into a shrine. Photographs of a happy Beheram stood upright on his dressing table. A small oil lamp burned in front of them. An agarbatti burned on each side of the dressing table sending spirals of incense into the haze above.

There, for many hours each day, she would go to pray. Sometimes me and Dilnawaz would hold her hands and pray with her. At other times it would be Papa and Keki praying with her. When there was no-one to pray with her, Mama would sit Chrissie on her lap.

As Mama prayed, the baby would fidget, trying to grab the burning agarbattis. But holding the baby gave Mama comfort.

Mama's hair turned white overnight. She abandoned her expensive clothes and jewellery and all her make up. She became a simple woman. She just couldn't get over Beheram's death. Mama also began drinking.

As Parsees, alcohol is not forbidden to us and all of us enjoyed an occasional glass of weak white wine. But someone had told Mama that a drink of brandy would help her cope with her grief.

So we would find her sitting alone in the sitting room with a glass of brandy and a half-empty brandy bottle. Papa or Keki would quietly remove it. Through a slurred voice, Mama would then rebuke Papa, saying,

'Why did you have to break the Murti? Look what you've done to us.'

She'd then take another sip of the brandy before carrying on,

'Poor. Poor. Beheram. How he must have suffered, being smashed against the rocks at Sandspit.'

'No he didn't suffer,' replied Papa. 'He was already dead. He would have died very quickly.'

Mama was not open to reason. She just could not cope with her grief. And it was always the same conversation. It went on for months. Like a gramophone record which had got stuck.

After one such episode, Papa made an announcement.

'Mama is not getting any better. We need to move away from here.'

'I agree,' said Dara. 'We need to sell up and go back to India. It's a shame. We were so happy here.'

'I wasn't thinking about India. I was thinking about England.'

'England?'

'Yes. I was there during the War. And Shirin works at India House. So we've got connections'

I interrupted.

'I don't want to go to cold horrible England. What about my friends?'

'You'll make new friends. You're always making friends,' said Dara.

'I don't want new friends. I want Kurshid.'

'You can still keep in touch with Kurshid. You can write letters to each other.'

It was another three years before we actually made that move to England. Before Papa could sell Faridabad House he first needed to win his case with the Pakistan Government and clear out our unwanted guests,

Meanwhile Mama had become obsessed about meeting the sadhu who had foretold Beheram's death. She wanted to know why the sadhu had told Beheram he was going to die. She sent out servants to look for him. But the problem was that at that time there were so many sadhus in Karachi, sitting on the ground. Eventually one of them said to our servant Abdul,

'Give me some money and I'll point him out to you.'

Abdul pressed a few rupees into the sadhu's hand and was introduced to the sadhu who had been Beheram's friend. The sadhu cried when Abdul told him how Beheram had died. He then reported back to Mama.

Days later both Mama and Abdul went back to meet the sadhu. Both Mama and the sadhu cried together.

'Why did you tell my son that he was going to die?' she asked the sadhu.

'It was written in the palm of his hand. I hoped that by telling him he might be able to avoid it. But it was not to be. I loved Beheram as my own son. The sandwiches he gave me every day were too much for me to eat. So I shared them out with my friends.'

Because Shirin was working at India House, she missed Beheram's funeral. My geologist brother Soli was also absent. He worked in America. But it was a subsequent telephone discussion between Shirin and Soli, which aroused Shirin's suspicions around the circumstances of Beheram's death.

Up to then we had only the official explanation as told by Douglas. That, whilst swimming in a heavy current, Beheram had disappeared and that although Douglas and the launch-skipper did what they could to save him, they could only watch as his head slipped beneath the waves. None of us believed that Beheram's death could be explained away so simply.

'In the telephone conversation Soli had explained that at the date of Beheram's death he had been on board the Polish liner 'Batorie'. Whilst half-asleep, he had seen Beheram facing him through the window of his cabin. But the Beheram he saw through the mists of his semi-consciousness was smiling. He spoke to Soli, saying only,

'What have you brought me?'

Then he waived to Soli as he faded from view.

Soli added that, whilst still aboard ship, he had received Papa's telegram giving the bad news about Beheram's death. He then remembered his vision and was taken aback to discover that it had happened two nights after Beheram's disappearance on 29th June 1953. That discovery turned to astonishment when Soli asked ship's captain where the ship had been that night.

'We were off the coast of Sandspit'.

3 The Séance

The five sat around the wooden trestle table on the roof-terrace of our palace.

In front of them was an Ouija board. In the middle of the board, surrounded by the letters of the alphabet, was an upturned glass tumbler on which each of the participants placed a finger. Spirits were then summoned.

These were purely social occasions. They would ask the spirits for horse racing tips. When a tip came through, someone would jot it down.

At the next meeting of the Karachi Race Club, the five would go along to the race course as a syndicate. Bets would be placed. When a horse won a race, they would celebrate at the Gymkhana Club.

As tipsters the spirits had no more inside knowledge than the tips you might find in the racing pages of an English newspaper. Sometimes the horse would win. More often it did not.

Whilst my brothers and their friends were busy calling spirits, Dilnawaz and I would play carrom inside the dome. Carrom is a table-game similar to snooker but using wooden counters instead of balls. By flicking a larger disc, the aim is to move the counters into one of the four pockets at each corner of the square table.

Sometimes Freyni and Helen would join us. Between shots we could watch our brothers and their friends calling spirits and hear the murmur of their voices.

There were no tips at all on one Saturday night as the five sat huddled round the table resting their index fingers on the upturned glass. They watched it expectantly. It did not move.

It was Freyni who first noticed Shirin. She tapped my arm.

'Farida. Look! There's your sister.'

I looked out of the window and saw Shirin walk towards the Ouija table. None saw her approach.

'Hello! Can I join you?'

They jumped, knocking the table over.

'Hello Shirin,' said Dara, picking up the table and putting everything back in position. 'I thought you were in London.'

'I arrived back this morning. I was sorry to miss Beheram's funeral. But I came as soon as I could. I'd like to join you if I may.'

'Yes of course. Pull up a chair.'

Shirin walked across to where two year old John was asleep in his pushchair. She picked up a chair standing nearby and brought to the table. She sat down.

'How are you Shirin?'

She sighed.

'Devastated.'

'Shall we put this away?'

'No. I want you to carry on.'

'Are you sure?'

'Yes. I want you to call Beheram.'

The conversation stopped. Keki whispered.

'Shirin. Why do you want to disturb Beheram?'

'I want him to tell us how he died. How he really died.'

There was further silence as they thought about the suggestion. Then Chaudhrey spoke.

'Would it be better if Joseph and I left?'

'No. Please stay with us,' replied Dara.

Dara re-set the table. Six index fingers now rested on top of the upturned tumbler. Keki looked at his watch. It said quarter past midnight.

'Beheram. Are you there?' whispered Dara into the stillness. Nothing.

They waited. Waited.

Keki looked at his watch. 'It's five past one.'

'Beheram. Are you there?' Still nothing. Still they waited. The only sound was the faint clicking of counters from our carrom table.

Keki looked at his watch again. 'It's twenty eight minutes past two.'

Chaudhrey yawned and covered his mouth.

'Shall we give it up for tonight?' said Dara.

'Give it just a little longer. Another half hour,' said Shirin.

They waited. More clicks from the carrom table. Dara exhaled.

'Beheram! Are you going to come – or not?'

He was trying to make a joke of it.

Shirin glared at him.

There was sudden pressure within the glass. The five exchanged glances and pressed down harder with their index fingers. The glass resisted and began to move toward the letters.

'Is that you Beheram?' asked Shirin.

The glass zigzagged across the table pointing out the letters '-N-O '

'Damn!' said Keki.

'Then please leave us,' said Shirin.

The glass zigzagged again.

'-Y-O-U..H-A-V-E…..C-A-L-L-E-D …M-E…A-N-D   I …W-I-L-L …S-T-A-Y …U-N-T-I-L…I…..G-E-T…W-H-A-T…..I W-A-N-T.'

'Who are you?' said Dara.

M-U-S-T-A-P-H-A A-L-I

'What do you want?..'

P-R-I-S-O-N. E-X-E-C-U-T-E-D

'I'm sorry.'

Y-O-U M-U-S-T H-E-L-P M-E P-R-O-V-E M-Y I-N-N-O-C-E-N-C-E

'No. We can't do that. We are a Parsee family trying to contact our brother. We are sorry that we have disturbed you. Now please leave us as we want to speak to our brother.'

The glass zigzagged faster, pulling the six index fingers along with it.

'N-O! Y-O-U W-I-L-L T-A-L-K T-O M-E. O-R I H-A-U-N-T Y-O-U F-O-R-E-V-E-R'

Dara laughed.

'What do you want us to do?'

G-O T-O M-Y B-R-O-T-H-E-R A-S-I-F. T-E-L-L H-I-M T-H-A-T I-T W-A-S KA-R-I-M W-H-O K-I-L-L-E-D H-I-S W-I-F-E M-U-M-T-A-Z N-O-T M-E I A-M I-N-N-O-C-E-N-T T-E-L-L H-I-M

'Why would Asif believe us? And anyway. What would be the point?'

W-H-A-T D-O Y-O-U M-E-A-N ?

'Think about it. You're already dead. So what does it matter whether you are guilty or innocent? They're hardly going to bring you back to life.'

Dara's teasing did not go any further. The pressure within

the glass increased. The fingers pressed down harder. The glass raced wildly between letters. Suddenly the glass broke free. It flew into the air. A moment later there was a shriek from John when the flying glass smashed into his face.

Keki rushed over and cradled the screaming child in his arms. He saw the angry red mark on John's cheek and the broken tumbler lying on the floor, a yard away from the pushchair.

A chill wind blew up, knocking over the furniture and the pushchair, and scattering everything on the floor. Keki rushed downstairs into the building with the sobbing toddler. The rest of us followed, wasting no time to collect our belongings. From within the building we heard the whirlwind overhead and the ratting of items being blown about. It seemed to be blowing stronger.

'Wait here. I'll find a dastur,' said Shirin.

She left and after 25 minutes returned with a yawning dastur. The wind on the roof raged unabated, whilst the rest of Karachi was calm. The dastur looked at them in horror.

'What have you done?'

After taking a minute to compose himself, the dastur said a short prayer for his own safety and made his way towards the roof terrace. The rest followed a safe distance behind. He stepped onto the roof terrace and into the midst of the whirlwind, his white robe pulled tightly around him. Then raising the palms of his hands he began to chant amongst the chaos.

The wind continued to blow about him as he chanted and increased in intensity. Then after fifteen minutes solid chanting, the wind dropped and there was calm.

The dastur came back downstairs and wiped his brow.

'The bad spirit is gone. What you did was very dangerous. Don't do anything like it again. Promise me. '

Dara thanked the dastur and pressed money into his hand.

The following Saturday at quarter past midnight the Ouija table was set up on the roof terrace as it had been the week before. Now there were only four people round it: Dara, Keki and Shirin. And my other brother, Rusi. Another white-robed dastur sat downstairs sipping mint tea from a glass. Before the table was set up he had said prayers for their safety. Keki had already mentioned to me and Dilnawaz that they intended to call Beheram's spirit.

'Whatever happens, don't come out of the Dome,' he warned.

Three fingers touched the top of an upturned tumbler. Keki sat back with a pencil and a shorthand note-book. Shirin spoke into the night.

'Beheram are you there?'

Nothing. The four looked at each other and waited. Shirin looked at her watch. It was now five to one. She spoke again softly.

'Beheram, if you are there, please contact us. We love you Beheram. We don't want to disturb you. But we need to know how you died.'

It was Rusi who first sensed gentle pressure within the glass, He glanced at Shirin.

'It's happening.'

Shirin spoke to the glass.

'Please identify yourself to us.'

The glass slowly marked out the letters: 'B-E-H-E-R-A-M'

Her eyes widened.

Keki pencilled a note of each letter as it was spelt out.

Shirin spoke again.

'Thank you Beheram. Please tell us how you died.'

The glass moved slowly and deliberately.

'M-U-R-D-E-R-E-D'

'How?' said Shirin.

'D-O-U-G-L-A-S H-I-T M-E W-I-T-H A R-I-F-L-E B-U-T-T-

'U-N-C-O-N-C-I-O-U-S

'P-U-S-H-E-D M-E O-U-T T-O S-E-A

'D-R-O-W-N-E-D'

Over the next two hours, Beheram explained how he had come to be at Hawkesbay Beach with Douglas and Conchita. He explained that the three had intended to go to the hunting grounds at Sindh. But that heavy rain that afternoon had made hunting impossible. So they had decided, at the last minute, to go swimming at Hawkesbay Beach.

He had been sitting on the 'wall' with Conchita and teasing her by throwing sand down her back. Douglas had gone back to the jeep to move it. When Douglas returned and saw what Beheram was doing he became angry.

'I asked you to look after my girlfriend. Not steal her from me,' he had shouted.'

It was when Conchita giggled that Douglas flew into a jealous rage and hit Beheram across the temple with the butt of the hunting rifle. His last conscious memory was the smack of that rifle butt.

Then, looking down from the ether, he saw the panic in the faces of Douglas and Conchita as they argued about what to do. His body lay flat on the stones, facing upwards. He saw the bloody red mark on his temple where the rifle butt had smashed into it.

Conchita wanted to take him to a hospital. Douglas lied that he was already dead, even though he had seen the rise and fall of his breast. He saw Douglas pull his unconscious body to its feet, so that it was standing between the two, with his head lolling on Douglas's shoulder. They then tried walking with him.

But it attracted attention. Several passers-by wondered what was wrong with him and offered help. After ten minutes they sat him down, propped upright so he appeared to be staring out to sea. Then Douglas ran back to the jeep and returned with a stretcher. They both rolled him onto it. Then with Douglas at the front and Conchita behind, they carried the stretcher to a more remote part of the beach.

'It's OK he's just had a little bit too much to drink, so we're taking him to the medical centre,' was what Douglas told anybody who enquired.

Beheram saw in the distance a young Pakistani couple with children. They too stared at the two figures carrying a stretcher with something on it. And watched as they pushed the stretcher and its load into the sea.

He was still breathing as he saw his body lifted off the stretcher and pulled away by the current. He regained consciousness as the water covered his face and gasped as the waters entered his lungs. It took several agonising minutes for him to choke to death. Then his body floated lifeless. There was no skipper. No rescue launch.

Over the next three days he had watched his own body being tossed towards the rocks of Sandspit. At one point a huge shark nudged towards it and, after a moment's hesitation, chewed flesh from its thigh. The release of blood drew other sharks to feast, until bloodless and lifeless, the half eaten Beheram was pushed against the rock where it was eventually found by Minwalla's men.

Beheram confirmed that, from the seas off Sandspit, he had seen his half-asleep brother Soli through the porthole of the passenger liner and waived his goodbye.

As the glass moved, Keki continued to make his notes. But after two hours, the hands were tired and the four had learned what they needed to know.

'Thank you Beheram for what you have told us,' said Shirin. 'You may go back to your rest. And remember that we will always love you.'

The glass moved again.

'T-E-L-L M-A-M-A I L-O-V-E H-E-R.'

'I will.'

'D-O-N'-T A-S-K M-E T-O G-O B-A-C-K. I W-A-N-T T-O S-TA-Y W-I-T-H Y-O-U'

'Beheram. You must go back.'

'N-O'

Shirin whispered to Keki, 'Call the dastur.'

Keki went downstairs and awoke the dastur, who had fallen asleep in the chair where he sat. Keki explained the situation and returned to the table with the dastur. More prayers were chanted and Beheram's spirit went back to rest. There were no more séances after that. Keki gave Shirin his pencilled notes.

4 The Confession

Every old year's night the Gymkhana Club threw a dinner dance.

December 31st 1953 was no different. Shirin had booked a table for herself, Dara, Keki and Rusi. Mama and Papa were still too broken up to see in the new year. But I and Dilnawaz came along. Other guests included American military officers as well as Karachi's richest families.

Dinner had finished by eleven. The cabaret began with the resident band playing, 'I Get a Kick Out of You.' Three tinselled dancers high-kicked in front of the audience. Amongst them was Conchita.

Although none of us were really in the mood for celebrating, Shirin and my brothers sported grins and moved along with the music. If Conchita recognised any of us, she did not show it. The new year was seen in with Auld Lang Syne.

Shirin and my brothers joined in the hugging and shaking of hands. Then the cabaret continued until its scheduled break at 12.30am. It would then resume at 12:45am and continue till 2am. At five and twenty past twelve, Shirin quietly left the table.

Five minutes later the dancers left the stage to freshen up. Shirin followed Conchita and tapped her on the arm.

'Can I speak to you for a minute?'

Conchita turned towards Shirin but did not recognise her.

'Yes'

'I just want to say how much we are enjoying the show. Is there somewhere we can speak privately? It's important. It'll only take a minute.'

'I have to be back on stage in ten minutes. Come with me to the dressing room.'

I saw Shirin follow Conchita into the dressing room and close the door. It was Shirin who told us word-for-word what happened next.

Once inside the dressing room it was Shirin who opened the conversation.,

'Conchita.'

'How do you know my name?'

'I'm Shirin. Beheram's sister.'

Conchita's mouth dropped open.

'I need to know how he died. You are the only one who can tell me.'

'It was a tragedy,' said Conchita. 'I live with it every day.'

'So do I. Now tell me what happened.'

Conchita took a deep breath.

'I was with Beheram and my boyfriend Douglas. We'd wanted to go hunting. But it was raining.'

'Yes.'

'So we went to Hawkesbay Beach instead. We went swimming in the sea. But we couldn't find Beheram.'

'That's very strange. He was a champion swimmer.'

'So we asked the skipper of a launch to help us find him. We saw Beheram's head come up several times. Then we lost him.'

She paused and sobbed into her handkerchief.

'It was so sad... I'm so sorry for you and your family'

Shirin's face remained frozen. She looked at Conchita.

'Liar!'

'It's the truth.'

'Remember you're in Pakistan. Also remember who you're dealing with. We could have you kidnapped. Taken to the quicksands of Sindh. No-one will ever notice your disappearance. Now tell me how my brother died.'

Conchita trembled.

'I've told you what happened. As I've told the Police a hundred times. You must believe me.'

Shirin paused.

'Oh yes. I believe you.'

Shirin reached into her handbag and pulled out a revolver. She pushed it against Conchita's head and cocked the trigger.

'Please Shirin. Don't do it. Please. Give me another chance. I'll tell you how Beheram died. Oh God!'

Shirin slowly released the trigger and pulled the gun away. With her other hand she pulled from her handbag a black biro and a writing pad.

'Here! Take this.'

Conchita took it.

'Write down everything that happened. Tell the truth and you may leave here alive. Try to deceive me and I will shoot you down.'

With her shaking hand, Conchita wrote – and wrote – for three foolscap pages. When she had finished she showed it to Shirin.

'Now sign it!'

Conchita signed it. Shirin knew the statement was true as it matched exactly with what Beheram's spirit had told her. Conchita gasped as Shirin picked up the gun and again pointed it at Conchita's head.

'Now wait here.'

Still pointing the gun, Shirin opened the door to the dressing room.

Keki, Dara and Rusi were by this time standing outside the door. With them was Adil's police friend Omer. Another young police officer accompanied him. The five entered the room. Turning to Omer, Shirin said:

'Here is Conchita's confession.'

He took it from Shirin, read it, folded it and put it in his pocket. He then handcuffed Conchita, saying: 'I'm arresting you for the murder of Beheram Manekshah.'

We saw the two police officers lead Conchita away. The next day the police arrested Douglas, who also confessed, and the guilty pair were arraigned for murder before Karachi's High Court.

The second half of the cabaret started forty five minutes late – with only two show girls instead of three. In the audience there was a table with the remains of a meal and six empty chairs.

5 The Bargain

Chopra hadn't told Papa about the Government's requisition order on Tinnani's Palace. Why should he?

Let the sale go through. Let the Parsee enjoy his bargain. He, Chopra, just wanted to sell up and get his family out of Pakistan as quickly as possible. He and his family had lived a good life in Karachi – as had his parents before him. But the British withdrawal from India had changed all that. Living there had become too dangerous for wealthy Hindus. There had already been threats against his life and the lives of his family. Some of his friends had already been killed.

Every day there were reports of trains being attacked. Of passengers being burned alive in their carriages. Sometimes it was Muslims attacking trains full of Sikh or Hindu pilgrims. Sometimes it was the other way round. It didn't matter who incinerated whom. The whole world had gone mad. He placed an advertisement in Dawn Newspaper.

'FOR SALE. Tinanni's Palace, Gooru Mandir, Karachi. Offers invited.'

Jetwani, saw the advertisement. He was a Sindhi who still had connections in Pakistan. He was also a friend of Papa and knew that Papa was looking for something grand in which to invest the money he had made from the Rembrandt and Vandyke Photographic Studio and his glass factory at Andheri.

Since leaving the British Army at the end of the War, Papa had gained a reputation as a portrait photographer amongst his ex-army colleagues. That's how he might have stayed if he hadn't married Mama.

She had been the younger and more beautiful of two sisters who were born in Isfahan in Iran but later adopted by my Jal Uncle and Mehera Aunty and taken to India. It was they who asked a caaj woman, or marriage broker, to find a suitable husband for Mama's elder sister, Sherazad.

Papa had already let it be known that he was looking for a wife and was seen as a likely prospect for that marriage.

The caaj invited Papa to dinner at her house at Grant Road, Bombay, where the couple could be introduced.

'I want you to meet a young woman who would make a good wife' she said. But it was not the older sister who caught Papa's eye.

'Who's the other woman? The one serving the food?'

'She's the younger sister. But it's the other girl I've brought to you to see.'

'I'm not interested in her. I want the sister. Can't you speak to her parents?'

By the end of the evening the deal was done. A marriage was arranged between the shy young woman and the older man. Many of Papa's ex army friends attended the wedding as well as his Parsee friends and family.

Mama had a pale face and brown eyes. Unlike Papa she was traditional in the way she dressed and preferred wearing an Iranian jubbah and blue headscarf than western clothes. It always annoyed Papa.

But it was using money borrowed from Jal Uncle and Mehera Aunty, that Papa was able to buy a rundown photographic studio above a big department store at Hornby Road in Bombay's prestigious commercial centre. The existing owner was glad to get rid of it. He sold it to Papa for next to nothing

Papa took over the dead horse, dressed it up, and brought it back to life. He called it 'Rembrandt and Vandyk'. Above the studio was a little office which Papa partitioned off and sublet: using the income to buy photographic equipment. But Mehera Aunty would never have lent him the money if she had known how he would cheat on Mama. Jal had never really liked Papa from the start.

Like many men of his wealth and culture, Papa wanted it both ways. He wanted a dainty Persian wife to stay at home and be a mother to his family. And he wanted fashionable English women to fuck. It was just too bad that those English women happened to be married to other people.

6 Daisy

Amongst Papa's clients were the English wives of older army officers, whose husbands were away. Many of them had married because they had wanted to see the East. But they became unhappy and their marriages were doomed. In fact it seemed that most of Papa's regular customers were young British women who came to Rembrandt and Vandyke to have their portraits taken. And I'm sorry to say that Papa's relationship with these bored housewives sometimes went beyond that of a top photographer and his clients

Papa's favourite was Daisy, the twenty eight year old wife of Alex, a middle aged army colonel. He had a frumpy moon-face and had once been Papa's commanding officer.

Daisy looked like Gone With the Wind actress Vivien Leigh. She didn't have any children: at least not until Papa got his hands on her. Back in England she'd been a waitress until she married Alex.

On transferring to India the couple first lived at Mamlashwar, which is famous for its Hindu Temple. It was also a fun place and its Gymkhana Club was the headquarters for parties. It was a clubhouse with entertainment to which English ladies went with their husbands. Mama, Papa and Dara also went there with servants for the occasional weekend. It was a couple of hours drive away from our Studio.

But the couple had since moved to Panchgani, where the army barracks were situated. Like other officer-wives living in Panchgani, Daisy had nothing to do except go to Coloba to spend her husband's money shopping for designer frilly clothes.

She was bored. She'd married Alex for a good time but the relationship had soured. Alex seemed to care more about the little terrier dog which never left his side. In fact Alex and the dog seemed to spend most of their time asleep together. So now she was going to fuck him up.

Daisy had found Rembrandt and Vandyke Studio when she went there to get some photos to take back to the UK. Now she became a regular visitor. Instead of going back to barracks after a day's shopping, Daisy went instead to Rembrandt and Vandyke Studio. Papa encouraged her visits. But Mama found it odd. One day whilst developing photos, Mama said to Papa,

'Why does Daisy keep on coming?'

'Because she's bored living in Panchgani'

Papa added, 'Why don't you make her feel at home?'

Mama did not enquire further. As the visits continued Mama became friendly towards Daisy.

Daisy told her husband that she went to the Studio to see Mehera my mother. She didn't tell him that she and my father were lovers. But it was whilst Mama was seven months pregnant with Dilnawaz that she saw Papa in his true colours.

He didn't see Mama come into the studio with an appointment book. But she saw Daisy sitting on an arm-chair, legs crossed and wearing a white silk flapper dress which was hitched up around her thigh. Papa was crouched in front of her, his left hand on that thigh and his fingers beneath her pink silk garter.

'Jehangir! What are you doing?'

Both turned to look at Mama. Papa feigned annoyance at the interruption. 'I'm adjusting my client's pose so that she can be photographed.'

'With your hand on her thigh? Here – I came to give you this.'

She handed Papa the book.

'Mr and Mrs Schroff are coming in at ten tomorrow with their children.'

Mama walked out, holding back her tears until she was outside the studio. Her worst fears were confirmed. She had already noticed that Papa always carried lots of little cards around with him with telephone numbers. She also found it strange that whenever Papa bought her jewellery, he would always buy a second set for Daisy.

'I got both for the same price,' he would lie. 'So I gave one to Daisy.'

Two weeks earlier Mama had been going through the drawers of Papa's oak bureau. At the bottom was a small drawer in which she found a pile of letters from Papa's satisfied customers. The more flirtatious were from army wives. But there was one particular letter that caught her eye. It was from Daisy. It spoke about a weekend which Papa had spent with her in Shimla. Mama remembered that five weeks previously Papa had gone to Shimla to close one of his many 'business deals'.

Mama never told Papa that she had found the letters. Instead she suffered in silence. Two months later she gave birth. Still the affair continued.

Whenever Papa wanted privacy with a favoured client, he would lock the Studio door and put up a 'Closed' sign. His assistant Bheekhoo helped Papa to keep up the pretence. After one fuck, Daisy surprised Papa by saying,

'Jehangir. Why don't you leave Mehera and come away with me?'

Papa said nothing. They dressed in silence. Then Papa turned and put his arms around Daisy. He whispered,

'I can't leave Mehera. You know I can't.'

A month later a less welcome visitor arrived at Papa's studio. It was Alex. With him was the dog. The door was locked. The 'Closed' sign was displayed. Alex banged on the door until Bheekhoo opened it. Alex smiled at Bheekhoo.

'Call Jehangir. I'll surprise him.'

After a ten minute wait, Papa appeared. The conversation was short and matter of fact. Alex looked Papa in the eye and said,

'If you want Daisy, she's all yours. I can't keep her because we've drifted apart since we've lived in Panchgani.'

Papa's response was equally brief,

'You must be joking. I couldn't leave my wife and children for Daisy. She puts up with me and looks after the children. She's the lady of the house. I'd be lost without her.'

Daisy's visits to Rembrandt and Vandyke stopped. The next we heard, was that she had divorced Alex and was marrying another Parsee called Feroz. Daisy sent all of us an invitation to her wedding. None of us went.

As well as taking photographs, Papa had another skill. He was a hypnotist. It was a gift he'd discovered whilst working as an army officer in Agra. He'd already earned a reputation as someone who could cure someone's phobias or redirect a young lady's passion towards her husband or to a future husband which her parents had chosen for her. It was the latter for which Papa's skill was most in demand and which was most lucrative.

Many of Papa's hypnotism customers were anxious parents whose sons or daughters had fallen in love with the wrong person instead of their intended spouse. Or the customer might be a husband whose wife had fallen in love with someone else. And Papa always had the perfect bedside manner.

'Just relax' he'd say to the frightened wife or daughter.

Smiling and touching their forearm, he'd guide them to a beige armchair within the Studio. The ritual was always the same.

Hanging from Papa's right hand was silver disc, of about one and a half inch across. In the middle of the disc was an emerald cut glass. It sparkled in the half-light and swung gently. Within two minutes the woman was entranced. Gazing into her eyes, Papa spoke softly,

After fifteen minutes Papa slipped the silver disc back into the pocket of his black shewani. He snapped the patient awake. Then continued his gentle patter.

'How are you feeling?'

'Fine! I think… I must have fallen asleep.'

'Only for a moment.'

After the treatment the grateful father or husband would push money into Papa's hand before leaving the studio with the love-smitten wife or daughter. Mama hated it.

'What you are doing is evil,' she told Papa.

In spite of the temptations of the officers' wives, Papa's photography became a successful business in which others in my family became involved. Keki, Dara and Shirin also became expert photographers. It was the income from that and the hypnotism business which enabled Papa to buy a small glass factory at Andheri. Papa knew nothing about glass blowing but saw it as an investment. But in spite of the wealth which Papa was now accumulating as a photographer and businessman, he still had a mean streak.

Within the grounds of our estate at Andheri there was a

well. It provided more than enough water for our own use. And for as long as I could remember, a stream of beggars also came to the well every day to draw water. The beggars sang as they heaved up buckets on a rope. For the rest of us it was a cheerful sight. But it didn't please Papa.

'I'm going to stop those beggars coming on to our property,' he said. Mama disagreed.

'God has given that water for everyone. They may only be beggars, bringing us nothing but their blessings. But send them away and they will curse you.'

Papa told our servants to chase away any beggars seen coming to the well. This happened whenever Papa was at home. But as soon as Papa was away, Mama would get Bheekhoo to invite the beggars back to fill their jugs.

This game of hide and seek continued until one day Papa came back unexpectedly and heard the beggars singing as they drew water. Papa said nothing. A week later we awoke to see workmen installing a high wire compound around the well and with a locked gate. Only Papa and my elder brothers had keys to that gate.

The singing stopped. The beggars drifted away. When my brother Dara next tried to use the well, it was dry.

Within two days the fencing was removed. A week later the well had filled up. The singing resumed.

7 Taking the Bait

In the years following the 1947 partition of India and Pakistan, Papa had noticed a large number of properties coming on the market north of the border in Pakistan. Some of them were grand mansions which were being sold off cheap by their wealthy Hindu owners. Papa let it be known amongst his friends and customers what he wanted. One day Jetwani came into the Studio holding a copy of Dawn Newspaper. He pointed to a small box advertisement.

'Look at this. If I was not a Hindu I would get it myself. But I can finance you if you want to buy a palace. You could make it into a bed and breakfast.'

Papa took the bait and the same day sent a telegram to the advertiser expressing his interest. Within days a letter arrived for Papa containing a small black and white photograph of an impressive building. There was also a handwritten letter.

'Dear Mr Manekshah,

Thank you for asking about Tinanni's Palace. Enclosed please find a photograph of this magnificent building. It's been in our Chopra family for more than half a century and has given us much happiness. But now we have decided to move to India and I am looking for a quick sale. Come and see it. Then we'll talk. Yours sincerely, Chopra.'

Within days the deal was done.

Papa advertised for someone to look after his photographic studio and the glass factory whilst he was away. Then Mama and all my brothers and Shirin flew with Papa to Karachi to see our new home. It was also the fulfilment of a destiny.

In his younger days Papa had worked as an administrative officer at RAF Cambridge. One day Papa was travelling by train to Cambridge when he found himself sharing a carriage with a smartly dressed Indian barrister about twenty years older than himself. The man explained that he had been involved in the struggle for Indian independence but that he was currently working in England.

Papa said that that he needed legal help to win back ownership of an antique painting which had been stolen from him.

'I'll help you,' said the barrister.

And he did. The painting was recovered. As a result the two men became lifelong friends. The barrister's name was Mohammed Ali Jinnah.

'Congratulations on your achievement,' Papa wrote in a letter to Jinnah on his appointment as Pakistan's first Governor General.'

'Thank you Jehangir,' replied Jinnah. 'I hope that you and your family will come to live in my new country. And if you do, please send me a telegram to let me know. You are welcome to see me at anytime.'

Papa showed the letter to Mama.

'Look Mehera. If ever we move to Pakistan we'll be people of influence.'

Sadly Jinnah never survived to see Papa take up his invitation. He died a year after independence.

Papa and my brothers shuffled backwards and forwards between Andhery and Karachi shifting our belongings. I was seven years old when I eventually made that journey with Dilnawaz and brother Hira.

8 Karachi

Karachi in the 1950s was a most beautiful place. Pakistan was a young country which was at peace with itself. It was very modern and its people were full of optimism for the future. It was like Tenerife, with its streets lined with palm trees and small cafes. It was hot like the desert. It was over 100 degrees Fahrenheit during the day but cool at night.

Settling into Karachi was easy. The first thing which Papa did was to rename Tinnani's Palace as Faridabad House after me, the apple of his eye. Papa quickly enrolled Dilnawaz and me into the Mama Parsee High School, the Karachi equivalent of England's Rhodean.

It was founded in 1918 to provide Karachi's Parsee women with an all-round education. It was then still in the ownership of the founding Mama family, its then proprietor being Zubin Mama, a dashing young man with a love of beautiful women and fast cars, who had inherited the school from his late father. He was the favourite would-be husband for rich beautiful Parsee girls, who would often be seen next to him in his two-seater sports car. He always wore a black velvet cap, which blew off from the top of his head the moment he accelerated away. Women would rush to pick it up. But that was as far as it went.

Zubin was not into marriage but was fun to be with. Then it was too late. Whilst racing along in one of those two-seaters, Zubin crashed his car and died.

Every morning Ummar, our deaf and dumb chauffeur, picked us up from Faridabad House to take us to school. And each afternoon Ummar would return to the school to take us home. It was always the same car: a 1947 American silver grey Buick. Keki had seen it advertised in Jama Jamshed, a Zoroastrian newspaper circulating in India and Pakistan. He immediately arranged for it to be shipped from the USA to Karachi.

Three months later we watched as it was unloaded at Kemari Dock.It was the same Ummar, who, in his sign-language, was later to warn Mama of an assassination plot against Papa.

Other girls, whose mode of transport was more modest, would tease the 'posh' Manekshas. So much so that we asked Ummar to take us to school in one of the several motorised rickshaws which Papa owned and would rent out. This was another of Papa's many businesses.

Although in the 1950's the school still primarily catered for Parsee girls, the Mama school also provided an education to the offspring of an increasing number of wealthy Muslim families, as well as some of the remaining Hindu girls and my two Baha'i friends. The dress codes were strict and divisive.

Muslim girls had to wear their traditional shawal kameez. Whilst Parsee girls could only wear the School's western style uniform comprising the type of green jacket and calf-length pleated skirt that you might see at an English girls' public school. On one occasion, on the last day of term before the summer vacation, Dilnawaz and I went to school wearing identical green shawal kameez which Mama had made specially for us. As soon as she saw them, one of head teachers, Shirin Bhai, sent us home to change into our regular school uniforms.

'You are not Muslim. So don't wear Muslim clothes'.

Those of my brothers who were still of school age were enrolled in the Bai Virbaji Soparivala Parsi High School. As our rickshaw passed that school daily on route to our Mama School, we would look into the windows and watch Parsee boys exercising and wearing their black felt religious caps.

Papa wasted no time in joining the Gymkhana Club situated at Club Road where wealthy Muslims and Parsees went to socialise and be entertained. Amongst its members there were English people working in various companies. There Papa was able to meet and make friends with influential people and establish himself amongst Karachi's business community.

9 Trouble in India

Whilst we were enjoying life in Karachi, things were not going so well in Bombay. At that time our parents and brothers travelled like gypsies between Karachi and Bombay, where Papa still had his businesses.

There were firstly problems with bhaiya squatters encroaching on our land at Andheri, which resulted in a series of on-going court battles.

Andheri was known as a factory place. It was a commercial site out of Bombay. Back in the fifties there were no made-up roads in Andheri.

Roads only existed for cows. A farmer would come along with a herd of goats and cows chained together with horrible pieces of wood and a paraffin lantern. Sometimes a bus or a lorry would inch along. But it was a dangerous journey.

The roads were narrow and with sharp bends like a snake. You couldn't see what was coming in front of you. On either side were steep ravines and I would see the remains of vehicles which had tumbled down.

The word 'bhaiya' means 'brother'. But these people were not our brothers. They were thugs. Criminals. Like Mafiosi they carried around lots of money which they would lend to you at extortionate rates of interest.

'Ghundas' Papa called them. They were heavily built men with shaven heads and a tiny pigtail hanging from the back of their scalps, like those worn by western Hare Krishna converts

Then there were Papa's issues with Patlo, a property investor who owned vast chunks of Bombay real estate including the flat in which we lived when staying in Bombay. It led to Papa's arrest.

Other than the fact they both Parsees, Papa and Patlo couldn't have been more different. Papa was the forty-something entrepreneur with an eye for the main chance. Patlo was the older orthodox Parsee, with his walking stick, his black velvet cap and his white linen shirvani and loose white trousers hanging from his body. In fact the word 'patlo' means 'skinny' so perhaps it wasn't his real name. But it was what we called him. He was like a Charlie Chaplin but with a 'Groucho' painted on moustache.

Papa and Patlo didn't like each other. Patlo didn't like any Parsee who lived in Pakistan.

The animosity began when Papa rented from Patlo a flat in the prestigious Manek Mansion at Colaba. Papa wanted somewhere from where he could daily commute to his photographic studio.

Patlo was forever putting up the rent. And he was forever coming round to check up on us.

On one unannounced visit he saw my brother Aspi with his pants down and about to urinate in the front garden.

'Hey. What are you doing?'

'I need to go to toilet.'

'Then why don't you use the toilet inside?'

'Can't. I'm locked out of the building.'

'Then run and get your father.'

Aspi pulled up his pants and ran off.

'Jehangir! Can't you teach your boys some manners? This is still my property you know.'

'Don't I know!'

'I've come to tell you that I'll be putting up the rent from next month.'

'Again? You are the owner of the whole Manek Mansion yet you treat your Zoroastrian family so meanly? That's why I hate your guts.'

'Yes. I've been letting you having it too cheap, according to my accountant. I'll be increasing the rents on all my properties. If it's too much for you to afford, perhaps you would like me to transfer you to somewhere cheaper.'

'Then you'll have to deal with my wife Mehera. I'm back to Karachi next week. She'll be here with the children. And by the way, she's six months pregnant. So she won't be going anywhere. Now go back to the charitable house where you belong!'

In fact Mama was not pregnant. Just fat. But Papa frightened him by saying that.

Three weeks later Patlo came back to the flat and knocked on the door. Mama opened it, her stomach bulging beneath her loose smock. Patlo saw that Papa wasn't joking. He said, 'Meherabai. How many months are you pregnant?'

She didn't know what he was talking about.

'Can I speak to Jehangir?'

'He's not here. He's gone to Pakistan.'

'When is he coming back to Bombay? I've come about the rent. His cheque didn't arrive.'

'I'm sorry. I'll let him know when he contacts me.'

Mama closed the front door. Patlo banged his stick on the ground and walked off. Patlo came back the following week. And again two weeks after that. But Papa was never there. He knew how to make himself scarce. Whenever he knew Patlo was coming he would go out for a drive to his studio to check up on his customer appointments. One day I was at the Studio when two policemen came to arrest Papa. One policeman spoke to me.

'Where's your Papa? We need to speak to him.'

'Can I help you?' interrupted Adil, who had walked in from the next room.

'We need to speak Mr Jehangir Manekshah. We have a warrant for his arrest.'

'Arrest? For what?'

'We've received a complaint that he owes two months' rent.'

'And you are arresting him for that?'

'When someone absconds without paying two months' rent, we have no choice. Now where is he?

'If you'll excuse me a moment, I'll try to find him.'

Adil left the room and quietly entered the 'dark room', where Bheekhoo was busy developing photographs which were stretched out on a piece of string. Putting his hand on Bheekhoo's shoulder, he whispered.

'Go to Papa and tell him that Patlo has sent two policemen to arrest him – saying that Papa owes him rent. Tell Papa to get a solicitor to sort Patlo out.'

Papa had always complained to Patlo about his dirty flat, saying that he was about to send a solicitor's notice to get the rent reduced. In fact it wasn't dirty at all. But Papa wasn't going to say that.

Bheekhoo cycled back to our home, where Papa was sitting outside on a wicker chair reading Times of India.

'Sir. Don't go to the Studio. There are two policemen waiting to arrest you. They say you owe money to Patlo. Adil has said that you must get a solicitor.'

Papa folded the newspaper and put it on the table beside him.

'Why should I stay away from my studio? Call Dara.'

An hour later and Papa and Dara arrived together at the studio. The two policemen were still there drinking mint tea.

'Now what's this about?' said Papa.

'We are sorry Mr Manekshah but we have a warrant for your arrest. It's about unpaid rent. If you can pay us the money now, we can leave.'

Papa gave them each a Five Rupee note saying 'This is for your trouble. I'll sort it out.

'Thank you sir. We'll tell him that you're still working in Pakistan.'

The two policemen left. But that was only the start of Patlo's vendetta against my father. He wanted us out of his property.

Patlo knew of the on-going dispute which Papa had with trespassing bhiayas and exploited it. He visited them and offered them the help of his own lawyers in their dispute with Papa. One bhiaya boasted to Papa that he had the 'law on his side'.

Keki and Adil followed Patlo and checked his movements. One evening they caught Patlo walking alone. They crept up behind him and pushed him into nearby bushes.

Keki grabbed his left arm. Adil grabbed his right arm, snatching his walking stick from his hand. Patlo struggled.

'Who are you?'

'We'll tell you in a minute. Just think of us as thugs from Pakistan. '

'What do you want? You want to rob me? I haven't got much money on me. '

'Your money? We don't want your money" said Adil.

'We are from Pakistan and we've got a friend who will

kidnap and make mincemeat of you. He'll do a qurbani on you. We can make you disappear. No-one would ever know. What do you think Patlo?' Adil drew his right arm back and forth as if he was sharpening a blade.

Patlo looked into the two faces and recognised my two brothers.

'Yes. You know who we are,' said Keki.

'I'm an old man. Let me live out my final days in peace.'

'You're not so old as you make out to be,' said Adil. 'Shut your fat mouth.'

'See this blade! I'm going to take your moustache off. And when I've done that, I'll shave your skin off.'

Patlo shook with fear. My brothers released him.

'Leave us in peace, old man,' said Keki. 'Next time there won't be a happy ending."

Patlo never again called at our house or tried to do deals with our enemies. He was frightened of my brothers. They strutted like turkeys as if waiting to sort him out. But it was more than co-incidence that two months later I saw the same two policemen come to our studio and arrest Papa and take him away: this time for alleged tax evasion. The truth was that Papa never paid his taxes: at least not when he was in India. Adil and Bheekhoo were again at the studio when it happened.

'Bheekhoo. Get Rusi,' said Adil. 'Quickly!'

Fifteen minutes later Rusi arrived. He slapped Adil's face.

'Why did you let them take Papa away?'

'What could I do? They were the police.'

What happened next brought home to me the importance of having friends in the right places. Rusi telephoned Darius Modi, the wealthy owner of Bombay's Regent Hotel, who also happened to be a friend of a local chief of police.

The three of them then went to the Police Station at

which Papa was being held and met the police chief. After a hushed discussion, during which money changed hands, Papa was quickly released and all charges dropped. Not to appear ungracious Papa also left a 25 rupee tip for each of the two officers who had arrested him. It was a lesson which I saw repeated time and time again during my childhood.

Two months later, we moved out of Patlo's house at Manek Mansion and into a luxury flat nearby. It was owned by Cox, an ex-officer colleague from Papa's army days whom he had met in England and where they had got to know each other. With his big glasses and stylish appearance he looked like Dr Stephen Ward, of Christine Keeler fame. It was a good deal. The house was big and it was pristine. From the first floor balcony we could look across the sea and watch the ships passing by and coming into Appolo Bunder Beach. It was only half the rent we had been paying to Patlo.

But if Papa had had to deal with problems in India it was in Pakistan that a bigger bombshell was about to drop.

10 Requisitioned

It was a Tuesday afternoon when an official came to call at Faridabad House to tell Papa that the Pakistan Government had requisitioned our palace. People were moving in the following week.

Over the next few days Papa and my brothers met with government officials to try to get the requisition order overturned. Money was offered. This time to no avail. It was too late. The Order had already been made.

One consolation was that we were not being evicted entirely. Only from the ground floor. It just meant that we would have to move upstairs.

The other consolation was that the people coming to our house were not peasants. They were diplomats from countries across the globe. They included members of the Saudi Royal Family. And we would be their host.

The servants spent the next week clearing our furniture out of the ground floor of our palace and moving our things to the first floor accommodation which the Pakistan Government had reserved for us. A week later the first guests arrived. They were Mr and Mrs Jaap from the British High Commission.

We stood back and watched as the Jaaps got out of the limousine and walked into the building: in awe of the splendour in which they would be living. Meanwhile removal men began unloading furniture from two camel carts and were taking it through to the Jaaps' accommodation.

Like so many European couples living in India and Pakistan at that time, Jaap was an older man married to a much younger woman. Jaap was overweight, about 5'7' tall and balding. I guessed that he was in his mid-forties. His wife, Angelina, was in her twenties and looked stunning in her loose floral dress. Papa would be pleased. So was handsome Adil, whom I could see exchanging glances with the lovely Angelina. It was a liaison which would have disastrous consequences for the Jaaps.

Motorbikes were Jaap's passion. He had two sparkling chrome and black motorbikes with apehanger handlebars like American Hells Angels.

 When he was not roaring down dusty roads, they were being stripped down or polished. Like Arizona, the roads in Pakistan were ideal for motorbikes. Adil spent much of his free time with Jaap 'talking bikes': discussing the latest models and how they performed. So did Dara and Keki, who had just imported their own motorcycles from the BSA factory at Birmingham England.

Two days after the Jaaps' arrival came Murray, an overweight Scottish diplomat with a stomach spilling over the belt of his trousers. He was younger than Jaap and did not have the luxury of a pretty wife. Instead he lived at our property with his mother, a beanpole of a woman in her sixties, who also worked in the diplomatic service as a secretary. Murray was not into bikes, cars or anything else as far as we could see. They were a strange couple who kept to themselves and we didn't like them. Amongst the British delegation there was also Patrick O'Reilly and his anglo-indian wife Mary, who always seemed slightly drunk. She often liked to take me to church in the evenings.

Of more interest to us was the arrival of a traditionally garbed Arabian couple with their two girls and a small entourage. He was Al-Hamid, Secretary to the young Prince Faisal of Saudi Arabia, to whom he was related. He had an attractive wife who had some gold teeth and whom we knew only as 'Aunty'. With them were their two daughters, six year old Mahue and her seventeen year old sister Maluck. They were a family with whom we were to grow close over the next couple of years.

Like Anne Boleyn, 'Aunty' could produce daughters but not the son which her husband craved. It was putting a strain on their marriage.

Mama said to Aunty, 'I'll pray with you and give you my blessing. Every night I'll pray for you on my balcony that you'll get pregnant. Next September you will have a boy.'

Every evening Mama said the same prayer:

'Make that woman pregnant with a boy child. So she doesn't have conflict with her husband.'

Mama also took her prayer on her many trips to the Zoroastrian fire temple in Karachi

The following September Aunty gave birth to her son Hussain. After that she was in awe of Mama, thinking that Mama had a great spiritual power. The grateful couple threw a party for us at Beach Luxury Hotel,

The following year, during the festival of Eid, Prince Faisal himself visited Pakistan and all of us were invited to a function at Clifton in his honour. Clifton was – and still is – the posh part of Karachi. Being amongst so much Royalty and powerful business and political leaders, we felt like the poor relations. But we enjoyed the occasion. And there was an unexpected spin off.

A week after the party, Al-Hamid mentioned to Papa that his 17 year old daughter Maluck had fallen for the natural charm of my brother Rusi. He asked whether a marriage could be arranged between Rusi and Maluck.

Rusi had been in the habit of buying chocolates for six year old Mahue. But Mahue was always holding the hand of her seventeen year old sister.

One day after Rusi had given sweets to Mahue, Aunty pulled him to one side and whispered:

'Maluck likes you.'

Rusi smiled and went upstairs to our quarters. But he noticed Maluck looking at him.

Aunty had already said to her husband:

'I want you to talk to the Parsee. Maluck loves him. If he wants to become Muslim we will give him the hand of our daughter Maluck. He won't regret it as he knows we are very rich.'

Maluck, who had overheard the conversation, said to her father, 'I don't want to marry anyone else. I love him.'

'The Quran doesn't talk about love'

'Yes it does Abbaa.'

Two days later Al-Hamid knocked on our door. Papa answered it.'

'Can you come down?' said Al-Hamid.

Mama said, 'Why do you want us to come down?'

'Not you Mehera,' said Al-Hamid. Only Miya Jehangir must come down. We are going to have a feast'

Mystified, Papa followed Al-Hamid down to their living quarters.

'This is a celebration. We are taking the hand of Rusi for our daughter Maluck. She loves Rusi. Here! Have some naan bread.'

Papa paused to take in the news. Then gently shook his head.

'We are all Zoroastrian. Non-Muslim. We can't get married in a mosque.'

'But you don't have to get married. It will be Rusi who gets married. He will wear a gold cloth around his head. But in his heart he will still be Zoroastrian. And I'll make sure you get your house back. Remember that we are related to the King of Saudi Arabia. And I'm Secretary to his son Prince Faisal. So you let Rusi marry my daughter. She's always praying in the Quran that she'll marry Rusi. That he's got quality as well as looks.

'I'll talk to my wife' said Papa.

Papa knew what Mama would say. There had been too many young Parsees marrying Muslims. Though usually it involved young Zoroastarian girls falling in love and eloping with Muslim boys, who were friends of their brothers at Karachi's Sopariwala Parsi High School. Their families didn't like it.

But first Papa spoke to Rusi about Al-Hamid's proposal.

Rusi was amenable as he also liked Maluck as well as the prospect of marrying into a royal family. To his disappointment Mama was not. She did not want any of our family to turn Muslim. So Papa's answer to Al-Hamid had to be,

'We are honoured by your proposal but unfortunately our religious differences would make such a marriage impossible. We hope that you will understand.'

Al-Hamid was embarrassed and humiliated. Referring to the Pakistan Government's requisition of our home he said,

'You people have deserved everything you've got. My wife loved your wife. Maluck loved Rusi. But...'

He shrugged his shoulders.

'But it was not meant to be.'

In spite of his disappointment Al-Hamid was not one to

bear a grudge. We were still invited to their parties. Al-Hamid's wife still revered Mama and many times said to her, 'May Allah bless you.' Rusi still brought chocolates for Mahue.

In fact it seemed that every night Al-Hamid threw a party. And every night my brothers would go downstairs to sit and listen to the Arabian music and watch belly dancing. All except Gustad, who preferred to stay upstairs in our kitchen and cook for stray dogs.

Amongst the diplomats living at Faridabad House there was the Iranian ambassador, Darshad Burjode Khan, and his wife: a small pretty young woman with green eyes and a pale complexion who helped Darshad with his work. Her name was Godafrie Rukhshanah and she wore ankle length skirts with gold sandles poking out at the bottom. On being introduced to Papa and my brothers, Darshad said:

'We are brothers from Iran. I am Muslim and you are Zoroastrian.'

There was another young Iranian lady living in our mansion. She was married to another diplomat, Phiroz. Before mini-skirts were invented, she wore a turquoise satin short skirt when she was in the house. She also loved sewing and, when she was not flirting with my brothers, she would make me clothes. One day Mama said to her:

'My Farida is always with you. What are you doing with her?'

'I'm teaching her to stitch. Look at this lovely frilly table-cloth she's made for you.'

Her drawback was that she struggled to speak English. It meant that the only person with whom she could really hold a conversation, apart from her husband, was Mama, who could communicate with her in Farsi. We got to know her as 'Chi Chi' but were never sure why? Perhaps it was because of the strange noises she made when trying to communicate in her broken English. Or perhaps 'Chi Chi' meant something in her Iranian language.

Finally there was Mohammed Aga, the spoilt young son of a millionaire Afghan businessman and a French mother. He was only 25 years old. And with his golden hair and green eyes he looked like an older version of the Hollywood actor James Dean. He drove a black Mercedes.

Freyni, loved him. Not least, because Aga always remembered to buy her chocolates. But he was also someone whom Papa grew to hate. Unlike the others Aga was not a diplomat.

Sometime somewhere the palm of some government official had been sufficiently greased to enable Aga to come onto our property on the coat tails of the other diplomats. Aga took over a concrete air raid shelter in the grounds of our palace which he refurbished with carpets and drapes until it looked an Arabian Kasbah. It became his love-nest to impress the many different women which he brought home each night when he was not away on business. Sometimes I would hold one of his hands, whilst Dilnawaz held the other, as he led us down into the shelter to show us what it had become.

11 Fighting Back

There was a report in Dawn newspaper about our issue with the Pakistan Government. It was as a result of that publicity that Papa was approached by a young lawyer.

'I'm Mohamed Somji. An Advocate of the High Court of Pakistan. I've seen your case in the Dawn Newspaper. And I believe that I can get your property back'

Somji's office was small, old fashioned, and on the first floor of a building in Sadda.

At their first meeting Papa explained to Somji our situation. The fact that we bought Faridabad House intending to start our new life in Pakistan, only to have it snatched away by the Pakistan Government

Somji looked at the papers.

'It is difficult. We will be taking on the Government of Pakistan.'

'So I've lost everything?'

'No. I said it's difficult. It's not impossible. Whilst the Government may be corrupt, there is one thing in your favour. Most of our senior judges are Englishmen who worked for the British Raj. They will at least give you a fair trial.'

'So I've got a chance?'

'Yes. But there is something else.'

'What's that?'

'We need to get the case on quickly before the judges transfer back to England. After that you will be lost.'

Papa sometimes took Dilnawaz and me with him when he had meetings at Somji's office. We did not want to go with Papa. Sitting staring at piles of dusty files, whilst Papa and Somji talked to each other, was so boring. We would much rather have sat outside in the car with the chauffeur or gone out to buy kulfis.

Whilst Somji declared war on the Pakistan Government, we opened up a second battle front against our unwanted guests – or at least those we didn't like.

Papa fired the first shot by paying a company to demolish the air-raid shelter and fill in and level the ground, so there was nothing to show that it had ever existed. Coolies, employed by the company, picked up the debris. Papa then arranged for all of Aga's belongings to be collected together and deposited outside the front gate of our property.

We waited to see Aga's reaction when he returned after one of his month long absences. He was heartbroken

Aga complained to the police. But Somji and Papa had already done their homework. The Government's requisition order only related to the ground floor of Faridabad House. Not to anywhere else in the building. And certainly not to a derelict air-raid shelter in the grounds of our palace.

'Speak to my lawyer,' said Papa to the police officers who came round in response to Aga's complaint.

Every year during Eid, butchers called at Faridabad House, Usually Mama would politely send them away, explaining that we were non-Muslim. But on this occasion Dara and Keki opened the door.

'Have you any Qurbani?' asked the butchers.

'No. But if you go downstairs and knock on the door, there is a big fat dhumba 'said Dara. Dhumba means a sheep. Dara then directed the two butchers to the downstairs flat where the Murrays lived.

'Knock on the door.'

One of the butchers knocked. Murray answered it with his big fat stomach and bull neck supporting his crew-cut head. He always wore ugly green shorts.

'We have come to slaughter your dhumba.'

'Dhumba? What dhumba? I don't know what you are talking about.'

'He keeps it out the back', shouted my brothers from the veranda. 'But it's very aggressive. So you'll need four or five people to handle it.'

The butchers just stood there.

'Go away!' shouted Murray. My brothers laughed and shouted down to the butchers. Pointing towards Murray they said, 'Hey stupid! That is the dhumba. It's standing right in front of you.'

The butchers looked at fat Murray and realised they had been fooled. They shook their fists at my laughing brothers, saying, 'Stupid Parsees.'

In spite of Papa's difficulties with the Pakistan Government we made the best of our new life in Karachi. Papa kept his photography studio in Bombay and our lands at Andheri. He and Mama would travel several times a year between India and Pakistan. Dilnawaz and I only went with them to India during school holidays. We didn't like Mama leaving us behind. To avoid tearful goodbyes, Mama would tuck us into bed as normal. But by morning we would discover that she and Papa had gone – leaving us with the servants and my elder brothers and sisters.

Adil liked Jaap's wife Angelina. But he'd grown to hate Jaap. He hated the liberties which Jaap took with our property.

Before his tragic death, Adil would often play tennis with Beheram on our front lawn. But Adil hated the pungent grease-smell wafting across from the customised motor-bike which Jaap had stripped down. Jaap did his stripping down on the enclosed mosaic patio which formed part of the ground floor which the Pakistan Government had allocated for the diplomats. And Jaap seemed to strip down his bike every day.

Motorbike parts rested on a stone bench supported on two stone vase-shaped supports, whilst oil dripped onto the mosaic below. One afternoon Adil put down his racquet and walked over to Jaap to complain,

'Why can't you go somewhere else to strip down your bike? Look at the mess you've made on our patio.'

'This is not your patio. It's ours for at least three to five years,' replied Jaap. 'We didn't choose to be here. It's where your government put us British Embassy workers. And besides, when I've finished what I'm doing, the servant will come and clean it up.'

He paused,

'Adil. Why do you hate us so much? I don't have this problem with your brothers.'

'I am not soft like my brothers.'

Adil stormed off. But the issue rankled with him.

Adil was tall and slim. He was the champion boxer at his school and would later win medals fighting on board ship. Just seeing Jaap made Adil angry. In fact Adil was always angry when he came home in his school uniform. He would throw things around. But maybe there was also a hint of jealousy.

When Jaap was at work, Adil would come round to visit Angelina. And they would flirt. Angelina adored handsome Adil and they would spend time hugging each other. But as she was six months pregnant with Jaap's child, there couldn't be anything else. Sometimes Jaap would return home from work to find Adil sitting in his lounge with Angelina. Often Adil was wearing only his pyjamas. Jaap hated it.

One afternoon he came home earlier than expected and saw Adil sitting indoors with Angela and holding her hand. He squared up to Adil.

'Get out of my flat. Now!'

Adil refused to move, and replied,

'It's not your flat. It's our flat. I'll come and go when I like.'

Jaap moved towards Adil, his fists clenched.

'Then I'll throw you out!'

Adil glanced at Angelina. Then back at Jaap. Then he got up and walked quickly out of Jaap's flat. Jaap smiled. But Adil wasn't in retreat. He ran upstairs, opened his satchell and put on a pair of mauve boxing gloves. The glove-clad warrior then ran back downstairs and stood in the doorway of Jaap's flat facing the couple. Both stared at him in astonishment.

'Let's settle this outside.'

Man and boy then stepped outside and squared up to each other. It was gloves verses bare knuckles. We watched from our upstairs veranda.

Jaap swung a punch. Adil ducked. Then Adil caught Jaap with a flurry of punches to the head. Jaap fell to the floor. But Adil wasn't finished with him.

Pulling Jaap's head up by the hair, Adil continued punching - punching – punching - until our cook, Khansama Ali, pulled Adil away. Jaap lay still. Ali checked to see if Jaap was still breathing. He wasn't. And there was no pulse. Ali whispered to my brother in Urdu,

'You've killed him. But I'll be your witness. It was Jaap who started the fight.'

Police and an ambulance came. Jaap's body was taken away. Adil was arrested. Things looked bleak. Papa phoned Somji.

Two days later and to our relief the police released Adil pending further investigations. Two weeks later the police came again with the news that the medical examination had shown that Jaap had died from cardiac arrest. Adil had not caused his death. Jaap already had a weak heart due to his overweight and It was just unfortunate that he suffered a fatal heart attack on the day he fought Adil.

In the weeks following Jaap's death, Angelina gave birth to a boy. Then as soon as she was able to do so she resumed her work as a stenographer at the British Embassy. After a respectable interlude, Adil's visits to the widowed Angelina also resumed but had to be more discreet.

'If people see us together they'll talk,' warned Angelina.

12 The Verdict

One evening Somji phoned Papa with an important message,

'Your case is on tomorrow. Be at court at ten.' By 9.00 am the following morning we were already assembled in the court foyer. Papa tapped his fingers on his black briefcase as we waited. At 9.40 Somji bustled in cradling a pile of papers. He smiled at Papa.

At the scheduled ten o clock start time we were still waiting. No-one from the Pakistan Government had arrived. The court usher looked at her watch and said, 'I'll speak to the judge'.

The usher disappeared through a side door and reappeared five minutes later.

'The judge will give the Government lawyer until ten thirty to present himself at court,' she said. 'Otherwise he'll hear the case without him.'

At 10.29 a panting Government barrister arrived with his papers. He whispered something to the usher. She disappeared again through the side door: reappearing ten minutes later at the entrance of the courtroom. She opened the door and led us into the court room.

As soon as we were all seated a court clerk exited through another side door behind the raised judicial bench. He returned a minute later and beckoned us to stand up, saying, 'The court will rise.'

Justice Brown entered and stood facing us. He bowed before taking his seat.

It could have been any court in England. Brown was a middle-aged Englishman: a thin clean-shaven colonial type. He had a kindly face. But he also looked weary. The clerk was the first to speak. 'We've had a request for an adjournment from the Pakistan Government. They need another month to prepare their case.'

'Thank you Mr Husain.'

The judge paused.

'If I'm to adjourn this case, it will have to be rescheduled before another judge. At two o clock this afternoon I'll be flying back to London. This is my last case.'

The announcement shook Somji. He looked round at Papa and back to the judge.

'Could I have five minutes with my client?'

'Granted.'

The judge bowed and walked out of the room.

Somji walked over to Papa and put his arm round his shoulder.

'Jehangir. You have a good case. But if it is rescheduled before one of the new Pakistan judges, we are lost. They won't go up against the Pakistan Government. The case has to be heard today.'

After ten minutes the judge returned. He again bowed and sat down.

'Yes Mr Somji.'

'Your honour we oppose the adjournment. The Pakistan Government have had more than two years to prepare their case. But they know and we know that if the case is adjourned today, my clients, the Manekshahs, will never get justice. And they are still grieving the loss of a son. All they want to do is to sell their property and start a new life in England. But they can't do that whilst this case is pending. So we ask you – please – to hear our case to today.'

'I will adjourn for 15 minutes.'

The judge bowed and left the room, taking the court file with him. Fifteen minutes stretched to thirty minutes. Then to forty minutes. Papa paced the courtroom. Somji went into the foyer for his third cigarette. Then the court usher came over and called Papa to one side. As a Katchi, a follower of the Aga Khan, she could speak to us in our native Gujarati.

'You are going to win,' she whispered to Papa.

'I know, because I get on well with this judge and he talks to me about his cases. He is shocked by all the corruption which lies behind the requisitioning of your property by the Pakistan Government. He's also delayed his flight so that he can finish the case. He is the last of the English judges to fly back.'

After fifty four minutes the judge came back.

'The court will rise,' said the clerk.

Everybody rose and bowed to the judge and sat back down. The judge spoke.

'I'm going to give my decision on this matter today. I've read the papers and am satisfied that the Federation of Karachi's requisition order is wrong for reasons that are apparent to me from the documentation. I therefore give judgment to this respectable Parsee family and order that the whole of their property be returned to them within 15 days. Is there anything else?'

'We would ask for six months to comply with the Order,' said the Government lawyer.'

'No. The diplomats must vacate within fifteen days.'

The judge knew that granting any longer period would give the Government a chance to get his order overturned. And he wasn't going to allow that.

'Then we will appeal,' said the Government lawyer.

'There will be no appeal. My decision is final.'

So for the first time in almost two years our family had something to celebrate. Somji thanked the judge and shook his hand. He then took the written judgment which Brown had just signed off. He pushed his way through the front doors of the courthouse and stood outside at the top of the steps. Then, like Neville Chamberlain, he held the document aloft and spoke to the waiting reporters.

'Today justice has been done. This poor Parsee family who were tricked into buying this requisitioned property, have now had that property returned to them.'

We had already left the court by a side exit as Papa didn't want us to be photographed by waiting photographers. It was as a result of Somji's victory in our case that he established his reputation as someone to be reckoned with. Everyone wanted to use his services.

Over the course of the next two weeks all our unwanted guests moved out until the whole of the ground floor of Faridabad House was vacant. In fact the house seemed empty without them. As soon as the last diplomat vacated, Papa made plans to sell Faridabad House and make a new life in London.

13 The Sale

Shirin wasted no time in advertising our palace in Dawn newspaper. Her advertisement read:

'House like a palace to sell in Karachi.'

She received various replies, but none worth following up. But it was a chance meeting with a French nun at Lourdes, which led to Faridabad House being sold.

Shirin had received a catholic education at Bombay's famous St Xavier's College. It had been founded by German Jesuits in 1869. And although Shirin never left our Zoroastrian faith, she felt able to combine it with whatever Catholicism had to offer.

Shirin was also a devotee of St Bernadette, the fourteen year old miller's daughter who in the 1860's had repeated visions of the Virgin Mary in a cave in the southern French village of Lourdes. Shirin's job at London's India House made it easy for her to cross the Channel and visit Lourdes, whenever she needed to pray for a miracle.

On one of these trips, Shirin was in a slow queue of people waiting their turn to be immersed into an ice cold bath. Standing next to her was a middle-aged French nun. She smiled at Shirin.

'And what brings you here?'

Shirin opened up.

'To find peace. I lost my brother Beheram. He was murdered on a Karachi beach. And it's broken us up. We want to move out of Pakistan. I've been working in London and have taken the chance to come here and pray for myself and my family.'

The nun looked at Shirin in silence. After a long pause, she said.

'I'm Paiva. I'm also here to pray. We want to land a shipment of food-aid in India. But we are being prevented from doing so by Indian government officials. Without paying a hefty bribe to these corrupt officials, we can't get our papers stamped. But we are not prepared to do that. And if we don't land our perishable cargo, it will all go to waste.'

'Maybe I can help?'

'You can help by praying for us.'

'I can do more than that. I work at London's India House and I am dealing every day with the Indian Government. I will get your papers stamped.'

Paiva's face lit up.

'Thank you. What is your name?'

'Shirin.'

'Tell me a little bit more about you and your family, Shirin.'

Shirin reached into her leather handbag and pulled out a brown photograph. She showed it to Paiva.

'This is our home in Karachi. Papa named it Faridabad House after my sister Farida. She has always been the apple of his eye.'

Paiva looked at the grand rectangular building in the photograph, with the dome at one end.

'Isn't it beautiful?'

'Yes. It is beautiful. But it has not brought us happiness.

That is why we want to sell it and start a new life London.'

'Have you found a buyer?'

'Not yet. But I've advertised it and I've had a few replies. But I haven't had a chance to follow any of them up.'

'It would be ideal for what we want.'

'What's that?'

'We want to open an orphanage in Karachi. And we've been looking round for suitable premises. But we haven't been able to find anything. Until now. Can we come to see it?'

'Of course. But first let's get your shipment landed.'

Instead of flying back to London, Shirin flew instead to India and went to see the Indian official who was refusing to stamp Paiva's document. She explained what it was about and asked for the stamped document. But the official was unmoved.

'Then you won't have a job' said Shirin.

Through her work at India House, Shirin had made important contacts within the Indian Government. She got onto them immediately to get clearance for Paiva's ship to land. Within a week the papers were stamped and the news telexed through to Paiva's organisation. The following day Paiva's ship landed and the food was unloaded for distribution to the people who needed it.

In the meantime Shirin carried out her own private detective work to make sure that Paiva and her missionaries were as genuine as they seemed and that they really wanted and were able to buy Faridabad House.

Although Shirin liked Paiva, she was also a shrewd business woman and would never be anybody's fool.

Shirin then telephoned Paiva and invited her to Karachi. She arrived with a small delegation. After Papa had shown them Faridabad House. Paiva said,

'That's exactly the type of house we are looking for. Fifty

rooms up and fifty rooms down. And with acres of extra garden and a huge balcony.'

Papa asked Paiva how she would arrange the money. Paiva offered French currency. Shirin insisted that all the money was paid in cash. She also told Papa not to hand over the keys until we received confirmation from our bank that all the money had been received from the French missionaries.

We then moved to rented accommodation in Karachi for three months whilst all financial matters were sorted out. We stayed at 'Raza's House', which Papa saw advertised in Dawn Newspaper.

It was a recently built luxury house on Drigg Road in the American Colony. The Raza family lived on the ground floor and we rented the first floor four bedroom apartment whilst we prepared for our move to London. In the meantime Papa asked Shirin to look out for a suitable property in London to which we could move.

We moved to London in September 1957, when I was twelve years old. It was a painful process for me as we had to leave behind our beloved pets. These included several Alsatian dogs which we owned and which we gave to another Parsee family. We had bred Alsatians to sell as puppies to the 'Nawabs' – or 'Royal People' as guard dogs. But my favourite pets were the four geese we gave to the zoo in Karachi. My last wish before flying to London was to visit my geese at the zoo.

They weren't at all happy with the other strange exotic birds with which they were living. Keki said that I could visit them every week until I left Karachi to fly to London. The zoo manager also said that if I wrote to him from London, he would give me all the good news about my geese.

14 The Shrine

'Before we leave Pakistan we must go to Quaid e Azam Dargah to pay our respects,' said Papa.

Quaid e Azam Dargah translates literally to 'shrine of the great leader': the leader being Papa's old friend Mohammed Ali Jinnah. It was the last time we were to be together as a family before leaving Pakistan.

In 1957 Jinnah's tomb was not the grand mausoleum it is today. But it was still impressive. It was a large white marble slab raised and surrounded on each of its four sides by three marble steps. Each of those steps was wide enough for a person to kneel down and pray. Displayed on each of the steps was the Holy Quran. An armed policeman stood guard at each of the four sides of the dargah.

As we arrived, a policeman directed Papa and my brothers to one side of the dargah – whilst Mama, Dilnawaz and myself were directed to another. He gave us scarves to put on our heads.

Papa had been brought up in a Muslim school and immediately began praying into the Quran. When Papa had finished praying, he reached for the hands of the brothers on either side of him. Then Papa began to speak to the tomb itself.

'Why is Papa speaking in English?' I asked Mama.

'He and the Quaid e Azam always spoke to each other in English.'

As Papa spoke I could see him begin to shake. My brothers held him steady. Then, still shaking, Papa reached into his pocket for a handkerchief and wiped his brow. It seemed to go on forever. Then the shaking stopped. Papa and my brothers said a closing prayer.Then with a final bow Papa and my brothers stepped back down to the base of the dargah.

'What happened?' said Mama. 'You were shaking like a leaf.'

Papa's words tumbled out.

'The Quaid e Azam's spirit came to me. He was wearing a white religious cap. I'd told him that I had done a very bad thing when I broke the Murti and that I had lost my son because of it. He said that I had done everything I could for Beheram whilst he was alive. And that now Beheram was smiling down at us.

'He said that he had prayed hard to get our palace released from the requisition order. And the fact that our palace has been released showed that Allah Miya has forgiven me. He also spoke about the night we went to Piccadilly and ate chestnuts in Leicester Square. And he sends his love to you Mehera. He also said that our sons have been coming often to the Dargah to pray for the release of our property.

'He wished us well for our move to London and said that he and I will always be brothers.'

One of the policeman overheard Papa's conversation with Mama. But he didn't seem in any way surprised.

'Since he died the Quaid e Azam has become a saint. His spirit comes to everyone with a problem who prays at his dargah,' he said.

It was a year after our move to London that Papa said that he would be travelling back to Karachi for the Quaid e Azam's death anniversary on 11th September. But Mama said,

'No. We have moved to England and we must leave the past behind.'

15 London

I cried as I boarded the Quantas plane to London. My only company were the two Australian air-stewardesses whom Papa had paid to look after me on the journey.

I had not wanted to leave Raza's house and had told Papa that I would not be leaving. Papa replied.

'Then you stay here on your own Farida. Raza's family will not look after you. We are all going to London.'

My parents had previously left for London, leaving me in the care of my brothers. Now, a month later, it was my turn to fly to London. Papa had not wanted us travelling together in case something happened to the plane. On the evening of the flight, Keki drove me to the airport.

I was going to miss Karachi very much. The only reason we were going to London was because Mama was still very depressed at losing my brother Beheram. In fact I still believe that the only mistake we ever made was leaving Pakistan.

On the way to Karachi Airport, Keki took me back to the zoological garden to see my four geese for one last time. They came over to the fence when they saw me looking at them as if to say, 'Please take us home.'

I continued to cry as at 11pm the propellers on the red and

87

white plane spun into life and it took off for my one-way flight. I just could not stop crying.

Seeing my distress, the stewardesses took me into the cockpit to meet the pilots, which cheered me up. This was repeated several times.

We broke our journey at Rome, where the stewardesses tried unsuccessfully to get me to eat something. Then it was back into the plane and off to London.

I got another shock after landing at Heathrow, when I stepped out of the plane into the cold London air. It was March 1957. When I had got through Arrivals, I saw my parents waiting for me. But I pushed Papa away saying,

'I don't like it here. I'm going back to Pakistan.'

'Then you'll be staying with Miss Gathi,' said Papa.

Miss Gathi was a beanpole of a woman who was a teacher at Mama School. She was in charge of the residential block where the boarders lived when they were not in lessons. Papa wouldn't have wanted me living on my own with the Raza family because they had teenage sons. So I accepted my lot and went with my parents to the two bedroom flat they were renting at Turnham Green. We could not afford anything else at that time because the Pakistan Government would not let Papa take his money out of Pakistan. We were just allowed enough cash to live on.

It was sour grapes on the Government's part because Shirin had had the foresight to have the proceeds of sale of Faridabad House transferred to an account with a British Bank with offices in Pakistan. It meant that we were at least with a bank which would take our side in any issue with the Pakistan Government. He also retained the services of Somji to fight through the courts for the release of our money.

'I won't even charge you,' said Somji. 'You are like a brother to me.'

Whilst we were crammed in the Turnham Green flat, Papa applied for my enrolment at Hogarth Boys and Girls Comprehensive School, Chiswick.

Miss Mackenzie, an assistant head, came round to our flat to meet me. But I was in no mood to co-operate. I stamped my feet and argued with my parents in our native Gujarati. Miss Mackenzie looked at me over her glasses.

'She seems very unruly Mr Manekshah. Could we go into another room?'

'I don't want to go to Hogarth School,' I shouted at Miss Mackenzie. 'I want to go back to Pakistan.'

Miss Mackenzie looked at Papa in astonishment,

'She speaks English?'

Following a private conversation with Papa, Miss Mackenzie left. She came back at 10 am a week later to take me to school. I saw her first.

I ran into the toilet and locked the door. I refused to come out. Coaxing failed. So they played a trick. Instead of calling for me to come out, everyone stayed quiet. Miss Mackenzie hid behind a door. After ten minutes I called out,

'Has she gone?'

'Yes,' said Mama.

'Then swear on Bharam Izzard that she's gone.'

That caused Mama difficulty. Bharam Izzard is a Zoroastrian angel, on whose name Parsees call out in distress.

'Go on. Swear,' said Papa, who was not religious at all.

'No. I'm not going to swear,' said Mama. 'Just come out Farida.'

'If you don't come out, I'll get a carpenter to take down the door. Then I'll pull you out,' said Papa.

After a further wait, and when it seemed safe to do so, I crept out of the toilet. Miss Mackenzie grabbed me immediately.

She bundled me into her car and took me for my first day at Hogarth School.

'This is England and you have to go to school,' she warned me. 'If you don't, you'll be taken to a remand school and then you won't be coming home in the evening.'

On the second day, Mama took Dilnawaz and me to school by bus. We were wearing our new school uniforms and It was the first time that I had been on a red London bus. We were sitting on one of the long seats at the back of the bus. Sitting facing us on the long seat opposite were two middle-aged men. One of them caught my eye. He smiled. Mama elbowed me in the ribs. She spoke to me in our language.

'Look down. And close your legs. If I see you smiling at them I'll slap your face.'

'But Mama they're only smiling.'

'I know what they're thinking. They're dogs like your father.'

'No Mama. I think they're smiling at you. They're smiling at your Irani headscarf and that big smock you're wearing. They're wondering why you look so old fashioned.'

'Don't be so rude.'

'Even Papa says that he's going to put your headscarves in a pile and set fire to them.'

Mama saw that two seats behind the driver had become free. She hurried us to the front of the bus and we sat down. It meant that no men would be able to look at us whilst we were travelling. After that she always looked for empty seats towards the front of a bus.

As it was, my first days at Hogarth School were not as bad as I had feared. The other girls were nice. There were also a couple of Pakistani teachers who took me under their wings. But they also reinforced the message which Miss Mackenzie had given me.

'We can take you to a remand school to meet other Pakistani girls who didn't want to go school. But you won't like it very much.'

For the first time in my life I also had the chance to meet boys.

There was the baker's boy, who would come round on his bike to give us freshly baked buns. There was Steve, who worked in a butchers and brought cooked sausages. They were still at school but worked in the evenings and at weekends.

There was another boy whom I sat next to in class. His name was Geoffrey and we became friends. The two of us would also sit on the same table at lunchtime, whilst Dilnawaz sat with other girls. Then Dilnawaz told Papa. He was most distressed but didn't say what he was about to do.

As our money began to come through from Pakistan, Papa was able to put aside enough from our monthly quota to buy a house at Elmwood Road, Chiswick. Shortly after moving in, Dilnawaz and I met our next door neighbour..

Whilst peering through the window of the next door house we'd noticed a young lady reading aloud from a script. She suddenly looked up and caught our peeping eyes.

'Boo!'

We jumped back. The lady laughed.

'Hi! I'm Wendy Craig. I'm just a struggling actress just trying to learn my lines. You must be Farida and Dilnawaz.'

'Yes.'

'Your father spoke to me about you. I understand that you're both going off to boarding school.'

Our faces dropped.

'Oops! I'm sorry I shouldn't have said that. I thought you already knew.'

But we didn't. And - yes - it was true. Papa was not happy

about us mixing with boys. And there was another reason why we had to go. It had to do with money. Somji had said to Papa,

'If you want to increase the girls' monthly quota, you must demonstrate that you need the money to send them away to school. You are entitled to do that.'

So we were taken out of Hogarth School and enrolled at a private boarding school near Ipswich. Keki drove us there at the beginning of each term and collected us when the school broke up.

'But it's only for a little while,' said Mama. 'Just until the money comes through.'

As it was we were there for barely three months. Somji got our monthly quota increased. Then Papa took us out and enrolled us at Oxford College.

Contrary to what its posh name would suggest, Oxford College was just a large house in Marlborough Road, Chiswick which was run by two middle aged spinsters. They were both sisters and we called them both, 'Miss Fowler.'

Papa was happy because Oxford College was just for girls. We were happy because it meant that we could come home after lessons. It was whilst we were at Oxford College that Papa met someone who would help him to become very rich by investing in and renting out property. His name was Husain. We met him one afternoon when we were on our way to the Zoroastrian House at Hampstead. Husain already knew about Parsees and as soon as he heard us speaking Gujarati, he knew that we were Parsees. He wasted no time introducing himself.

'I'm Husain. When I settled here from Pakistan fifteen years ago I struggled. But now I'm a millionaire. I've got a dozen houses which I rent out across West London. When I arrived in England I got myself a job as an administrator with BOAC. I saved enough from my earnings to buy my first house.

My wife and I lived in part of it and we let out the rest. Then I used the income from that to help pay the mortgage on another house. By doing that I've become very rich. If I wanted to I could give up my job tomorrow and live on the income from my properties. I'll show you how to do it.'

Papa was impressed. He wasted no time selling our house at Elmwood Road and used the money as a down payment on two houses in Chiswick High Road. We lived on the top floor of one of the houses and rented out the rest. It was the income from those two houses which enabled Papa to buy his next house at Cromwell Road, Kensington. Very soon he also owned properties spread across West London.

We also visited Husain and his family at their lovely large house at Sutton Court Road, Chiswick. One day Husain invited us to an Eid party at his house. To his surprise Papa politely declined.

'I've already been invited to an Eid party at the Pakistan Embassy.I want to go and tell the Pakistan Ambassador how I won my case against his horrible Government. I want to embarrass him.'

Papa's attitude to the Pakistan Ambassador worried Shirin. She was about to start a new job at the Pakistan Embassy. It paid a lot more than her previous job at India House.

'I'll lose my job if you do that,' she told Papa.

In fact it was Shirin who got us the invitation to the Eid party at the Pakistan Embassy. And every year after that we got another invitation.

After more money came through Papa enrolled us in Our Lady of Sion Convent School at Notting Hill Gate. It was very different to any previous school I had been to.

We had a school uniform comprising a pale biscuit coloured skirt and jacket, which contrasted with our green ties and we had to obey the rules of the convent, which were a lot stricter than any rules I had come across before or since. For instance, when sitting down in the dining hall we were not allowed to reserve seats for our friends.

It was whilst we were at Our Lady of Sion, that Shirin got us parts as film extras at Pinewood Studios. She knew Mrs Seine, a Burmese lady, who had a film agency. Film companies used her agency when they wanted foreign ladies.

One of the first films in which I made an appearance was the 1963 epic, Cleopatra, starring a young Elizabeth Taylor. Although the film was not released until 1963, filming had started several years earlier at Pinewood. Me and Dilnawaz were two of Cleopatra's handmaidens.

Look. You can see us in the background standing guard at the entrance to Cleopatra's chamber. We're both standing facing each other on either side of the door wearing Egyptian headdresses and holding our plastic spears. No man must be allowed to enter.

But we first needed to take time off school to go to Pinewood Studios. Shirin fixed that by telling the nuns that we needed to take time off school to attend prayer meetings. Nobody queried it.

It was whilst we were filming Cleopatra that Dilnawaz and I became friendly with a young Pakistani actor called Raza, who lived local to us.

When we were supposed to be in the games class, we would quietly slip away from the school tennis courts and go to Raza's flat to watch Indian films and eat the spicy snacks which he had prepared for us. But there was never anything more than that. We had noticed that he seemed to prefer the company of men and was never seen out with a woman.

Papa asked the nuns to inform him immediately if either of

us did anything wrong: when he would deal with us. They wrote to Papa querying why we were not attending games lesson.

'We've been going to Raza's flat to watch films and eat Indian food,' Dilnawaz told him.

'What! You've both been going alone to a man's flat?' shouted Papa.

'Don't worry,' I said. 'He doesn't like women. He's an hijro.'

Hijras are Indian eunuchs who dress in womens' clothes and earn their living by dancing at parties. My answer cooled Papa down.

'Anyway,' he said. 'I don't want you going to his flat anymore.'

16 This is England

'As soon as school has finished, you have to come straight back home. There is to be no hanging around after school with friends.'

Very soon I had no friends at all. I could not go out or see anyone. Papa was an old Victorian minded man. He wanted discipline and respect.

It seemed that all the other girls in the school had young boyfriends coming to visit them during the lunch break. It was not just the girls. One of the nuns, Sister Teresa, also had a regular visitor. He was a young priest.

Thinking no one would notice, the pair would quietly slip into a back room and lock the door.

'They must have something very important to discuss,' I told one of the girls.

Every lunchtime Dilnawaz and I stood alone inside the gym room looking out of the windows and watching the other girls meeting their boyfriends. They hugged. They giggled. They kissed.

Once when the girls saw us watching, one of them waved and called us over to join them. We walked over to them. The girl who had waved then said, 'Saturday night we are having a birthday party. Would you both like to come? Don't worry about boyfriends – because there will be quite a few boys there.'

We didn't go to that party. Worse still, Dilnawaz told Papa about the conversation. He was most distressed. He kept even more of an eye on me and said, 'If there's any hanky panky, I'll sort you out.'

Not to be put off, I managed eventually to meet some of my classmates after school. I lied to Mama:

'After school I'm going to June's house. She's a welsh girl. And her mother has just lost her husband. June wants me to go to her house for tea. It'll cheer her mother up.'

It was true that I was going to June's house. But it was not to cheer up her mother. Instead I met June's handsome seventeen year old brother Keith, He was quite taken with me and said nervously,

'Would you like to come out with me to the cinema next Saturday?'

His question took me by surprise. I had to decline saying, 'I'd like to but I can't. There is no way I would be allowed out in the evening, because my father is very strict.'

'I'm sorry but I don't understand. All thirteen and fourteen year old girls go out with boys of that age. This is England. You should tell that to your father.'

Keith saw the shock on my face.

'I could never do that. My father would get very angry and beat me up.'

Keith pondered about for a moment.

'Then would you like to come to the park with me on Saturday afternoon?'

I thought about it, took a deep breath, and said, 'Yes.'

The following Saturday morning and before leaving the house I said to Mama,

'Don't worry. I'm going out at one o'clock to meet June.'

To my disappointment she replied:

'I'm sorry. You can't go. But why don't you ask June to come over here?'

As soon as Mama's back was turned, I sneaked out of the house past my father, who was asleep in the garden. I went to a red public telephone box. I would deal with the consequences later. There I made a quick telephone call.

'June. Can you come over to my house? Just stay for a few minutes and we'll go out together. Tell Keith to meet us at Richmond Park.'

Half an hour later June arrived. After ten minutes we left the house together and went to Richmond Park, where Keith was waiting. Then June went home, leaving Keith and me together.

I really liked Keith. He held my hand as we walked through the park. I wanted to marry him that day. Just to get away from my family. It seemed as though a cloud had been lifted.

But at half past three Keith had to take me to the bus stop to see me off home. It brought me back to reality. Even though I wanted to spend the whole day with Keith, an anxious family would be waiting for me at home.

My fascination with Keith also had other consequences. I started losing interest in my lessons. My next school report was bad.

Each Thursday afternoon was given over to sport. In the winter months it was gym. In the summer: tennis. But I was never attending those lessons. Instead I was seeing Keith.

The nuns soon noticed my non-attendance during gym lessons and sent a note to Papa. He asked me what I was doing on those days. I replied:

'I go to June's mum to have tea and cakes and to spend the afternoon with her.'

'Is June in your class?'

'Yes.'

'Was June also there with her Mum?'

'No. She wasn't.'

'Then what about Dilnawaz?'

'She always goes to the gym. I asked her to come with me to June's mum but she was not interested.'

To my surprise, Papa accepted my explanation. It meant that I could see Keith more and more. But that happy situation didn't last long as I soon discovered that Dilnawaz had been telling tales about me to Papa. Dilnawaz was very goody goody when it came to telling tales. It was a very painful discovery.

On returning home from seeing Keith one Thursday afternoon, Papa greeted me with several hard slaps round the head.

'You will get up to your room,' he shouted.

I did as I was told. As soon as I was inside, he closed the door and locked it. There I stayed until Mama came home that evening and opened the door. She beckoned me to come down to the dining room and eat something. There Papa was waiting for me. Pointing his finger at me he said:

'I want you to eat your meal and go upstairs again. The whole week you are going to be in your room locked up.'

I cried my eyes out. But Papa was not to be put off. He said:

'We are going to check the times of all the buses between here and Notting Hill Gate. Every 15 minutes. I want you to be back in Chiswick by 4.30.'

Papa also asked the nuns to give him daily information as to what time I was at school in the morning. I felt like a prisoner.

Dilnawaz and I were ordered to go to and from school by bus. Fortunately my elder brothers now had their own jobs and could not follow me during the week. But they made up for it at weekends.

Every Saturday I went shopping to Woolworths and Marks and Spencer. But I was never alone.

Rusi, Keki and Dara would wait outside the shop in a white Riley saloon. They gave me twenty minutes to go in, do my shopping, and come back to the car.

It was claustrophobic. My social life was shattered. I no longer had any friends. Papa had become very strict. One day June saw how tearful I was. She spoke to me quietly.

'Farida. They can't keep you as a prisoner. This is England. You are entitled to go out and have friends. Just like the other girls. The way you are being treated is against the law. The next time he hits you, promise me that you'll speak to someone who can do something about it.'

I promised.

'Here! Take this!'

She handed me a piece of writing paper with a telephone number written on it.

'This number will take you straight through to the Children's Welfare Office. They'll speak to your father. Then everything will be all right.'

I forced a smile. Put the paper in my pocket and forgot about it. But I remembered it a fortnight later when my bus was cancelled and I was an hour late home from school.

Papa greeted me with a slap and sent me to my room. The next day I mentioned it to June.

'So what are you going to do about it? I've given you the number to telephone.'

'Papa will kill me.'

'No he won't. And if you are worried about seeing the welfare officer, I'll come along with you.'

I thought about it. Then nodded.

'Come on. Let's make that call.'

We both walked to the red telephone box and squeezed inside. Trembling, I dialled the number, secretly hoping that no-one would answer. But after two rings, the phone was picked up. My heart thumped.

'Children's Welfare Office'

I stood there. Not knowing what to say.

'Hello! If you don't answer I'm going to put the phone down.'

I handed the phone to June.

'Could you speak to her?'

'Hello. My name is June. I'm with my friend Farida. She's being ill treated by her family and she's very frightened.'

June did the talking for me. She explained how my family was ill treating me. An appointment was made for me to see the Children's Officer at Chiswick Town Hall. Again June came with me.

We saw a Miss Jackson, a portly middle-aged lady wearing a pearl necklace over a floral dress. June did most of the talking as Miss Jackson took notes. The whole process took an hour. At the end of the interview, Miss Jackson folded her notes and said:

'Thank you. You've told me everything I need to know.'

'What happens now?' said June.

Miss Jackson looked at me and said, 'I'll pay a visit to your father and talk to him. He needs to understand that he can't keep you a prisoner. You are entitled to go out and have friends.'

Miss Jackson saw the alarm on my face. She touched my arm and smiled,

'Don't worry. It'll be all right.'

I smiled back. Then June and I picked up our things and left.

I was at home the following week when Miss Jackson arrived at our house carrying a file. Our Goan servant John answered the door.

'Is Mr Manekshah at home?'

'Yes. I'll find him.'

As I watched from a discreet distance, John went and found Papa. He came to the door.

'I'm Manekshah. What do you want?'

'I'm the Children's Officer for Chiswick. I've been contacted by your daughter Farida. She's complained that she is not allowed out and that you and her brothers have been hitting her. Is there somewhere we can speak in private?'

Miss Jackson moved towards the front door as if to step inside. Papa barred her way. He scowled at her and said:

'You fat lump. How dare you come to my house telling me how to bring up my family. Get away from my house!'

Miss Jackson stood her ground.

'How rude you are Mr Manekshah. No wonder Farida is unhappy. A complaint has been made and we have to investigate it. Don't you know that you can be prosecuted for child cruelty?'

'Child cruelty! How dare you! We are a respectable family. And I'm not going to have my daughter going out with boys and getting a bun in the oven because you say she should have more freedom. Now fuck off!'

'I beg your pardon!'

'I said fuck off. If you don't, I'll come down and throw you off my property.'

As Papa moved towards her, Miss Jackson turned and scuttled down the steps, her papers flapping. Papa called after her:

'Why don't you go on a diet and lose some weight? You fat old bag. Don't come back here!'

Papa didn't know that I had seen his exchange with Miss Jackson and he didn't mention it to me. But his attitude towards me became increasingly frosty. The next week Papa had another visitor: a tall skinny middle-aged man. He was clean shaven and wore a grey wide brimmed trilby hat. He spoke sharply to Papa.

'I'm the Children's Officer for Chiswick. Last week my assistant Sylvia Jackson visited you to investigate a complaint that you've been ill treating your daughter Farida. I'm here to follow up that investigation. Can I come inside?'

Again Papa barred his way and spoke in his best Oxford English:

'Am I supposed to discuss my daughter's affairs with a man wearing a cowboy hat? I don't think so.'

'Then I'll have to report you for prosecution.'

'You do that!'

Papa closed the door. Two months later a magistrates court summons arrived for Papa. It was dropped through the letter-box and charged Papa with child cruelty towards me. Papa set about finding a lawyer.

Mr Marks, who was Papa's bank manager, recommended Craig Scott of Scott and Co solicitors, which was based in Chiswick High Road. Scott and Co was a one-man band with a musty office situated above Lloyds Bank. It reminded me of Somji's office in Karachi. There were files all over the place. But what Scott and Co lacked in tidiness, Craig Scott made up for in court.

Miss Jackson attended Brentford Magistrates Court with the Council solicitor and gave evidence about my complaint and her attempt to speak to Papa. She had previously asked me if I would give evidence in the case against my father. Fearing for my safety, I had declined. Under Scott's cross-examination, the Council's case fell apart. Other than my initial complaint to the Childen's Officer, they had no evidence to prove that Papa had ever hit me or ill-treated me.

The magistrates warmed to Papa as he explained the circumstances of how he had come to live in England and how he had brought up my elder brothers and sisters, one of whom had become a geologist and others who were studying law. The magistrates dismissed the case against Papa and wished him well. He left the court smiling that day, whilst Jackson and the Council solicitor picked up their papers and left without a word.

Papa's smile disappeared the moment we arrived home.

'Look what you put me through,' said Papa, before giving me the beating of my life.

17 The Music Lesson

After I moved on from Lady of Syon to the Technical College, I developed a crush on my music teacher. He was Tony Mikos. He was half Greek, about thirty years old and tall and clean shaven. In fact you could say he looked a bit like the actor Cary Grant.

I had gone there to learn hairdressing. Not just hair dressing. Papa also enrolled me in other courses such as cooking and embroidery. He also paid for me to have private music lessons.

Mikos was head of the Music Department. I went to him for singing and to learn the piano. I also knew that he was a bachelor and that he had an eye for the girls.

Mikos would often bring into the school lovely Greek cakes which his mother had baked and which he would share with us. After one lesson, Mikos said to me,

'I see you like cakes Farida. There's a place in Leicester Square where they bake the loveliest cakes. Shall we go there together?'

I agreed. We arranged to meet after College outside the cake shop. To his disappointment I brought along my Irish friend Liz. She was also studying hairdressing but dropped out from College after six months when she got a job in a supermarket.

'Why have your brought your friend along,' said Mikos.

'Because she is my best friend and we go everywhere together.'

In fact Liz had wanted to come along, thinking that Mikos would bring another man along for her.

So the three of us went into the shop and had cakes. They were lovely Greek cakes. Cakes with pecan nuts. Cakes filled with custard. Cakes topped with peaches. Liz looked at Mikos and then at me.

'Why are you holding her hand?' she asked.

'Because I'm her teacher. And she is my star pupil.'

I was fifteen and Mama had now started trusting me. My elder brothers were no longer chauffeuring me everywhere in the car and waiting for me whilst I did my shopping. Instead Dilnawaz and I would go out with Mama to Woolworths. As Mama did her own shopping, I would disappear, saying that I was going to another counter and that I would meet her outside Woolworths. This subterfuge gave me at least half an hour to meet Mr Mikos for a little chat.

Every Saturday morning he was in Chiswick High Road doing his shopping. He was always by himself. I could see that he liked me from the way his eyes followed my every movement. And I really fancied him. But I thought that he only liked me in the way that a teacher likes his pupil. The truth was his crush on me was as intense as mine was for him.

Having returned home from college one afternoon, I saw Freyni. I said to her,

'Where is Mama?'

'Mama has gone to Kensington High Street with your father.'

'Oh. That's good. You don't mind if I just go out and meet a school friend.'

'They will be back by eight. I hope you come back by eight.'

Dara was sleeping. Dilnawaz was playing Ludo with John and Chrissie. So I quickly dressed up and slipped out of the house and went to meet Liz at Chiswick Park. After an hour with Liz, we said goodbye and went our separate ways. As I walked home along to Chiswick High Road, a car horn bipped. I turned round. It was Mikos sitting his white Triumph Sports car, which was parked in the High Road. He waived and I ran back towards his car.

He opened the passenger door and said, 'Come in. It's so nice to see you.'

'Mr Mikos.'

'Don't call me Mr Mikos. Call me Tony.'

'Tony.'

'Would you like to come for a drive?'

'No I can't. I'm going home.'

'What time are your parents coming back?'

'Eight o clock. But I really have to be home by half past six.'

'All right. We'll just go for a drive.'

I climbed inside the vehicle and he drove off. We drove through Chiswick and out into open countryside.

'Where are you taking me?'

'To a place called Lovers Lane.'

The area was unfamiliar to me and I'd never heard of anywhere called Lovers Lane.

Mikos turned right into an unmade road and we bumped along for about half a mile. Mikos stopped the car.

'We're here. This is Lovers Lane.'

I had thought that Lovers Lane was going to be open fields. But we were in the middle of nowhere. We were amongst big trees and bushes. I saw a few other cars parked in the distance. But I didn't know why they were there. Mikos reached across me and opened the passenger door.

'Shall we get out and take a walk?'

I got out of the car. He did likewise. And we started walking. We walked – and we walked. It seemed never ending.

It was worse because thistles started going into my legs. Mikos held my hand and led me along. After twenty minutes I said to Mikos, 'We're walking a long way.'

He replied, 'We will sit down and have a little chat.'

I sensed that something was wrong.

'No. I'm a little frightened and the car is miles away.'

'It's only a little further.'

'OK Tony. Just a little further and we'll go back to the car.'

I trusted him. We walked on a little further until we came to a small clearing.

'We'll sit down here,' he said.

I thought for a moment then replied.

'No Tony. I want to go back to the car. My parents will be waiting for me.'

'Sit down!,' said Mikos, like a teacher commanding his pupil. 'I want to talk to you.'

I stood where I was.

Mikos tried to push me to the ground. It was hard ground with straw and mud and rubbish strewn about. And it was out of the bushes and away from his car. Then Mikos started pulling at my blouse.

'No! Don't do that!'

'Why not? Don't you like me?'

'Yeah! I do like you sir.'

'Then let me open your buttons.'

'What for?'

'I want to put my hands on your lovely breasts.'

I started to cry. Mikos held my arms and whispered:

'Don't be upset. All the girls like their teachers doing that.'

'I don't like it.'

'Well if you like me, you must let me do it.'

I pushed him away and started to run: leaving one of my sandals behind on the open ground. I ran for my life.

But I fell and he caught up with me. Before I could get up he was on top of me. He tore my blouse and started kissing me. Then he opened his trousers, pulled out his penis and started trying to make love to me.

I was absolutely shaken up. The straw dug into me and I was crying my eyes out. But Mikos couldn't care less. He held me down with his weight. He was between my legs but had not yet got his penis inside me. With my one free leg I drove my knee into his stomach and pushed him away. As I did so, he ejaculated, showering me with his sperm. In that moment I was up and running. This time luck was on my side.

I reached a narrow road and saw coming towards me a morris minor. I waved frantically. To my relief it slowed down and stopped beside me. Inside was a middle aged couple. They saw that I was in distress. I was crying and they saw my torn blouse. My feet were also bleeding, where one of my sandles had been left behind. The wife got out and put her cardigan on me.

'What happened?'

'A man. My teacher. He touched me and pulled me about'

'Did he rape you?'

'He nearly raped me.'

'Then we'd better take you to a police station.'

I was still very upset.

'Come and sit in the car.'

I went into the back of the morris minor and sat down.

Meanwhile the husband got out of the car and looked for

Mikos. He saw Mikos in the distance peering round looking for me. At that moment, Mikos spotted me with the couple and quickly returned to his car. We watched him drive off.

The wife said to me, 'Do you know the man, because I couldn't get his registration number?'

'Yes. He's my music teacher.'

'Then that solves the problem. We'll take you to the police station.'

I panicked.

'No! No! Please don't take me to the police station. My father will hit me for coming here.'

'You have to go to the police. If you don't, he'll do the same thing to someone else.'

The husband chipped in. Eyeing me up and down he said,

'What a beast! He's torn your blouse. How are you going to go home?'

'If you could just take me home before eight o clock... before my parents come home... everything will be all right.'

So they sat there with me until I calmed down. The wife was very kind. She got out her handbag, pulled out a comb and combed the straw out of my hair. Then the couple drove me to their house. There the the wife found me a blouse and a skirt and stockings. The clothes fitted me well enough. Then she said to me:

'Do you want us to go back and look for your other shoe?'

'No! No!'

'Well I've got a spare pair of sandals. You can take them.'

'Thank you.'

'But you must let us ring the police.'

'No! No! You don't understand,' I pleaded. 'I'm from a very orthodox family. My father will kill me because he will say 'I told you to keep away. You always wait for a chance to get out".

They continued to press me to let them phone the police. I continued to refuse. Eventually the couple relented and drove me home. It was seven thirty when I arrived and Freyni was waiting for me. She smiled at me.

'Did you have a nice time Farida?'

I forced a smile.

'Yes.'

'I can see that. You're covered up with all straws in your hair.'

Freyni paused and looked at me.

'I don't remember you wearing that blouse.'

My smile vanished and I started to sob. Freyni was sympathetic.

'What happened? Didn't the chap turn up?'

She tried to make a joke of it. I could hold my emotions no longer and grabbed Freyni as I broke down. She was very close to me and I told her everything which had happened that afternoon. As she listened her eyes widened with shock.

'Oh my God! I hope he hasn't done anything he shouldn't have.'

'What do you mean?'

'I think you'll have to see a doctor. Just in case.'

'But he didn't go right in. He just put it over me. He pulled my knickers down and was right on top of me. But I pushed him away before he could go any further into me.'

'That's a most disgusting thing. Who was it?'

'My music teacher.'

'I hope you get your next month's period. Because if you don't your father will kill you. I'll also take you to the hospital just to make sure everything's all right'

At Freyni's insistence I went with her to West Middlesex Hospital. A doctor and a nurse then examined me. They said that my virginity was still intact. After I had got dressed and was about to go home a young policeman walked in. He said that the police always had to be notified if someone was taken to hospital because of a sexual assault. The doctor told him the result of his examination.

'Do you want us to arrest him?' said the policeman.

'No. My parents mustn't know anything about it. They'd say it was all my fault and stop me going out.'

It was true. Dara was always saying that if I kept going out alone, people would think that I was a prostitute.

'All right. As you've still got your virginity, I'll put in a report to say that nothing happened.'

I smiled at him.

What Freyni hadn't noticed when she took me to hospital were the angry red marks on my neck where Mikos had bit me. To cover it up I wore a big white shirt. But Mama noticed next morning at breakfast.

'What are those marks on your neck?'

'Nothing. It's because my school uniform is very tight.'

Mama was so stupid that she believed me. But it was the bites of that animal teacher of mine. I didn't want to go to school the next day but I had to, hoping all the time that I could avoid coming face to face with Mikos. He saw me first.

'Hello Farida. I want you to come back after your classes are over. Come and see me in the music room.' He spoke to me as though nothing had happened. I turned and replied, 'No. I'm not.'

'I have to talk to you.'

'If I come to see you, I won't be coming alone.'

'Don't be silly. The evening classes will be coming in at six. So you can just come in.'

At six o clock, as the first evening students were coming

into the school, I went to the music room. Mikos was there waiting for me. I stood by the door. Mikos beckoned me into the room saying,

'Come in and shut the door. Don't be a chicken. I'm not going to do anything.'

I went in and shut the door.

'Did you go to the police?'

'No I didn't'

'That's good. Because if you had, I would just say that you went to the police because you were frightened of your father and had wanted me to sleep with you.'

'Sleep with me? I don't want to sleep with anybody. I've got my own bed.'

'You stupid cow. Don't you know what men and women do when they get married? Or even when they are not married?'

'Yes I do. My mum told me. But I don't want to sleep with you.'

'Well that's what I wanted to do to you. But you acted very badly. If you do go to the police - let me know – so that I can go to see the Principal of the College.'

'Look here! I don't want to talk to you. I don't want to see you ever again. And I don't like you anymore.'

I walked out of the music room, closing the door behind me. I never entered it again and avoided Mikos whenever I could. The following month I got my period, which meant that I could put the episode behind me.Then June told me that the policeman had contacted her wanting to see me. I met him at her house. He said that he'd like to keep in touch with me and take me out as soon as I turned sixteen. I said,

'That would be nice.'

He also showed me a collection of newspaper cuttings about girls who had been raped.

'You need to be careful who you meet when you are out,' he warned. 'I don't want anything happening to you.'

Three months later Mikos was suspended because there was a court case against him. It was said that he had raped a Turkish girl at the school in the same way that he had tried to rape me. But this time she had actually been raped. To my relief, he was convicted and sent to prison. I never saw him again.

As the case was about to come to trial, the police came to me saying that they wanted me to give evidence in the case. I refused.

After things had blown over, I sent a nice card to the couple who had rescued me, thanking them for what they had done. From my pocket money I got the wife a lovely big box of chocolates, which I posted to her at Chiswick Post Office, along with the card. I'm sure that if I wasn't for them, Mikos would have caught up with me, forced me into his car and raped me – or perhaps worse.

18 Young Love

After I finished the Tech, I went on to do a course at the Morris School of Hairdressing, in London's West End. But I failed my hairdressing examination. I told Papa that I was not interested in going anymore to College.

'So what do you want to do? Bum around? Or do you want to go back to College and do a different course?'

'I want to go out to work.'

'You can't go to work.'

I insisted. I left the hairdressing course to get a job at Woolworths in Chiswick High Road. It was from 9am to 5.30pm six days a week. At first I liked it. I was in the chocolate department and later on the ribbon counter. But I soon got fed up because I didn't like standing behind the counter for long periods when there were no customers. So during my lunch breaks I started looking for other jobs.

Waitrose was advertising for a full time supermarket cashier. I saw the manager, who asked for references. And I got the job.

I started working as a cashier and filling shelves as required. I enjoyed it but then left to earn more money at Prima Supermarket in Earls Court. Papa was concerned at me changing jobs and again suggested that I go back to college and keep re-sitting my exams until I passed them. But it was not for me.

I travelled each day from Chiswick Park Station to Prima Supermarket at Earls Court. They were even paying my fare. I enjoyed the job and would have stayed. But it ended when I got sacked.

I was always chatting to customers. It distracted me from my work. I forgot to change price-tickets: which meant that goods were sold under price. On one occasion I mis-priced Class 1 tomatoes at 2d per lb. Staff wondered at the long queue of customer for tomatoes until the reason was discovered.

That afternoon I went home crying, having been given one week's notice. Shirin was unsympathetic:

'It has been decided that you will go back to college'.

I would have none of it. There followed an argument with Papa in which I maintained my refusal to go back to college. Instead I got a job in the make-up department of Barkers Department Store, where I was a relief assistant. It was a huge store situated next door to Kensington High Street Underground Station. It was like Harrods but without the Royal connection.

I soon progressed to the ladies hat department and then to the stocking and jewellery departments. I started at 8.30am and left at 4.30am. It meant that I was home by 5.30pm. I worked Saturdays as well.

There I met a beautiful Zoroastrian girl called Noile Anklesaria. She was an air hostess with a Middle-Eastern airline and a friend of Shirin. She had recently graduated from Imperial College.

Shirin met Noile when Shirin advertised for a flat-mate, where she was living in Earls Court. Although Shirin helped manage Papa's properties, she also wanted her own independence.

Noile answered the advertisement and Shirin was pleased to discover that she was Parsee like herself. Shirin mentioned to Noile that I had a nice assistant's job at Barkers. It was where Noile was always doing her shopping.

One day Noile came up to me at the make-up counter and said, 'Are you Shirin's sister?'

It was the first time I had set eyes on her. With her white skin, dark brown hair and black eyes, she reminded me of a Japanese woman. I had no idea that she was Parsee like myself. She also looked elegant in her blue air hostess uniform. She said, 'Would you like to be an air hostess?'

I laughed.

'I have done a hairdressing course and now work as a shop assistant. And now you want me to become an air hostess?'

'Yes. You're beautiful. You should be an air hostess instead of wasting your time working behind a shop counter.'

'I don't think Papa would like it.'

'Then I'll talk to your sister to arrange a meeting with your father. I'll talk to him. He'll see what you're missing.'

Noile went on.

'Look! I'm only twenty one. But I'm already earning good money and have my own flat. Best of all, I'm seeing the world. Why don't you join the airline with me? I could fix you up.'

At that time I was growing up to be an attractive young woman. Lots of customers were coming up to my jewellery counter and chatting to me: especially men. There were men from the middle-east, Norwegians and from everywhere else in the world. I said to Noile;

'I'll have a word with Papa and give you a call.'

Noile parted with the words, 'I'll come back to see you next week on my day off. I'd like to invite you and your family to my twenty-first birthday party, which is in three weeks' time.'

Invite us she did. We all went, including Soli; Keki, Rusi; Gustad, Shirin and Dilnawaz. It was the most beautiful birthday party I had ever known. It was at a church hall in Earls Court. At the age of fifteen it was also my first experience of going to a birthday party. But something else made it extra special for me.

I was sitting with Shirin when I saw a young man looking at me. I looked back. He looked away. Then, as soon as my head was turned, I caught him looking at me again. I smiled shyly. He was tall and handsome with blue eyes and pale freckled skin.

He came over to me and asked me to dance. I replied that I had never danced in my life. He pulled a chair across and sat with me. He introduced himself saying,

'Hello. I'm Janusz. I was in the same college as Noile.'

'I'm Farida. Where are you from?'

'I'm originally from Poland. But now I'm at Imperial College, studying for my Bachelor of Science degree. Would you like to come to the pictures with me?'

I just looked at him.

'I'm sorry for asking. But how old are you?'

'Fifteen.'

Janusz looked me up and down. With my make-up, high heels and nice clothes I looked much older.

'I thought you were nearer twenty.'

Before I could answer, Noile came over and said, 'I see you have become acquainted with my classroom friend.'

I said to her in my Guajarati language, 'He's very nice. And I quite like him.'

She replied in the same language, 'If he wants to take you out, why don't you go out with him?'

She winked at me.

Rusi saw us chatting. He came over from the other table

where he and my other brothers were sitting. He broke our conversation. Speaking to Shirin he said,

'Why did you let Noile introduce Farida to that man? I don't like the look of him.' Noile replied to Rusi saying,

'He's graduating in two years' time. You must let Farida see him. She's fifteen. If he wants to take her out. So what?'

Rusi replied, 'Papa would never allow that.'

I later discovered that Noile and Janusz had met as students at Imperial College.

Janusz had wanted to take her out. But she had put him down saying, 'I want to meet and marry a rich man who can look after me. Not a penniless student.'

But she invited him to her party in the hope that he would meet someone else. Though sadly for Noile she never did get to marry her millionaire. Instead she fell in love with a married American pilot. But when his marriage broke up he didn't fall into Noile's arms. Instead he started seeing other women. It broke Noile's heart and she committed suicide at the age of twenty three.

Janusz stayed with us until the end of the party, after which we went our separate ways. Next day Janusz phoned Noile saying, 'I must see Farida.'

Noile passed the message to Shirin and the two of them agreed that Noile would pass Shirin's telephone number back to Janusz. Noile suggested I and Janusz could go out as a foursome with Shirin and her boyfriend Tom. But Shirin still had her reservations.

'I don't know,' said Shirin after she had spoken to me and raised my hopes. Shirin was always changing her mind about things and having second thoughts. I said,

'What a shame. I would love to go out with him. He is so handsome.'

Even at that young age I always went for a man's looks. The following Saturday evening, to my delight, Shirin phoned me at home.

'Meet me tonight at the Cromwell Road house at half past seven this evening. But don't say anything to Mama or Papa. I've got something to tell you.'

The Cromwell Road house was Papa's letting house which Shirin managed for him.

'What is it?' I whispered.

'I've arranged for Janusz to take you to the pictures.'

I cupped my hand over my mouth to hide my joy.

'Thank you. Thank you. Thank you so much.'

I was over the moon. I couldn't thank my sister enough.

That evening the four of us went to the Classic Cinema at Bayswater to see a movie, The Great Escape. Janusz held my hand. I trembled as no boy had ever held my hand before. Inside the cinema Janusz and I sat in the back row, whilst Shirin and Tom sat in the seats immediately in front of us.

As Janusz and I snuggled in to each other to watch the film, I felt his hand creep under my skirt and onto my knee. I gently lifted it off and told him that I preferred to hold his hand on the arm of the seat. Janusz obliged. After the movie, we all went to the Kon Tiki Coffee House Shop in St Mary Abbots Place, just off Kensington High Street. As we were sitting drinking our coffees, Janusz put his hand on my shoulder and told Shirin that he liked me a lot. He said to Shirin,

'I was dreaming about her after I saw her in Noile's party. I liked her in that turquoise blue sleeveless dress with her long hair and that fringe. I thought, *That's the girl I want to have as my girlfriend*.'

Shirin became serious. She spoke quietly to Janusz saying,

'Our father is a very orthodox chap. He would not want you

to see Farida as a boyfriend.'

Janusz was stunned. But he was not to be put off. Thinking quickly, he replied,

'In two years I'm going to finish my Bachelor of Science degree. Perhaps Farida can get engaged now at fifteen and we can then wait until she is seventeen to get married.'

Shirin said, 'No'

I saw my happiness slipping away and burst into tears. Shirin put her arms around me and relented. She said:

'Don't be distressed. You can see Janusz every Saturday.'

My tears dried up. I kissed Shirin.

I fell for Janusz that night. The rest of the world was blinkered to me without him. I thought about him all the time. It affected my work at Barkers.

I started giving the wrong change to customers and soon got sacked. Janusz was the first love in my life. I lost weight just thinking about him.

One day Janusz seemed annoyed about something.

'What is it,' I asked.

'I don't like you wearing that dress. It's got German swastikas on it.'

He pointed to the pattern on my dress.

I didn't understand what he was talking about. To me it was just a traditional Indian design. Janusz explained.

'When I was only four years old I escaped with my father from a German concentration camp. But my mother didn't make it. My father had to put his hand over my mouth to prevent me screaming out as we watched her being shot.'

I didn't wear that dress again.

I saw Janusz every Saturday evening for the next nine months. Not alone of course. We were always chaperoned by Shirin and her boyfriend Tom. It did not matter to me. We were together. But it mattered to Janusz.

One Saturday evening we were sitting in the Kon Tiki Coffee Shop when Janusz had some bad news for me. Shirin and Tom were at the counter ordering coffees and pastries. Janusz and I were alone.

'I'm going to Torquay to do a course,' he said.

I thought about it. Then replied:

'Why can't you do it in London?'

'I can't. I've been sent by the Government to do it in Torquay.'

For the first time in our relationship I became jealous. I pushed my food away and refused to speak.

Janusz was upset at my reaction. In frustration he said to me,

'Why can't I ever see you without your sister coming along as a chaperone?'

I couldn't understand the problem.

'At least we can see each other.'

.'I want more than 'seeing'. I want to take you out by myself. Like to a party.'

He looked at me and held my hand. 'And there's something else.'

'What's that?'

Janusz took a deep breath.

'I want to sleep with you.'

His face reddened as he saw the shock on my face.

'You can't do that.'

Janusz then recited to me the lines he had memorised:

'I've been seeing you for nine months. If you love me you must let me sleep with you.'

'I'm sorry. But I can't do that.'

There was nothing more to say. We sat together in glum

silence.

Shirin and Tom came over with the coffees and the eats. Janusz and I both forced smiles.

'Janusz is going to Torquay to do a Government course,' I said matter of factly.

'How exciting!' said Shirin. 'Tell us more about it.'

I took little part in the subsequent conversation and worked hard to hide my anxiety until Janusz pecked me on the cheek and left us. Tom left at the same time and I went home with Shirin.

Inside the house, I said nothing to anybody and went straight up to my room.

'What's wrong with Farida?,' said Mama.

'Young love,' laughed Shirin.

Two months later Janusz went off to Torquay. Before doing so he made one last attempt to get me into his bed.

One afternoon after work he met me alone at the Kon Tiki. He brought a bunch of red roses for me. Over coffee he said to me.

'You know I don't have to go to Torquay. I could stay here with you. Which is what I want to do. Because I love you'

I reached across the table and held his hand.

'And I love you.'

Janusz smiled.

'Then you can take an afternoon off from work and come over to my flat. It's where I live with my father. I have my own bedsit where we can be alone together.'

I took my hand away.

'I'm sorry. I couldn't do that.'

'Then I'll be going to Torquay. But I'll be keeping in touch. And maybe...'

The following week Janusz took the train to Torquay. I

stood with Shirin and Tom as we saw him off at Paddington Station.

Three days later I got my first letter from Janusz telling me about his journey to Torquay and how much he missed me. I wrote back saying how much I missed him and wanted him to come back to London. The letters came every week. Sometimes twice a week. Often these letters came with presents, such as lovely bracelets. It made me miss him even more.

I became distressed when Janusz began ringing Shirin and I was having to go to her house at Earls Court to receive his calls. During those telephone calls Shirin was good enough to leave the room, quietly shutting the door behind her as I sat huddled over the telephone. Janusz and I shared our emotions with each other. But one morning our love affair came to an abrupt halt.

Papa received a surprise telephone call. It was from Janusz's father. It was a surprise because Papa could not even recall who Janusz was, having met him only once many months previously at Noile's birthday party. And he had never seen or spoken to Janusz's father.

But Janusz's father had found all my love letters to Janusz. From my letters he was able to trace Papa's telephone number and address from the GPO Phone Directory. He told Papa that Janusz had failed his exams. And it was all because of me interfering with his studies. He told Papa that I was trash.

Papa became angry. He rounded on Janusz's father, shouting,

'I would not let my daughter spit at your son. My daughter is a diamond to me. You say that my daughter is trash. I think your son is trash. My daughter is innocent. I don't believe she sees your son.'

'If you don't believe me, I will post all Farida's love letters back to you.'

As yet I knew nothing about that telephone conversation. But I was still very distressed and missing Janusz. In the meantime I received a letter from Janusz saying that he had failed his exams and that he wanted to meet me.

I took half a day off work and was waiting for him at Charing Cross Station when he arrived. Mama had wondered why I had looked so happy when I returned home from work at lunchtime to get dressed up. I lied that I was going to be attending a buyers' function at Pontings Department Store, where I was then working and that we had all been told to go home to get dressed.

Again Mama believed me and I made my get away. As I saw Janusz getting out of the train I ran towards him and we fell into each other's arms. I had my first passionate kiss.

I knew that Janusz had previously spoken to Shirin saying that he wanted to get engaged to me and that he intended to retake his examinations in London. Shirin had then suggested to Mama that we could get engaged as Janusz was an educated man who had said that he intended to settle in Switzerland. Mama reminded Shirin that she herself had married Papa at the age of sixteen. Before Mama could mention anything to Papa, the letters arrived through the post.

Papa took the bundle of correspondence and sat in the dining room. As soon as Papa discovered what they were he called Mama into the dining room. Both of them then read the letters. Mama then told Papa about her conversation with Shirin concerning Janusz's wish to marry me. Whilst all this was going on I was happily doing my work at Pontings Department Store. But when I got home that evening, the atmosphere was frosty. Papa ignored me as I came through the door and walked into the sitting room.

I went upstairs to change into something more casual. I put my slippers on and came down to the kitchen to have my evening meal. Mama looked at me sadly. She said softly,

'Papa wants to talk to you in the sitting room.'

The way she said it made me very upset.

'Why? What is it about?'

Mama whispered,

'It's the love letters you have written. How could you write those letters? You didn't tell me you were going out with Shirn and meeting that chap.'

'He's a college student. Not a barrow boy.'

Mama went on,

'Janusz's father was very rude to Papa about you.'

My appetite faded away with shock. I put down my cutlery and made my way slowly to the sitting room and went inside.

Papa stood glaring at me. There was no small talk. Instead he fired questions at me, scarcely giving me time to answer.

'Where did you meet this chap? How long have you seen him? Who did you see him with?'

'Shirin.'

'Shirin! I'm going to deal with her. Where has she been taking you?'

'We only went to the pictures. Papa! ......This is England. ..... And I'm fifteen and a half.'

Papa paused.

'That trash....... You know what is trash?'

I nodded.

'I'm going to hit you for that.'

I remained standing and refused to flinch as Papa slapped me hard across the face. Then he slapped me again – and again – left and right – until I started to cry. Then he got his belt and struck me several times across the hips. Mama came in and intervened.

'Enough! Jehangir! Enough! She has now paid for what she's done. Now we must do something.'

I recovered my composure and said to Papa,

'I'm going to run away now, if you're going to keep doing that.'

'Run away? I'm going to make you a ward of court. You're not going to work anymore while you are up to this.'

I could not believe what I was hearing. I was so upset. Mama said to Papa,

'I married you at sixteen. Why can't we sit down with Shirin and talk about.......'

'Shut up! And keep out of it!'

Mama, poor thing, walked back to the kitchen – whilst I started to cry.

'Go up to your room!' said Papa.

Papa picked up the phone and started dialling a number. From my room I overheard the Papa and Janusz's father discussing me. I quietly picked up an extension phone and listened to the conversation. It became increasingly angry.

Papa said to Janusz's father,

'Look here! She's only fifteen and a half. She is innocent. Your son has seen the world. My girl has never been out with a man and is still a virgin.'

'Is she a virgin? I don't know about that.'

'I'll sue you for that. Because I know she is. She never had anything to do with your son. She only fell in love with him. And that's natural. And I'm going to put a stop to it.'

Papa went on:

'You can take your trash son. If I hear again from you on the telephone saying my daughter has done this ..... or my daughter has done that .....I will send you a solicitor's letter.

You Polish refugee. I'll have you in court.'

'You calling me a Polish refugee?'

'Yes… We people have character. You people are gutter refugees. I would never give my daughter to a refugee's son.'

With that Janusz's father hung up and we heard from him no more. No-one could beat my father when it came to shouting insults. I was crying my eyes out as Papa was arguing with that chap. To make matters worse, I couldn't find my letters. It worried me. I was sure that Papa had put them in his safe but I had no idea how to open it. I looked everywhere around the house for a key but couldn't find one.

Then Mama became ill and had to go to Hammersmith Hospital for a hysterectomy operation. Every evening on my way home from Kensington High Street I would break my journey at Hammersmith and take her fruit, flowers and boxes of chocolates. She would sit with me in the hospital. She was crying with pain from the operation and I did my best to comfort her. But there was one question which, through her tears, I needed Mama to answer:

'Mama. I'm sorry to ask you. But could you do me a favour? I want those letters back. Please let me know where I can find them.'

I started to sob and Mama wiped my tears:

'Don't cry Farida. I'll tell you. They're in Papa's safe. If you go to my cupboard you'll find a handbag. It's on the left hand side of the first shelf. Inside the handbag is the key to Papa's safe. You take the key. And only open the safe when Papa is sleeping or in the garden. Take all your letters and destroy them.'

I did as Mama suggested and replaced the key in the handbag. It was more than a month later, after Mama had recovered from her operation, that Papa was going through his safe.

'Mehera! Where are those letters?'

Mama quickly replied, 'I tore them up.'

'I was keeping them as evidence to see what Farida had written to that Janusz boy.'

Hearing the name Janusz felt like a knife to my stomach. I still missed him so much. I was losing weight.

About six months later I saw Janusz again. It broke me up.

He was with an Indian girl about the same age as myself. He had his arm around her. Neither of them saw the young girl in the distance crying into her handkerchief. That girl was me. As I turned away, I felt a gentle hand on my shoulder. It was an elderly lady. She smiled and said,

'Why are you crying my dear?'

I pointed at the couple in the distance and said,

'It's him. He was my boyfriend. My father and his father had a fierce argument about our relationship. And now he's found somebody else. I feel so alone.'

'I know how you feel. It happened to me when I was a young woman. But I had to come to terms with it and move on with my life. Like you, I am alone. I never married. But you will find somebody else. No man is worth your tear.'

I forced a smile.

'Come and have a coffee with me.'

I did.

It was the following year when I was sixteen that Shirin met her new boyfriend George. We were at Tiffanies Dance Hall. Shirin was sitting alone looking after the handbags whilst the rest of us were on the dance floor.

She noticed a tall handsome teddy boy casting shy glances across to her. He looked sad. Shirin smiled back to him. Having plucked up courage, the teddy boy came over to Shirin.

'Would you like to dance?'

'I'm sorry but I'm looking after these belongings.'

'Then can I stay and talk to you? I'm George by the way.'

'Please do.'

George pulled up a chair. He explained that he had just split from his girlfriend Elaine. Shirin was in the same position, as it was almost three months since she and Tom had last seen each other and she had been told that Tom had been going out with somebody else.

We came back off the dance-floor to find this teddy boy sitting with us. And he stayed with us for the rest of the evening.

When it was time to go, George and Shirin swapped telephone numbers. A month later they got engaged.

19 My Lovely Policeman

The following year at Pontings I met my new friend Mary. She was a work colleague who was about my age and from Ireland. She had cropped hair like a tom boy. We started going out together. Often we went to the pictures. At other times we went to Hammersmith Palais, which had a nice little ballroom. But we would always leave the Palais at 9.30pm so that I could be back home by 10pm sharp. Under my mother's influence, Papa was gradually allowing me more freedom.

'You can go out only with Mary and only until 10 o'clock,' he said, adding,

'But you will not go with any man. Or I will break your legs. Do you promise?'

I promised. It opened up my life.

I began to make lots of new friends at Pontings. Sometimes they would try to phone me at home. But Keki was always first to pick up the receiver. If the caller was a man, Keki would snap back saying,

'No. She's not coming out,' and bang the receiver down.

If it was a girl he would say,

'You'll have to come here and take her. She's not going with any blokes.'

It brought home to me the fact that I still had no real freedom. It also affected the way my friends reacted to me. They began to think of me and my family as being very orthodox. The phone calls stopped. It made me very distressed.

One day as I had just come out of Pontings to go home, a handsome young policeman caught my eye. I was at the bus stop when I saw him. He winked at me. I looked back at him and smiled.

Then I saw him walking over towards me. My face went red like a tomato. Then he spoke:

'Hello! Do you work here?'

'Yes. I work at Pontings.'

'What department? Maybe I'll come and see you when I'm off duty.'

'I'd like to see you – but remember that I'll be working.'

Stupidly I only thought that he wanted to see me when I was working. But he was so handsome that I couldn't get him out of my mind. He was about six feet tall, slim and with blue eyes. I thought, 'Oh my God. Isn't he handsome? I'd like to have a boyfriend like that.'

After two days I saw him again outside Pontings. I told him where I worked and said innocently,

'When will you see me then?'

'I'm off sometime next week. Could I take you for lunch?'

I told him that my lunch time was between 1pm and 2pm. He said,

'Then I'll try to be there at One. By the way I'm Mike'

'And I'm Farida.'

The next week at Pontings I had a nice surprise. Mike arrived dead at 1pm to take me to lunch. He was in his police cadet uniform but without his cap on. We walked to a Wimpey. As we walked, he told me that he was nineteen.

As we arrived at the Wimpey he squeezed my hand. I started trembling. He then asked:

'Can I take you to the pictures?

'Sorry. But I have to go home'

'What!' he said. 'How old are you?'

'Nearly sixteen.'

'What a shame,' he said. 'Can't you come out with me to the pictures tonight? We'll go to the Odeon at Kensington.'

'No. I can't.'

His face dropped.

'Can't you phone your mum and dad up?'

'You don't know my mum and dad. They're a bit old fashioned.'

'So you just want to see me at lunchtime. That's no good to me.'

'I don't mind seeing you at lunchtime. Because my parents don't know I'm seeing you.'

It was so frustrating for both of us. Because I wanted to go the pictures with Mike. I explained the situation to Mary. She agreed to come and collect me from my home.

One evening Mary came home from work with me and I told Mama that I was going out with her.

'Where are you going with Mary?' she asked.

'We're going window shopping.'

'Window shopping? I've never heard of window shopping. Anyway I'll let you go.'

Mary and left the house. I had arranged to meet Mike at eight o'clock at the Wimpey. As we approached we saw him waiting. Mary waived me goodbye. I went to the cinema with Mike.

As the lights went up for the interval I squeezed his hand and said,

'Mike. I've enjoyed being with you. But I've got to go now.'

'I don't understand. I thought that we had the whole evening together.'

'I know. But I have to be back home by ten.'

'Ok. Then I'll come with you.'

'Don't you want to watch Guns of Naverone?'

'On my own?'

'Look Farida. I need to tell your father how much I like you. Because I can't carry on like this.'

But Mike never had a chance to have that conversation with Papa. We met several times to go to the cinema. On each occasion the protocol was the same. Mary would come to my house to collect me. I would go to the Kensington Odeon with Mike. And we would leave half way through. We never saw the main feature. But eventually I had to give up Mike.

One evening I knew that Rusi had seen me in the cinema sitting with Mike. As soon as the lights came up for the interval, I ducked down and made my way towards the Ladies at the back of the cinema. I stayed there until the lights went down for the second half. Mike wondered what was happening. I could see him looking round for me. Eventually he got up and walked towards the foyer.

From the doorway of the Ladies toilets, I beckoned and hissed his name. Mike caught my eye. He looked behind him and then walked over to me with a puzzled expression on his face. 'Why are you calling me to the Ladies toilets?'

'It's my brother,' I whispered. 'He's here with his English girlfriend. We've got to leave.'

'Why do we need to leave? It's a good film. I want to see it.'

'Well I'll be going anyway.'

'Ok. I'll come with you.'

We crept out of the cinema and went across the road for a

Wimpey. As he finished a mouthful, Mike said:

'Can't you tell your father that this is England and that you should have a boyfriend?'

'No I can't. It's OK for English girls. But for us it's very difficult.'

'I'm sure your family won't mind if I see you.'

I laughed at his stupidity.

'My brothers and my father will kick you out as soon as they see you.'

Mike was not to be put off.

'I'll come and talk to them. I just want you to be my girlfriend.'

'Girlfriend is no good. My father expects me to meet someone to get married.'

He touched my arm.

'If I have a girlfriend like you, I'll want to marry her.'

We finished our Wimpy and went our separate ways. Over the course of the next few days I thought about Mike's offer to speak to Papa. The more I thought about it the sweeter the idea became. I liked Mike and began to imagine myself as the new Mrs Wilson. He had a police career ahead of him. We would get a nice little house together and bring up a family.

What could be wrong with that? And marriage to Mike would also be my escape route to freedom. I was sure that when Papa met Mike in his police uniform he would welcome him into our family. My work colleagues noticed the change in me.

'You're looking happy,' they commented.

The next week Mike came to see me at my work. We went to the same Wimpy bar for lunch.

Over a knickerbocker glory I coached Mike on what he should tell Papa when he saw him. In typical police style Mike took down notes of my instructions. Then it was time to say 'goodbye' as I looked at my watch and hurried back to work.

That evening after work I met Mary and we went to see West Side Story. At 10am I returned home.

Papa opened the door. He was not smiling.

'Can you come in?' he said, wagging his finger. I entered.

'Your brother says that he saw you with somebody in uniform.'

'That's rubbish.'

'You're lying. I can see it on your face.'

He paused.

'Either you tell me who it was or I will stop you going out to work. I'll make you a ward of court.'

I said nothing.

Papa forced a smile to put me at my ease.

'If you are seeing someone, I don't mind,' he lied. 'When I see him I'll decide myself about him. Because you are still growing up.'

I relaxed and returned his smile.

'He's a lovely police cadet called Mike.'

Papa's smile fell away.

'Police cadet? Where did you meet him?'

'When I was coming out of Pontings to go home. I've been seeing him for about eight weeks.'

'Hmmm! About the same time you've been going out with Mary. Does Mama know about this?'

'Yes. Mary also has a friend, and we go out as a foursome.'

Then came the killer blow.

'Well you're not going to be seeing that Mike anymore. Or I'm going to make you finish the Ponting job.'

I saw Mike one last time. He wondered why I was so tearful. Then I broke the sad news that I would not be seeing him anymore. He soon realised I was serious. I searched for something to salvage from our relationship and said,

'You could perhaps wait until I'm twenty one.'

Mike glanced at me in irritation.

'Wait till you're twenty one? You must be joking. I'm not going to wait until you're twenty one.'

'Then it's too bad if you don't want to wait.'

'So what will I do until you're twenty one?'

'We could still meet at lunchtimes and go to the Wimpey.'

'I'm not going to do that. I want you to be my girlfriend.'

'That's impossible.'

And that was the end of our relationship.

20 Jock

In October 1961 Shirin married George at Hammersmith Register Office. They had been together for a year. I was now sixteen and went to the wedding dressed in a pink sari. Dilnawaz was dressed in white. The whole family was there except for Papa. He didn't think that George was good enough to marry his daughter. He thought him uneducated and with little prospect.

George was a policeman at Hammersmith Police Station. He only became a teddy boy when he was off duty. He was above six foot and had a deep voice, a lot like Blakey in the 1970's sit-com On the Buses. But without the moustache.

If Papa had his doubts about George, the rest of us loved him. Shirin was the shrewd business woman who pledged jewellery to obtain bank loans to buy properties in need of renovation. George was handy with a paint brush. He was happy to let Shirin make the business decisions and happiest of all when sitting in an armchair smoking his pipe after a hard day's work.

Shirin bought the properties. George did them up. Then Shirin found the tenants. Shortly after they got married, Shirin persuaded George to give up his job as a policeman so that he had more time to work on the properties and then manage them after they had been done up and let. The strategy worked.

Within a few years the couple owned a portfolio of properties across West London which they let out. They were now living in a four storey house by the river near Hammersmith Bridge and were both millionaires. If only I could have married somebody like George. But I was still only judging men on their looks.

Before Shirin's wedding took place I had made her promise to throw her wedding bouquet towards me when they came out of the Register Office. She did. I caught it.

I was happy, thinking that I was also going to get married, even though I had no boyfriend. It had been a long and lonely three months for me. Not only had I lost Mike, Papa had also banned me from going out with Mary. But one afternoon Mama let me go out with her.

I explained to Mama that I already knew about the birds and the bees. – but that on this afternoon it was Mary's sister's birthday and that she had invited some friends to her house for tea.

'I'm sure there will also be some boys there,' said Mama.

'Don't worry. I'll be all right.'

But I went instead with Mary and her sister Nancy to Hammersmith Palais. But it was nothing like before when I had been to Hammersmith Palais with Shirin.

The place was packed with teddy boys of all shapes and sizes, each with their immaculate quiff hairstyles, drainpipe trousers, bootlace ties, brothel creepers, and their long jackets with padded shoulders and velvet collars.

There were teds standing in groups outside the dancehall holding drinks. From the hall itself came the pounding rock n roll beat of a five piece band playing Johnny be Good. Inside the dancehall, teddy boys danced. Some were with their girlfriends.

Others danced alone, impressing the audience with their steps.

My eyes lit up. What a lovely time I was having in London. I was sitting in the dancehall with Mary and Nancy when a tall extremely handsome teddy boy caught my eye as he walked into the room. He had a turned up nose and very good features. He saw me looking at him and winked at me with his blue eyes. I smiled back and then turned my head away in embarrassment as he walked across to the bar.

After a couple of drinks and some Dutch courage, the ted walked across to me and asked me to dance. I accepted and went with him onto the dance floor.

It was the first time I had danced to rock'n'roll but I let him sweep me around the dance floor to Elvis Presley's Hound Dog. Then it was finished.

'By the way, I'm Jock,' he said as we paused for the next dance.

I noticed his Scottish accent.

'And I'm Farida. Do you have a girlfriend?'

'No I haven't. I've just come down from Scotland.'

Then the band started up again playing Buddy Holly's Peggy Sue. Jock took my hand and we danced along – and again and again – to Cliff Richard; Little Richard and many others. As I was whisked around the floor I saw another teddy boy dance with Mary and another with Nancy.

During our snatches of conversation Jock told me that he was 24 years old. I told him that I was sixteen. Then he asked the inevitable question,

'When can I see you again?'

To which I had to reply, 'I'm sorry but I can't see you.'

Jock's face dropped.

'Please I must see you. I'm working in London.'

'What work do you do?'

'I'm a carpenter.'

'Oh!'

Jock laughed.

'Jesus Christ was a carpenter. So don't think bad about carpenters.'

Mary waved to me. I waived back.

'That's my friend Mary. And the girl sitting next to her is her sister Nancy. We've come here for Nancy's birthday.'

'Then wish her happy birthday from me.'

We both laughed.

'Tomorrow I'm going down to Brighton to look for a job. But I'll be coming back next week. Can I contact you?'

I scribbled down Mary's phone number and gave it to him, saying,

'Mary will give me the message.'

'What?'

'Really. I can't come out with you because of my brothers.'

Jock smiled knowingly.

'I think you are married. I think you want to have a fling with me. I know that in the east, girls get married at a very young age. How old are you? 20?'

I smiled back.

'I look older than you think because of my make-up and because of my dress.'

'I never thought that your family could be so strict.'

The outcome was that we agreed to meet the following Tuesday. Jock put off his trip to Brighton by a few days.

That Tuesday was the buyers' meeting at Pontings where I still worked. All staff had to stay late. When I eventually left at 7.30pm, I saw Jock waiting for me outside, wrapped up in a duffle coat. We went to the Hammersmith Odeon and saw a lovely German movie. When we sat down, Jock put his coat across my legs.

I then felt something like a mouse running across my knees. It was Jock's hand. It was running everywhere. I took it off.

'Spoilsport.' said Jock. 'I just wanted to feel you. I love that tight skirt you're wearing.'

I next met Jock outside Hammersmith Palais. Mary had arranged it for me. Mary came to my house at around 7pm after I had home from work. We took a bus to Hammersmith. Mary waited with me outside the Palais for that good looking scum called Jock. We were both frozen as we saw Jock arrive more than ten minutes later with a paper folded under his arm. He was wearing the same duffle coat. Mary smelt the beer on his breath.

'He's drunk,' she whispered.

'Hi girls! Sorry I'm late. I've been celebrating with my friend Sean. He's leaving his job to go to Australia.'

Mary then left and caught a bus to see her sister. As soon as she had gone, Jock unfolded the newspaper and looked at the entertainment page to see what's on. He pointed to something on the page.

'We'll go to a movie. There's Guns of Naverone at the Hammersmith Odeon. Do you fancy seeing that?'

'Yes.'

Although for me it was not so much 'fancy' as to be over the moon to be going out with the handsome hunk standing next to me. I didn't mention that I had already seen it with Mike.

He was scruffier than when we had gone to see the German film because he had just come out of the pub and was still in his working clothes. He hadn't had a chance to get dressed up. He was also a little bit tipsy as he said that he had spent the whole afternoon in the pub, 'celebrating' with his friends.

Although we were out of the cinema by ten thirty, I was nervous about how my family would react when I got home. We waited at the bus stop for about twenty minutes. No bus came. Fortunately a black cab came past and Jock hailed it. We jumped inside and Jock arranged for the cab to drop me off as we approached my house.

'I'd like to see you again,' said Jock, as the cab parked to let me out.

'I don't know what's going to happen when I get home,' I replied. 'But please ring Mary up. I will leave a message with Mary as to when I can see you again.'

'That's fine. I'm sorry that I was a bit tipsy. But it was only because my friend was going to Australia'

Already I had begun to have my doubts about Jock. It was obvious that he liked his drink. But my doubts vanished when Jock kissed me goodnight outside the taxi. After the taxi had dropped me off, it continued to Chiswick Park Station, where Jock got out and caught the train back to his bed-sit at Victoria where he lived with his friends. I arrived home alone. Rusi opened the door.

'It's twenty to ten. What happened?'

'We missed the bus. Mary and I.'

'Well you'd better go in the sitting room and talk to your father. Explain to him. Because you are coming later and later.'

I went into the sitting room, where Papa was seated in an armchair. He looked at me.

'What is the excuse for being late?'

'We went to the Wimpey for something to eat.'

'Didn't you eat here before you went out?'

'Yes I did. But I was still hungry. I decided to have something around nine to nine thirty.'

'If you're going to start coming home late, perhaps it's best if I stop you going out altogether.'

The conversation finished on that note.

The following Monday when I went back to work, Mary said that Jock had phoned up that Sunday. She gave me a telephone number.

'Could you phone this number at one-thirty this afternoon. It's the telephone box next to the building site where Jock is working. He will be inside the phone box waiting.'

During my lunch break I went to the red telephone box nearest my work. It was empty. I went inside and waited, looking at my watch. At exactly one thirty I dialled the call. I waited as the numbers slowly clicked through. There was another moment's silence as I waited for the ring-tone and for Jock to pick it up.

Line engaged.

My heart sank. I thought to myself, 'What a shame. I won't be able to talk to him.'

My heart beating, I waited a few minutes until I noticed a fat middle aged lady standing outside the box and waiting to go in. She glanced at her watch and peered through the glass to see what I was doing. I dialled the number again. It was my last chance.

This time I got the ring-tone and almost immediately the receiver was picked up. I heard a broad Scottish accent.

'Hi Free!'

I relaxed. Jock had started calling me Free.

'Can I see you Tuesday?'.

It was a short telephone conversation. We arranged to meet at seven o'clock on Tuesday outside the Palais. Then the money ran out.

The next Tuesday I went home early from work so that I could get ready to go out. Jock had said that we would go out to get something to eat. But Mama – as usual – had kept food ready for me. I politely refused saying,

'No thanks. I've decided to eat with Mary.'

At Mama's insistence I had a little nibble, and then washed, dressed and went out. She called after me saying:

'What energy you've got. You come here, eat and want to go out.'

I said, 'In this country we've all got energy to go out. We can't stay here and watch TV.'

Mama looked at me and said;

'You be careful because I think that I can see something in your face. What you are up to I don't know. But if Papa finds out he'll break every bone in your body.'

She just warned me. But I wasn't listening.

I put on perfume and started getting ready. I could see that Mama didn't like it.

I had bought myself a nice new check skirt with a white blouse to see Jock. I was over the moon with his looks. I travelled to Hammersmith as arranged. As the bus rolled to a halt. I saw through the window that he was waiting for me outside the dance-hall. Puffing a roll up, he walked backwards and forwards like a tiger in a cage. He wore an ordinary white shirt with a tie and trouser and the same duffle coat. His first words on seeing me were,

'Shall we go dancing?'

'Yes. All right.'

'Fine. We'll go dancing tonight.'

He ordered chips for both of us from the upstairs bar. Then the dancing started and we went into the dance hall. After around two hours I looked at my watch, It said ten o'clock. The music was still in full swing. I touched Jock's arm.

'I've got to go to work tomorrow morning.'

Jock took the hint and walked me to the bus stop. He got on to the bus with me and got out with me at my stop. We then had a quick kiss and cuddle under a tree. Then he left. He said, 'I'll see you on Saturday.'

The following Saturday I made the same arrangement with Mary.

She came to my house at five o'clock and said:

'Farida and I are going to the pictures.'

Papa said to Mary, 'What picture are you going to see?'

'We haven't decided.'

'Then look in the local paper. Let me know what time the picture is starting and what time I will expect Farida back.'

Mary gazed at the entertainments page and picked a film at random.

'That one. Guns of Navarone. After the film we're going to the Wimpey Bar.'

'No.No!' replied Papa, 'I don't want my daughter gallivanting about in the night time.' Then turning to me, he said:

'After the picture, you're coming straight home.'

Again I had this unhappiness in my heart. Again I wished I could be free. But little did I know that within nine months I would get the freedom I craved. Only later would I discover that that this freedom was a false illusion. In short it was in March 1962 that Papa found about me and Jock. And by June 1962 it didn't matter anymore because we were married. There was no engagement. Here is how it happened.

I had been going out with Jock twice a week: every Tuesday and Saturday. The arrangement was always the same. Sometimes we went to the Palais. More often we went to the pictures. One Saturday we went to see a movie at the Regal, Hammersmith.

Rusi was also there with his friends from the British School of Motoring, where he worked as a driving instructor. He saw me.

In the interval Jock got out of his seat went to the foyer to get some ice cream. A minute later, Rusi saw me sitting alone and came over. He said to me,

'What are you doing?'

'I'm bursting for a pee. I'm just about to go to the Ladies'. As I got out of my seat, Rusi held my arm.

'I want to introduce you to my friends.' He paused. Then added,

'Who are you with?'

'I came with Mary. We get a better view from the back seat.'

'That's good. We'll come and join you.'

'I'll be back in a minute.'

I pretended that I was going to the toilet and looked for Jock. To my relief he had not reappeared. The lights dimmed and the curtains opened for the second part of the performance. Meanwhile I saw Jock entering the auditorium through the doors at the back. I crept up to him and grabbed him by the arm and led him outside.

Jock couldn't understand why I didn't want to stay for the rest of this lovely movie. I whispered to him and the words tumbled out of my mouth,

'One of my brothers is here. He's very strict. And he is going to cause trouble with my father. He's in here with his friends. And I don't want any trouble. We'll have to see this movie again. Somewhere else.'

The message sunk in.

'Come on. I'll take you home.'

We went to a coffee bar. Then Jock left me near my house to face the music. I got home before Rusi and crept up to my room to change. My lipstick was all smudged from kissing Jock. Then Rusi arrived. He spoke to Papa, and I overheard the conversation.

'I was at the Regal this evening with a couple of my work friends. Farida was there.'

'She went out with Mary to see a film.'

'Yes. That's what she told me. But there was something very fishy.'

Rusi paused. Then he continued.

'When I saw Farida during the interval, she jumped out of her seat and said that she was going to the Ladies to see Mary.'

My heart was in my mouth. Then the phone rang. Rusi answered it and the earlier conversation was forgotten.

After we had been going out for three months, Jock asked me if he could see me more often than the Tuesdays and Saturdays to which we had become accustomed.

'I can't,' was my sad reply. 'You know why.'

'If I had the money I would marry you.'

When I heard him say that I thought to myself, 'This is the only time I could hook him and get out of the house.' I nodded my head in encouragement. Jock continued.

'I am a carpenter and share a bed-sit with a couple of Irish lads. But I don't have enough money. Whatever I earn – I drink - because I am a bachelor. But I would like to marry a nice person like you.'

I had to be honest with him.

'I really like you so much Jock. And I wish I could see you often. But my father is a little bit strict. And I don't think he would let me go out with you.'

It was after that heart-to-heart that our relationship became that little bit more intense.

I never went to Jock's bedsit. Instead we always went to an alleyway near Hammersmith Station. The first time I felt awkward as Jock opened the buttons on my blouse, wandering his hands on my breasts and kissing me. But my inhibitions soon fled and I immersed myself into the passion of the moment. Being groped in a dark deserted alleyway was my first experience of love. It seemed the natural thing to do. During one groping session, I squinted as light was shone in my eyes.

'What are you doing here?'

It was a middle aged policeman with a torch.

'We're only kissing officer,' I replied.

'Well move along then.'

One day Shirin told me she wanted someone to babysit her small child as she and George were going to the pictures. She knew I was seeing Jock, as I had secretly introduced him to her. One day Papa also found out and I knew that there would again be trouble. But this time I was determined to stand up for myself.

I told Mama the truth that I was seeing Jock. I also told her that I was sixteen and that if they did not let me continue seeing Jock, I would run away and live with my friend Liz.

She had previously told me that I could stay with her and her sister if my family was too strict for me to go out.

Mama knew that I was serious. She spoke quietly to Papa saying:

'He's a very nice chap. A carpenter. And if you don't let her see him she will just go.'

One day Papa said to Mama:

'I want you to meet this Jock. I hear that he's a very nice countryman. Apparently he's twenty four years old and earns a lot of money.'

In fact I had lied to Mama about the money. I hadn't told her that Jock was drinking all his money. Papa suggested that I invite Jock home one lunchtime when my brothers were at work. Papa made it clear that he was not happy and said to me,

'If I don't like him, you are not going out with him. And if you do, I'll make you a ward of court.'

I met Jock at Chiswick Park Station. His first words were,

'How come you look so much older now?'

'I've got make up on.'

I thought that if I looked older, Jock would keep going out with me.

He walked with me to the house. Papa opened the door and took Jock into the sitting room. Then the interrogation began.

Papa's first question was:

'How long have you been in London?'

Before Jock could answer.

'How much do you earn?'

'Twenty five pounds a week.'

'What work do you do?'

'I'm a carpenter.'

Jock soon tired of the questions and said bluntly to Papa.

'I'd like to go out with Farida.'

Papa replied:

'We don't do that kind of thing. If you want to go out with her, you must have the intention of marrying her within a few months.'

'But I've got no money.'

Papa's eyes widened. He took a deep breath before replying.

'You say you have no money?'

Jock said hastily:

'In this country we save up for years to buy a house and everything.'

Papa became angry.

'This is nonsense. Years and years? She can't wait years and years.'

Papa paused. Whilst I held my breath. Then I saw him relax.

'If you can't manage financially, I'll give you a flat. But only if your intentions are clear. She has been a real pain for us.'

'What do you mean?'

'Well – we don't want her coming into trouble or something. You can see her. Then we will sort out the wedding date. I'll give you a very cheap flat in Chiswick or Kensington.'

Jock's face broke into a grin at this welcome news. Mine did to.

'That's good. That's very good.'

Then Mama came into the room with tea and cakes. She was over the moon at the news.

For the rest of the afternoon Jock got on fine with my parents. Papa thought he was a bit of a country chap. He looked nice all dressed up. But Papa still expressed one reservation.

'I don't like her marrying someone in building work. Because of all the drinking.'

'No.No.No!' said Jock, 'I only have the odd one or two pints with my friends.'

If only that were true, I thought to myself.

It was February 1962 when I introduced Jock to my family. Towards the end of that month, Jock moved back to Scotland. But he continued travelling back to London to meet me every Tuesday and Saturday at around 5.30pm. It must have been exhausting for him. But if my parents had taken a shine to Jock, the same was not true of my brothers. They didn't like Jock at all.

In the meantime Papa got us a one bedroom flat in Kensington High Street. It was newly furnished. Papa got us bedroom furniture as a wedding present. Our wedding date was now fixed for 19th June 1962 at Caxton Hall.

One Saturday evening, Shirin asked me to babysit her daughter Brenda whilst she and George went to the Regal

Cinema at Hammersmith. They left Jock and me in their flat. Brenda was asleep in her cot. We watched TV together on the sofa.

I saw Jock produce something from his pocket. It was a small packet of Durex. Although up till then I had no idea what it was.

We snuggled closer and I felt Jock's hands wandering over my thighs. At that time there were no tights. Women wore suspenders.

Jock commented on my nice white thighs. Then he said to me:

'Please let me touch you.'

'No. Not until we are married.'

'I will marry you. But I don't want to wait until June to sleep with you. Just now and again.'

Then the threat.

'Or I will get fed up. And then I might not want to marry you at all. But just let me be the first person.'

I nodded my consent.

Jock then lay me on some smelly army blankets that were in the flat and took my virginity. It was painful and I was in tears.

The sex lasted about ten minutes. I started to smooth down my clothes whilst Jock pulled up his trousers. As we were doing this he laughed saying,

'I'm so glad I'm the first one.'

It was whilst we were still half dressed that the door opened and in walked Shirin.

'Oh!' she said in my language, putting her hand to her mouth. Then having recovered her composure, she continued in our language saying:

'Come into the kitchen and help me to make a bottle for the baby.'

I followed her. Once inside the kitchen Shirin rested a hand on my shoulder and said:

'You swear on Mama that Jock didn't touch you?'

I lied and swore on Mama. Shirin then looked me in the eyes and said,

'Still. I think you are a lying bitch. Papa will kill me. I think he's done something to you.'

Shirin was very upset. After wiping her eyes she said:

'I hope he marries you now.'

'Yes. We are going to get married in June.'

During the following weeks I worked hard to buy lots of clothes for the wedding. But Papa was now having his doubts. One day he said to me:

'I'm not happy about you getting married. I've changed my mind. The drudgery of young English girls who marry men like Jock breaks my heart.' Then the killer.

'So I'm not going to consent to you getting married.'

Remember that in 1962, 'coming of age' still meant reaching twenty one. As a seventeen year old I would not be able to marry without Papa's consent. And as he had said that he was not going to give it, I would be forever trapped.

I panicked and started to scream. I ran upstairs to my bedroom and locked the door. From within the locked room I shouted out to my parents,

'I'm going to kill myself. I've got a pen knife and I'm going to cut my wrists.'

I meant it. And they knew it. Mama shouted back to me saying,

'No. You can't do that.'

Meanwhile Papa rushed to the telephone and phoned Jock saying,

'Come over immediately. We want to get rid of her as soon

as possible. She wants to be with you and is threatening to kill herself.'

An hour later Jock arrived. He'd come by train and was all dirty from work. Papa looked at him and said, 'Never mind.'

Jock managed to persuade me to open the bedroom door and come out. Then a Polish lady doctor came round. She spoke to me quietly. And then she spoke privately to Jock saying:

'She's having a breakdown because her parents are very strict. Her father keeps changing his mind about marriage. And she is in love with you.'

The truth was that I was not really in love with Jock. But I was very fond of him. What I really wanted was to get out the family house and live my own life. But a month later I discovered a nasty side to my lovely Jock. It should have warned me off. But of course it didn't.

One evening as we were walking home I thought that I would tease Jock by putting my ice-cold hands on his cheeks. I laughed as I did so. But my laughter was short lived.

Slap!

Jock's slap was so hard that it left a red mark on one side of my face and gave me a blood shot eye. When I got home Mama said,

'What did you do to your eye?'

I had my answer prepared,

'A stone went into it. And I'm going to put a cold compress on it'

Mama thought for a moment. Then said,

'How could a stone hit you in the eye?'

'It's a windy day.'

Then Papa interrupted,

'Stop you're noise! I'm trying to read.'

With the conversation closed, I ran upstairs, crying. I had

changed my mind about marrying Jock. The worst thing was that Jock was not even drunk when he hit me. It was pure temper. The next day Jock phoned me up and apologised for his behaviour. He said that he had never done anything like that before. He did not tell me that he had once beat the life out an ex-girlfriend in Scotland called Mary. Later, and in a moment of drunken honesty, Jock told me about it. He explained that he had lost his temper with Mary because she had cheated on him behind his back and gone out with somebody else. And it led to him being charged by the Police because he had beaten her black and blue. But that was all in the past. And it would never happen again. So everything was fine. And it was on that basis that the wedding took place on 19th June 1962 at Caxton Hall.

Papa refused to come to the wedding because he was still not happy about me marrying Jock. But he was kind enough to send away to a Muslim company in Karachi for a wedding sari. It was the most beautiful silver and white sari made of Japanese raw silk.

But if Papa was conspicuous by his absence, I had all my friends from the supermarket. Keki attended the ceremony. At the reception which followed, I was also honoured by the attendance of Papa's bank manager and lawyers. Amongst the guests I also saw another familiar face.

It was Mike, the police cadet with whom I had gone out a year ago. My Elizabeth had whispered to him that I was going to get married. Mike came towards me saying that he wanted to kiss the bride. At that point, Liz started screaming and said, Jock!'

Jock laughed and said, 'As long as it's only on the cheek I don't mind.'

Liz started giggling because she had had a few drinks. She replied,

'No. He doesn't want to kiss the bride on the cheek. He wants a proper kiss.'

That comment so upset Jock. But the wedding passed off in good humour.

After the wedding we honeymooned in Scotland. Horrible Scotland. I was sick and ill all the time we were there. Mama took down the address of where we were staying, just in case I didn't come back. Papa also wrote to us there, wishing us all the happiness.

During the few weeks we were there I became homesick. I was also ill and lost weight. I also became spotty from lack of vitamins. The truth was, I missed my family. I was too attached to Mama.

21 When Bad Things Happen

As soon as we got married we moved to the penthouse flat which Papa gave us at Argyll Road, Kensington. Papa gave it to us rent free. It was just above the flat where my parents lived.

In return I agreed to act as Papa's housekeeper in relation to that property as well as another property he owned round the corner in Phillimore Gardens. Both were tenanted by students from Imperial College.

At the time we moved in Papa was already having a problem with our next door neighbour, Lady Kell. She was always complaining to Papa about the dirtier habits of our student tenants.

Attached to the outside of the building was an iron spiral staircase which the students had to climb to get to their parts of the building. But after a heavy afternoon's drinking they couldn't wait to get to their flat to empty their bladders. So they pissed through the railings and over the side. Sitting in the garden next door would be Lady Kell and her party guests.

Hearing water splashing they looked up to see our students peeing and laughing at them. She said to Papa.

'If you don't control your tenants I'll call the police.' And she did just that. A month later the police did arrive and passed on Kell's complaint. But if Lady Kell was feisty, her husband was mild. He didn't want any trouble.

One afternoon after an argument between Papa and Lady Kell, the husband came round with a bowl of fruit. Handing it to Papa he said,

'I'm sorry for my wife's behaviour.'

'You should keep your women under control like I do,' replied Papa.

Apart from the issues with Lady Kell, the first year of our marriage was bliss.

Jock was an enthusiastic lover. We had sex two or three times a week. I teased him by wearing nice petticoats. Soon I was pregnant. But sadly I miscarried. The hospital doctor told me not to conceive again for a year. But that did not put off Jock. He was a sex maniac.

Almost immediately I fell for a baby again. This time the pregnancy went the full term and I gave birth on 19th June 1964 in St Mary Abbots Hospital. It was exactly two years after our wedding. We named our son Billy in honour of Beheram, the dear brother which I had lost a decade before.

But it was during that pregnancy that Jock's drinking started to become a problem in our marriage. I hardly ever saw him. He was always down the pub.

We Parsees are a superstitious bunch. It was Beheram's death and the requisitioning of Faridabad House by the Pakistan Government which had forced our move from that lovely warm country to nasty cold England in 1957. Mama blamed that on Papa breaking up the Hindu Murti at the entrance of the property.

But it was something unforgivable which I did in London

after Billy was born which I blame for the subsequent unhappiness in my marriage. Or was it just my stupidity in marrying an aggressive man who liked to get staggering drunk every night?

There was an elderly Parsee woman called Zareen who called in to see Mama every afternoon for coffee. But for Zareen it was more than just a social visit. Zareen was a caaj.

She knew that Dilnawaz was still single, and wanted to find a husband for her – in return for payment of course. Mama was not really interested but was too polite to say anything to put her off. So every afternoon the coffees continued.

I hated Zareen because every time I came downstairs with Billy to see Mama, she would be sitting there. So I plotted a way to get rid of her.

A fitting act of revenge would be to get a large pair of scissors and creep up behind Zareen as she was showing pictures of eligible Parsee boys to Mama, and cut her white sari to shreds. But as I was crawling along the floor towards Zareen, a more attractive opportunity presented itself to me.

There on the floor beside her was Zareen's fat calf-skin wallet. I picked it up and crept back out of the room. I opened it up.

Inside the wallet were a couple of £5 notes; four green one pound notes and a brown ten shilling note. There were also a couple of florins, a sixpence and some pennies. In a separate compartment there were some religious medals and some curled black and white photographs. The medals and the photographs looked very old.

I left the house with the wallet, pulling Billy's pram behind me. I glanced back and saw Mama pouring Zareen another coffee. Outside the house, I took out the cash and put it in my handbag. I then picked up the wallet and threw it towards the basement of a nearby tenement block, its religious medals and the photos still inside.

As I heard it plop, a wave of guilt came over me. What had I done?

With Billy still in tow, I went to the Catholic Church at Kensington. The priest knew me as Mama went there a lot to pray privately. I put Zareen's money into his hand.

'I want to give this money to the Church. I want it to help someone.'

The priest looked at the money – and then at me. There were no questions.

'Thank you,' was all he said. 'And God bless you.'

I went home. The next morning the police knocked on the door. Papa opened it.

'We've had a complaint from a Mrs Mehta that her wallet has been stolen whilst she was here with your wife. She's not so much worried out the cash. It's the personal items in the wallet which she is most concerned about. Can you tell us who was in the house at the time?'

Mama replied,

'Only Zareen and myself. We were together having coffee. Oh! …. And there was our daughter Farida and my grandson Billy.'

'Nobody else?'

'No.'

'Then call Farida down. We need to speak to her.'

Papa called me downstairs. 'There's a problem about a missing wallet. The police are here and they want to speak to you.'

With my heart in my mouth I went downstairs to speak to the police. One of them spoke to me.

'You were in the house yesterday when Mrs Mehta was

here.'

'Yes.'

'What do you know about a missing wallet?'

Before I could answer, Papa interjected.

'Are you accusing her of being a thief? On the word of that senile old woman? We are a respectable family. My daughter would not do anything like that. She probably left it somewhere'

'We're sorry to trouble you. But a complaint had been made and we had to ask. Mrs Mehta said that your daughter was always staring at her. That it made her uncomfortable.'

It was true that I stared at her. I hated her. Who did this busybody think she was coming round to our house trying to marry my sister off?

Then the police left. Papa forbade Zareen from coming to the house anymore and nothing more was said about the stolen wallet. Except something which Mama said to me quietly after the police had gone.

'I could see from your face that you had something to do with it. What you did was very wrong and God will punish you for what you did to Zareen. You will never be happy in life.'

Jock's violence had always been part of our marriage. Although it had shocked me at the beginning, I had learned to accept it and hide it. Except when the injuries were so severe that they were obvious to everyone. Even then I tried to explain my injuries away. But no-one was really taken in.

Shortly after I had Billy, Jock caught up with Dodd, an old friend of his.

Dodd kept began coming down from Scotland to visit Jock at our home around once a month. But Dodd was different to Jock.

Dodd was educated and nice. But his frequent visits began to cause trouble within our marriage.

.

Every time Dodd came to our flat, Jock would quickly get dressed up, so they could go out together. Sometimes they would go boating at The Serpentine. More often they would go out to pubs. But I was never invited. I was left alone at home nursing Billy.

So I started leaving Billy with Mama and going out with Liz and some of my other girlfriends. But one day after Jock had returned home with Dodd from one of their many outings, he slapped my face and said,

'Where did you go?'

'Since you went out with your friend Dodd, I went out with Liz.'

Jock then pushed me upstairs and hit me very badly. I started to cry. Mama heard me from downstairs. She came up and said to Jock,

'If you ever touch her again, Papa will really sort you out.'

I had always been Papa's favourite daughter. But the beatings became more frequent. One day Jock banged my head against a wall because he wanted me to make him chips. Then there was the jealousy.

One afternoon as I came back with Liz, Jock asked me where we had been.

'We went to the Post Office Tower.'

He snarled,

'You and Liz are like a couple of tarts.'

'What about you and your friend?'

'We just went out for a couple of drinks. Not looking for men.'

'We didn't go looking for men.'

'Did you meet any men?'

'Lots of men were coming to chat to us. But I said I was married. They were only chatting Liz up.'

'You lying bitch. If I ever catch you chatting some men up, I'm going to sort you out.'

The jealousy got worse when Jock started working overtime and afterwards going to the pub. It was the pub which became his downfall. Drink always stoked his jealousy and his violence.

During the afternoon I liked to go with Billy to the Commonwealth Institute at Kensington High Street. But Jock always insisted that I must be home before he came home from work. And as soon as he had come home from work, he scoffed his dinner and got himself ready to go out again. For me it was a lonely existence.

Another thing I had noticed about Jock when I was heavy with Billy, was the way he stared at other women and in particular at their cleavages. He said that he was a 'boobs man'.

Our bedroom window overlooked a flat across the road which was occupied by three attractive Australian nurses. I had spoken to them once or twice in the street. Then one evening I saw Jock staring out of the bedroom window across to the flat opposite and smoking a roll up. He thought that I was in the living room watching television and did not know I was watching him.

The next night, whilst Jock was at the pub, I took his place at the bedroom window. Looking across, I saw the three Australian nurses. The curtains were wide open and the nurses were getting undressed. It was like a striptease. The girls laughed and joked as they walked around taking off their clothes before finally getting into bed. It was all perfectly innocent. They were completely unaware of the thrill they were giving a pervert across the road. The next evening, after they had come home from work, I knocked on their door. When they answered, I said,

'Excuse me. There is something I need warn you about.'

'What's that?'

'There is peeping tom in the neighbourhood. He watches you every night as you are getting undressed. So be careful in case he comes in and rapes you.'

They gasped. Then said,

'Thank you for telling us. We never knew.'

Two nights later Jock was again at the bedroom window, peering out at the flat opposite. A smoking roll up was in his hand. But there was nothing to see. The curtains were firmly shut. Jock took one last puff of his roll up and stubbed it out.

It was six months after Billy was born that Papa moved us from Argyle Road to the basement flat in his property at Chiswick High Road, Turnham Green.

During my pregnancy the baby was weighing heavy on me and causing me discomfort. Because of this my doctor gave me sleeping tablets and suggested that I slept on high pillows.

I was seven months gone when I started having a very bad pain in my legs. I also noticed that on my left leg there was a big broken vein. When I went to the Hospital the doctor told me that the vein was a bad sign which meant that that the baby was overweight. He added,

'My God. You're carrying a lot of weight. You must be very big. On what floor do you live?'

'I live on the fourth floor.'

'Then problems are caused because you are walking up and down with all that weight when you should be resting. As soon as you get indoors you need to put your feet up.'

The birth itself was difficult as the baby needed a forceps delivery. I needed 18 stitches, which later became infected. The district nurse made me sit in a hot baths of salty water, which eventually killed the infection. But it was a painful time, which was aggravated by my journeys to the fourth floor. I explained the situation to Mama and she mentioned it to Papa. He felt sorry and said to me,

'How about moving to Chiswick? I'm going to give you a basement flat, free of charge. You can be our housekeeper and keep an eye on the flats and my tenants'

Papa owned several properties in Chiswick High Road.

Jock was over the moon to get out to Chiswick and away from my family. He had hated me staying with my family. Living at Argyle Road had meant that each time Jock beat me and I screamed, Mama would come upstairs. Jock hated it.

I was also over the moon to be living at 351 Chiswick High Road because Dara's family lived next door at 349. I was particularly close to Chrissie and her younger sister Sherazad.

Before we could move in to the basement flat, Jock would first have to decorate it. Jock had also lied to Papa that he would decorate all of his Chiswick properties. But apart from the initial decoration of our own flat, he never did anything during the course of our marriage. He was instead working outside and getting drunk.

22 When a Little Flirting Goes Too Far

At the time we moved into the basement of 351 Chiswick High Road three hunky Scottish carpenters began renting the first floor flat.

Like Jock they also liked to drink. And at night, when they were drunk, they fought over cards. Sometimes they made so much commotion that one of us would have to go upstairs and separate them.

One of those carpenters was Alan Morrison. He was about thirty years old and looked like Robert Wagner. He was tall, brown eyed and handsome. He was muscular as well. I really fancied him. And I knew that he fancied me.

He told me that he had been in the French Foreign Legion. They'd wanted him to re-enlist but he'd had enough of fighting in the desert. So instead he came back to England to work as a carpenter.

Living in the same flat was another chap called Phil. Although I called him 'Tomato' because of his red face. There was a third chap called McBeal, who was tall and skinny. And when they fought, it felt as though they were actually killing each other.

So I would tell Jock to go upstairs to sort them out. To which he replied,

'There are three of them and they will kill me. You go and sort them out.'

Then I would to go halfway up the stairs onto the landing and shout,

'I'm going to call the police.'

McBeal and Phil were both very nice, at least when they were not fighting. Morrison was a thug.

Because Jock spent almost all his free time in the pub and would only come home drunk to eat or sleep, I'd already become bored in my marriage. I knew that men were attracted by my looks and decided to make the most of it. Amongst Papa's tenants were so many handsome men. So what could be wrong with a little innocent flirting?

I put in that little extra effort in the way I dressed, even when I was working. I made time to chat, to laugh, to joke and sometimes to tease.

It was Thursday 31st December 1964 that I was cleaning the staircase leading to the first and second floor flats. I was cleaning the lino edges of the staircase with hot soapy water. It was a sunny day and to keep myself cool when I was working, I wore only a blue sleeveless top and a pretty check skirt. Because it was New Year's Eve, I knew that the three hunks would be coming home early from work.

As I worked, I heard the front door open and the three men come inside. They stood talking to each other in the hallway. I saw them from the corner of my eye but pretended that I hadn't noticed them and carried on working. I kept my back towards them blocking the stairway. I'd make them wait.

I was rubbing the lino when I felt a pair of large hands grab my thighs. I turned round. It was Morrison. He laughed,

'How could I resist that?'

'Get your hands out. If my husband knows what you are doing he'll kill you.'

Morrison laughed again. Then he grabbed me and kissed me. And because I was not getting that kind of attention from Jock, I didn't mind. And it was also because Morrison appeared kind when he was sober. After our embrace, Morrison whispered to me,

'Each time you go out of the house, the three of us are looking down from our upstairs window. We say, 'How nice it would be to have a woman like Free downstairs.'

Like Jock, the three of them called me 'Free', not 'Farida'. He went on,

'We ask ourselves why your husband doesn't treat you nicely. He's always fighting with her.'

Then giving me a final wave, Morrison and the other two went up to their room and closed the door. I smiled and went back to my work.

It was during the afternoon of Friday 2nd April 1965, I was at home cooking dinner. Freyni was going to come over to babysit that night so that me and Jock could go with Chrissie to the American base at Yateley. Although winter had barely finished, the last couple of days had been unseasonably warm with temperatures above 70 F. It meant that I could wear the lovely brown floral dress which Chrissie had made for me. She had recently finished a course at the Technical College and was an expert dress-maker.

We'd been invited to a party by the GIs, one of whom was going out with Chrissie. I'd been expecting Jock home early that afternoon. But he hadn't arrived. I had previously said to Freyni,

'I'll make a very nice Persian dish for all of us when you

come over.'

I was alone in the flat with Billy when the doorbell rang. I opened it.

'Hi Alan'

He pushed himself inside. I could smell the alcohol in his breath.

'I've come home to pick something up. So I need to use your staircase to get up to the first floor and into my flat.'

I said,

'You're not allowed to. Haven't you got a key? I'll give you a key.'

'Too bad. I'm in now. Give me a cup of tea'

'You're very lucky. Because Jock will be coming now.'

Morrison replied,

'He doesn't come home until five o clock.'

So I made us both cups of tea. As we were drinking it the door opened and in walked Sherazad. She helped me clean Papa's properties and I gave her pocket money.

'Hi Aunty'

Then she saw Morrison.

'Oh!'

I opened my handbag and gave her ten shillings.

'Thank you Aunty. I was going to take Billy to the sweetshop.'

'That would be nice. I'll give you something extra.'

'Let me,' said Morrison, as he pressed half a crown in Billy's hand. The tiny fist closed around it.

'Don't rush back,' he said. 'Give the boy some sunshine.'

I felt a twinge of anxiety, not least because they would have to cross a busy road to get to Boyes sweetshop.

'I'm worried about my son. I'm sure he will be knocked down.'

'No Aunty, we won't get knocked down. I'll wait on the

pavement until all the cars have passed by.'

Before I could stop her, Sheri walked out of the door pushing Billy's pram.

We finished our tea. Then Morrison got up.

'Thank you. I'd better be going.'

But instead of using our internal staircase to get up to his flat, he walked across to the front door and put a chain across it.

'Why are you doing that?'

'I'll show you.'

Morrison circled his arms around my back and gently pulled me towards him until my face touched his. If only Jock would hold me like that.

I waited for a moment, expecting him to let go. Then we would laugh. He'd peck me on the cheek and go off to his flat. Only he didn't let go.

He kissed me full on the lips. And I kissed him back. We embraced. He kissed me again: this time a long lingering kiss. It had brought back into my life the warmth and the passion which for so long had been missing from my relationship with Jock. Here was someone who actually appreciated me.

And there was another reason why I hadn't pushed Morrison away. I was still angry at Jock for something he had done six weeks before on my birthday.

When Jock came home from work that Thursday evening he had pushed a large bunch of flowers into my hand. They were wrapped in newspaper.

'I got these flowers for your birthday'

'That's very kind of you.'

I took them out of the newspaper and looked at the wilting stems. Some of the stems still had roots attached as if they had been wrenched out of the ground. A clod of earth fell to the floor.

'Where did you get them?'

'There was a demolished house where I was working. And in the garden there were some lovely flowers. So I took some home for you.'

I threw back them at him.

'Don't take it like that Free. It's the thought that counts.'

So now I was getting my own back on Jock by kissing and cuddling with Morrison.

Then I felt Morrison's hands under my dress. It was then that I should have resisted. I should have pushed him away. Slapped his face. And shouted at him to, 'Get out of my flat!'

But I didn't. I didn't know what to do. Then it was too late.

Cradling me in his builder's-arms, Morrison lifted me up and carried me across to the long bench table on which we had our breakfast each morning. As soon as I knew what Morrison was about to do I said, 'You know if Jock comes home he's going to kill you and he'll kill me.'

'No he won't,' grunted Morrison. 'We may both be the same size but Jock knows that I am stronger than he is. That's why he sends you upstairs when we get too rowdy. '

'But all the same.'

'No buts. If Jock lays a finger on you I'll kill him.'

'Then I hope you're going to put something on. Because I don't want any problem.'

'I don't have anything with me. But it doesn't matter because I'll take it out. I won't come into you.'

There was nothing more I could do as Morrison laid me flat on the table. He was already naked from the waist down as he lifted my dress and pulled down my knickers. Then he was inside me.

The sex lasted about half an hour. But I couldn't enjoy it as I was scared that any moment I would hear Jock pushing against the door. Then he would force it open and catch me with Morrison.

With a final thrust, Morrison shot his load into me. It was what he promised he wouldn't do. He remained on top of me, Panting. Before easing himself away from me.

'I'm sorry Free. But I had to. I've always fancied you. And I'm leaving tonight to start on a new site in Luton'

There was knocking at the door. More knocking.

Morrison ran upstairs to his flat. I smoothed down my clothes and opened the door. It was Sherazad with Billy. They both came inside.

'Aunty. What happened?'

I garbled an excuse,

'I was just cleaning the flat. Somebody phoned up. And as I picked the phone up there was a funny man at the door. So I closed the door and put the chain on it.'

'It frightened me. Where is Alan?'

'Alan only got locked out. We had a cup of tea and he went upstairs.'

I put my index finger on her lip,

'You mustn't say anything to Jock that Alan has been here. Otherwise there will be trouble,'

'No Aunty. I'll not say anything.

Sherazad walked out leaving me alone with Billy.

I broke down. I had wanted to punish Jock. But not like this.

I was still crying when Chrissie came round.

'Aunty. What's happened? Why are you crying?'

I asked, 'Where is your mummy?'

'Mummy is doing shopping. Why are you crying?'

As Chrissie was old enough to understand, I told her what had happened.

She said,

'Oh God. I'm going to go upstairs and bugger him up. Aunty. You must at least go to the police.'

'No I can't do that. Jock would never believe me. He would kill Alan. And he would kill me. We were only laughing and joking. What am I going to do?'

Chrissie understood. Then another fear hit me.

'What if he's made me pregnant? He didn't wear anything when he did it'

Chrissie thought about it in her adult way and gave me golden advice.

'Then you must pass it off as Jock's. But Aunty. It may never happen.'

I rushed upstairs and vomited because I was so shaken up. I couldn't cook or do anything. Chrissie went out and got fish and chips.

Instead of going to the American base with Chrissie, I spent the rest of the evening sitting at home with Freyni. I was so frightened. I didn't know what to do. Going round in my head was the thought,

'How am I going to get rid of the baby if I'm pregnant?'

Next month I missed my period and began to suffer morning sickness. The doctor confirmed my pregnancy. But I didn't say anything to Jock. Instead I cooked up a plan.

As he was going out to work the following Friday morning, I tapped on Jock's shoulder. He turned round. Then with tightness in my chest I said to him

'I'll make a nice dinner and we'll go out tonight. And I'll wear my peach miniskirt for you.'

To my relief, Jock agreed.

I had a peach coloured miniskirt with blue prints. Jock loved me wearing it.

I usually wore it with tights, which had just come out at that time to go with mini-dresses. But that evening my legs and thighs were bare. Jock had said that he liked brown thighs with the peach trimmings which Chrissie and I had made. And it had tight puffed sleeves. It was his favourite.

So we went out that night. And when we came in, he was over the moon with me.

After we came home, Jock led me to the kitchen towards the same bench table on which Morrison had raped me nearly two months before. He removed the table cloth and a flower vase which was on top of it. Then like Jack Nicholson in the film 'Postman Rings Twice' Jock laid me, fully clothed, across the top of the table and made love to me.

There was no durex because I had thrown them away. Instead Jock said that he would pull it out when he was about to come. But he never had the chance. Because at the critical moment I wrapped my arms around his back, pulled him close and held on to him for dear life. And he came into me. I pretended to be angry and said to him,

'You went into me. Now I'm very worried. What am I going to do if I'm pregnant?'

Little did he know that I was already pregnant.

So after I missed my following month's period, I gave Jock the bad news. But he was over the moon as for several months he had been talking about us having a second child.

The truth was that in spite of what Morrison had done, I still had a soft spot for him. I made excuses to myself for his bad behaviour. Perhaps he had a little too much to drink. And he wasn't violent. And he had apologised. So perhaps it wasn't really so bad after all. And I was anxious about who would support the child if anything happened between me and Jock. So after Morrison came back from his Luton job he got in touch with me and we went out to a few cinema matinee shows. It was as though nothing had happened. I did not have to mention that I was pregnant. It was obvious.

We kept in touch by correspondence. I got on well with a local post-mistress and arranged for Morrison's letters to be sent to her post office, where she would put them aside for me to collect.

I was in the seventh month of my pregnancy when Dara was rushed into St Mary Abbots Hospital with a sudden heart attack. The doctors put it down to his heavy smoking. He was a forty a day man. But over the following weeks he seemed to improve. He was now getting around the hospital ward on crutches. But what the doctors didn't know was that Chrissie and John were smuggling in packets of Capstan cigarettes, with the occasional bottle of whiskey. I struggled in to see him whenever I could but mainly relied on my brothers and sisters to keep me updated as to his health.

One October afternoon I tried to phone Shirin but got no answer. I tried Keki. But got no answer. I tried Papa, Rusi and Adil. But I could not get hold of anyone. I phoned the hospital and spoke to the ward nurse.

'How is my brother?'

There was silence at the other end of the phone.

'How is my brother?'

After further hesitation the ward nurse replied.

'I think it's best if I get the matron to speak to you.'

'How is my brother?'

A further silence. Then a new voice.

'This is matron. How can I help you?'

'How is my brother?'

More hesitation then,

'Haven't your family told you?'

'Told me what?'

'Mr Manekshah passed away this morning. I'm sorry.'

I let the receiver drop. I became hysterical, banging my head against the wall. Jock, who was standing next to me, turned me round to look at him. He said,

'Think about the baby. If you carry on like this it'll be born with brain damage'

He had no words of sympathy about Dara. He was only forty two when he died that October.

Funeral arrangements were hurried into place. Dara's body was moved to Brown and Saunders: undertakers who specialised in Zoroastrian funerals. Then the obligatory five days of ancient prayers chanted by a team of black capped dasturs, whilst our family gathered round the open coffin

On the last of the five days Dara's body, now purified by prayer, was carried by Rusi, Adil, Soli and Keki and lowered into the back of a hearse so that it could be taken to the small Zoroastrian Burial Ground tucked away at Brookwood Cemetery, about thirty miles away near Woking, Surrey, where an open grave awaited.

Almost every race, religion and sect is represented somewhere in this vast international cemetery. Each has its own part. The Zoroastrian Burial Ground is situated at the back near the main railway line. To get to it involves negotiating your way to the end of a long narrow road winding past small Muslim cemeteries. Sometimes the road is blocked by the cars of other mourners as there is nowhere easily to park. The Zoroastrian burial ground itself was donated by Victoria to the Parsees in 1862 in return for their loyalty to the Great White Queen.

If you are travelling by train between Waterloo and Basingstoke, look out for the Zoroastrian Burial Ground as you pass Brookwood Station, close to the Shah Jehan Mosque.

You will see the backs of the distinctive Tata mausoleums. And if you visit the Burial Ground itself, look out for the grave of Dr Cawas C. Lalcoca, who died 1st July 1909 at the Imperial Institute, London, trying to stop an anarchist's bullets intended for Sir William Curzon Wylije. Both men died.

But on that drizzly day there was no time for sight seeing. And when my brothers arrived to carry Dara's coffin to its final resting place, the hearse was nowhere to be seen. Perhaps the driver had got lost amongst the maze of narrow winding lanes which separated each of the nationalities. Eventually the hearse did arrive and my brothers carried Dara to his grave. Then there were more prayers and burning sandlewood before Dara was finally laid to rest. As well as the newly widowed Freyni, there was someone else present at Brookwood that day: Dara's Irish mistress Yvonne.

We all knew that my handsome lady killer brother had been leading a double life. There was Freyni and her children. And there was Yvonne.

'Which one is the widow?' asked the dastur who was about to conduct the funeral. But if there was an unexpected guest, there was also a notable absentee: Chrissie.

She was in disgrace. Adil had forbidden her to come anywhere near her father's funeral. Like me, Chrissie was also expecting a child. But Chrissy was not married to anyone. The father was a school friend with whom she had had an affair. Adil in particular was not happy about it.

When Chrissie had first tried to enter Brown and Saunders funeral parlour to join in the prayers, Adil had blocked her way.

'Come any further and I'll kill you,' he warned. Chrissie took him at his word.

It was two months later that I went into St Mary Abbots Hospital to give birth. It was 31st December 1965. It required a caesarean because of the size of the baby and the fact that he was the wrong way up in my womb. I wanted to name him after my recently deceased brother. But Jock would have none of it.

'You are not going to call him Dara or any Parsee rubbish name. But to keep you happy you can call him Daniel.'

Morrison had also found out from the hospital that I had given birth. He wrote to me saying he wanted blood tests to find out whether he was the father. We arranged to meet outside Chiswick Park Station. He wanted me to bring Daniel. But I was frightened to do so in case he snatched him away. So instead I brought along some Polaroid photographs of the baby.

The resemblance to Morrison was plain to see. Then Morrison pushed £50 into my hand and asked if he could pay towards Daniel's support. He added,

'I'm living in Chiswick High Road. Would you like to come and see my flat? In fact why don't you just come away with me. I'm earning good money and I'd give up anyone else just to have you with me'

I accepted the money but declined the invitation.

'Jock gets drunk every night. So do you. So what would be the point of me coming away with you?'

23 The Bunny Girl

I hoped that things would change when Jock began taking driving lessons. Perhaps a more responsible Jock would emerge.

Keki was then a driving instructor with the British School of Motoring: and a good one. Under Keki's expert tuition Jock passed his test within six months and bought himself a car. But I never saw the car. He always took it with him to go out drinking. Or he would leave it parked up in the basement car park whilst he was working.

It was during one of Jock's driving lessons that a shiny red E Type Jag shot out of Phillimore Gardens and collided with our tatty old car. I was sitting in the back seat. An attractive blond got out of the E Type and walked over. I was jealous.

'You bitch! Look what you've done to our car.'

She giggled.

'Don't worry. Daddy'll pay for it. And I'm earning good money as a bunny girl. Which is how I bought this car.'

She smiled at handsome Keki.

'Is there anything else you'd like me to do?'

Keki whispered something to her. A dinner date was arranged. It also gave me food for thought.

It had been 1st July 1966 that Victor Lownes had launched

the Playboy Club in London's Park Lane amongst a blaze of publicity. So this was how bunny girls lived. I'd already seen advertisements for bunny waitresses. And as soon as those advertisements appeared again, I applied.

'Why do you want to be a bunny girl,' said Bunny Mother Sue, who interviewed me. 'You could be a model.'

I was accepted for the job of cocktail bunny, working in the bar and serving the guests with their drinks. But that posed another problem. How was I going to get out every night to do the job without anyone knowing what I'm doing? Again my niece Chrissie had the answer,

'Don't worry. I'll cover for you. Tell them that you're coming out to work at the Hammersmith Odeon with me.'

At 4'11' Chrissie was too short to be a bunny girl. So she worked instead as a cinema receptionist. Anyway the lie convinced my parents as well my horrible husband who was hardly ever home. So much so that Mama agreed to look after Billy and Danny whilst I was out doing my cinema work.

The main reason I wanted the job was to save up to buy a new Mini Cooper, even though I had yet to pass my driving test. And with earnings of more than £50 a week, including tips, it was not going to take me long. But it was my friendship with a German film actor which was to prove my undoing.

Amongst the Club's clientele was Curt Jurgens, who was always in demand to play the part of German military officers and would later star in the 1969 epic, Battle of Britain. When he was in the Club bar, he always asked for me to serve him. And if he wanted room-service, it was always me who was asked to bring the drinks up to his room. But there it stopped. As bunnies we were under strict instructions not to enter a guest's room. But that couldn't stop a chatterbox like me.

As I knocked on the door, he would always say, 'Come

inside.' And I did. We would chit-chat.

Other bunnies complained about me. They said that they were working whilst I was chatting. And after two warnings I was sacked.

24 The Clinic

After Daniel I didn't want any more children. At least not with Jock. Both my pregnancies had been difficult. With Billy it was a forceps delivery. And with Daniel a caesarean. So when after six months I again had morning sickness I said to Jock.

'I haven't had my period. And I think I'm pregnant. I can't go through anymore caesareans. I'm ill with your mother coming and going. So I'm not going through with it. I've also got a job waitressing- on and off.'

Jock thought about it and said,

'We'll have an abortion.'

We went to our Doctor Guerken and she gave me the name and telephone number of an Iranian doctor she knew in Earls Court called Phiroz. She told me he had a lovely surgery in Harley Street.

Jock contacted Phiroz and we went for a consultation in the basement of his Earls Court property. Sitting with Phiroz was an English doctor called Segal. They were doing abortions illegally for cash.

Phiroz told me to go to the address at Harley Street and see Segal, whom he said would be carrying out the abortion.

'It will be £150,' he said.

Jock then arranged the £150. Mama loaned him £100, even though she was very distressed at what I was going to do. Mama was dead against abortion. Attempting to dissuade me, she said,

'I will look after the baby. And you go on family planning.'

Jock's mother then came round. She was also very upset. Jock borrowed the remaining £50 from a friend.

Clutching our money, we kept our appointment at Dr Segal's Harley Street surgery. But we were to be disappointed.

As we checked in at 8am, Segal's nurse took us into a private room and said to me,

'I'm sorry. The sterilising machine has broken down. You cannot have the abortion here.'

I said,

'Oh my God! What am I going to do?'

She replied,

'It's not just you. Everybody has to go to Golders Green.'

So we drove to Golders Green. As there were lots of other ladies in the same position as me who didn't have a car, we took two of them in the back seat.

We arrived at a large dirty house in Golders Green. Upstairs on the first floor there was a nursing home. I was in tears. Then a doctor came over to me. He was a geriatric English doctor with big glasses and covered up hair. He reminded me of an old Doctor Jeckle. He said,

'Don't cry. No need to cry. It's going to be all right. What is your name?'

I glanced round at the shabby surroundings and said,

'I don't want to have an abortion here.'

The Doctor ignored my comment and carried on talking,

'Doctor Segal has arranged it. We cannot do it at Harley Street because the machine has broken down. So we are going to do it here.'

His creepy appearance made me even more frightened. Standing a few paces away from him was a nurse: an old bag wearing a green uniform and a green apron.

'Come along Mrs McDonald,' said the old bag. 'You're second on the list. No need to cry. It's all we could do. Now open your arms and I'll give you a little prick. And after we've given you that prick, you'll not know what has happened. Then we'll give you the abortion. After that we'll take you upstairs in the bedroom with two or three other girls. About three o'clock, when you've come round after a couple of hours, you will be coming down to the dining room to have a cup of tea and some cakes. Then if you're fit enough, you will go home.'

She gave me the prick. The abortion was then carried out. Two hours after the abortion I woke up in the bedroom vomiting because they had given me so much gas. I was ill. And my nausea was made worse by the drip, drip, drip of rainwater coming down through the roof into a small bowl which they had put down to catch it. Jock was sitting in a chair next to me. Ten minutes later Jeckle and the old bag came beside my bed and put a cup of tea on the table next to it. They smiled kindly at me. But those smiles dropped when I said,

'I'm feeling very weak. I don't want to stay here. I want to go home.'

Jeckle's face became hard;

'I'm sorry you have to stay here. Because we don't want a police problem. Suppose you go home and you have a haemorrhage? What are you going to do? Are you going to call the police? Or are you going to call an ambulance?'

Jock interrupted,

'I'll call an ambulance.'

'No. You can't call an ambulance because they'll call the police. And the police will ask, 'who carried out the abortion?' '

Jeckle gave Jock a card with a number on it.

'We want you to contact this number only. Speak to Dr Phiroz or Dr Segal and to no-one else. Do you understand?'

Jock nodded. I was so frightened as I had a deep pain inside me. Then they took me down to dining room. I shook my head,

'I can't eat.'

'Why?' asked Jeckle.

'Because I'm about to be sick.'

The nurse rushed to get a bowl. Too late. I was sick all over. And just as all the other women were about to have tea, jam and cake.

During the two hours I was unconscious after the operation the nurse received a stream of calls from Rusi and Soli, asking after me. In response to one call from Soli the nurse said,

'Who are you?'

'I'm the brother. How is Mrs McDonald?'

'She's still sleeping at the moment. We will see how she is. She is resting fine.'

Rusi said,

'She can't come home.'

'We will only send her home when she comes out of the anaesthetic.'

'How come she is here instead of at Harley Street?'

'The machine was broken down.'

I was relieved to return home after forty eight hours. But I was not well and my brothers were worried about my condition. I was still vomiting and my lips had become white. I went straight to bed. After a few minutes the bedroom door opened and Billy came running in. Rusi shooed him out saying,

'Get out of the room and leave Mummy alone.'

Rusi then spoke quietly to Jock,

'I don't think she's looking at all well. You have to call a doctor.'

I was still vomiting and I was still all white on my lips. So they had to phone Phiroz to call a doctor. An hour later another Iranian doctor called at the house and attended to me.

The next day Rusi stayed with me and got me soup whilst I rested. But the moment I got up I was bleeding like a tap. Years later I read in the papers that both men had been caught and sent to prison. Women had died at their horrible clinic.

Although abortions had since become legal in Britain, elsewhere in Europe it was not. So the pair had been advertising in Switzerland for abortions

25 Another Black Eye

Jock's behaviour became worse after we moved to Chiswick because he liked his drink. And also because I was not afraid to answer him back.

Jock said that Scottish women kept their heads down, their mouths shut, and bowed to their husbands. But I wasn't going to do that. Jock also did not hesitate to hit me in front of other people.

One day there was an incident involving one Rusi's tenants, who lived at his property at West Croft Square. His name was Raj. He was a Ceylonese who was married to an Irish woman. One day he came knocking at our door, saying that he wanted a spare key to his flat. He added,

'Mr Manekshah told me to take the key from you – as you are the housekeeper. I've locked myself out'

'Well I haven't got a key. Wait a minute while I speak to my brother.'

I phoned one of my brothers. He said that Raj would have to go to Kensington to get the key. Raj would have none of it.

'You're a lying cow,' was his charming response. I replied,

'Don't you call me a lying cow. You scum.'

Raj began screaming outside the front door of our house.

It was a Saturday afternoon. As this happened Jock arrived crawling drunk. He couldn't stand to see me arguing over a key to get in. Jock turned to the man and said,

'Fuck off.'

'No I'm not going to fuck off. Your wife was very rude to me.'

Jock then turned to me and said,

'Get in!'

'I'm not going to get in. I'm telling him that I haven't got a key.'

Jock turned back to the man.

'You've heard her. She hasn't got a key.'

The man replied,

'I'm not going to get out until I talk to another brother.'

From the coin box in the corridor of the house I phoned my brother Soli. Then I handed the receiver to Raj.

'We can't get into our flat. And It's cold.'

Soli replied,

'Then you will have to come over to Kensington so that I can give you a spare set.'

'I'm not going to go all the way to Kensington.'

'Then you can fuck off,' was Soli's closing remark.

The man started screaming again. I screamed back. Jock told him to, 'get out!' But the man carried on shouting. Jock then turned to me and said, 'Get indoors.'

'I'm not going to get in. I'm going to stay here because this is my father's house.'

Then Jock hit me in front of that man. He did it to stop me arguing and embarrassing him. Never mind that he humiliated me.

He hit me so badly that I had very bad bloodshot eyes. I started to cry and ran out to a phone box near Turnham Green

Park, leaving my two children alone in the flat with their drunken father. I made a reverse charge call to Soli. As Soli picked up I said,

'I'm going to leave him.'

Soli replied,

'Please go back.'

'You haven't seen my eyes. I can't even open one of them.'

'I'll send Adil along. Stay where you are. He'll meet you there.'

I stood shivering outside Turnham Green Station and waited for Adil. He arrived after half and hour.

As he got out of his car he saw that I was crying. He also saw the state of my face. He said,

'Open your eye.'

I could hardly open it. He put his arm around my shoulder and said,

'I'm going to take you to casualty. But before that, I'll fuck Jock up. How long has he been doing that?'

'A long time. That's why he took me to Chiswick. So he could hit me on and off.'

'Get in the car.'

Adil took me home. As we entered the front door we heard Jock snoring on the sofa. He opened one eye,

'Hello Adil. What do you want?'

'Have you seen her eye?'

'I don't intend to see her eye. She deserved it.'

Adil stabbed his finger at Jock and said,

'Look here. You know I killed a boxer in Karachi. This is the last time you do this to my sister. If you ever lay a finger on her again……'

He paused.

'…… I don't know what will happen. I'll kill you. Her

parents are not here. Rusi is in India. So I have to take charge. Now I'll have to take her to Casualty. And I'm going to make a report that her husband punched her in the eye.'

So Adil took me to hospital. They gave me a solution and a cold compress to put on my eye. But I was too embarrassed to tell them the truth about how my eye had become damaged. Instead I lied that I had fallen down and damaged it. They didn't believe me. But there was nothing else they could do.

I kept up the pretence when I went back to work the next day at the supermarket. Like the hospital staff, they didn't believe me.

After four days I removed the plaster. My eye was still bloodshot and I went to the chemist to get some more solution to put on it and get the bruise out. Adil asked me how I was. He then phoned Jock up and said,

'Last time you were drunk. But if you ever touch her again we will report you to the police. We will tell them that you were violent to my sister.'

Jock was not to be put off. He began hitting me more often. I would lay on the floor crying for hours. Meanwhile Jock would laugh, put his coat on and go out drinking. So we were already having serious problems in our marriage.

It also meant that I couldn't go back to work because of his constant drinking. And even though he was working I never got enough money from him to keep us. Even though Papa had given us a free flat, Jock never wanted to pay the bills

In winter he always took a half crown coin and discovered a way of putting that same coin fifty times in the gas meter for a whole week. And then he took the same coin and put it fifty times into the electricity meter. So at least we were warm.

Although our Chiswick flat had only one bedroom and a small living room, it had a very big corridor.

One day Jock got some timbers from work and some windows. He then set about converting part of our large corridor into a single room complete with bunk beds for Billy and Danny, who were now growing up. But it was about the only carpentry work he did for our family whilst he was living free.

Shirin knew that our marriage had run into trouble and she started coming round frequently to visit me. She and my brothers were already becoming impatient about Jock's lazy ways. One day Shirin discovered that Jock was not putting money in the utility meters and she tackled him about it.

'You're not even paying the bills. Farida's not working. She's got your two children. So you've got to start paying. You're not paying any rent – but you're going to be paying the bills.'

Then Shirin turned to me and said, so Jock could overhear,

'Mama is not going to pay your fatso's bill.'

'Fatso' was how they now referred to Jock. In the four years since we were married, Jock had put on at least three stone in weight. Perhaps it was my Parsee dansaks.

'Don't call me Fatso. You cow,' Jock grunted. But Shirin was not to be put off.

'Even though you're living here rent free, you don't do anything round here. If we need a carpenter we have to get someone from outside. If there's a job to be done, it's always my George who has to come round and fix things for the tenants. You are just drinking all day and beating my sister. And we are going to tell you to get out. Did you hear what I said? Get yourself a house. Save up and buy something!'

Jock grunted again and walked out of the room. But he was not to be let off that easy.

Keki started coming round to our flat and saying to Jock, 'How much have you saved?'

To which Jock's reply would always be,

'Nothing. I've been giving all my money to Free. And she's been spending it.'

In fact all Jock ever gave me at that time was £3 a week shopping money, Each time I wanted clothes for myself or anything for the boys, Jock's answer was always,

'Go to Kensington to your mother's bank.'

When he said this he was talking about the safe which Mama had in my parents' house. She always kept some cash in it. Whenever I needed money for something, Mama would always open the safe, pull out some cash, and give me what I needed. There was never an issue. But it broke my heart to keep having to ask her for money because my husband kept me short.

One day I broke down in tears and said to Mama,

'I made a mistake. I shouldn't have married him.'

Mama put her hand on my arm and said,

'Don't worry. He'll get better.'

Of course he didn't. He got worse. He never took me on holiday unless his old bag mother came along too. She was the most horrible dominating bitch I ever knew. And incontinent with it. And he never brought anything for the boys. I was so fed up.

26 The Greek Party

At the supermarket where I was working, I had got to know a young woman customer called Janis. She had gone to the same Hogarth School as me. She was only twenty five but was married to a sixty year old widower who worked as a long distance bus driver. He had adopted the child she already had by a previous boyfriend and she had given birth to a couple more children since her marriage. She also got me a job as a canteen waitress at Bush Radio, Power Road, Chiswick, where she was then working.

One lunchtime we had coffee together to celebrate the fact that she had just passed her driving test. It was then that Jan confided in me.

'I have these children but not one of them are my old man's. But he is so simple that he thinks they are his. Even though I was already pregnant before he even slept with me.'

Jan giggled.

'And guess what. Eighteen months later I said to the old fool, 'Oh darling. I'm going to have a baby again.' He was so chuffed.'

She laughed again, spraying me with her coffee. As I mopped it off my face she said,

'Would you like to come out with me tonight?'

'I can't. It's Jock's Friday night out.'

'What a shame. I've been invited to a lovely Greek party at a restaurant near the Post Office Tower.'

I looked at her sadly. She paused. And then said,

'Don't worry. I could drive. Now that I can drive I can bring my station wagon. You ask your young niece to stay overnight. You can change the boys and put them to bed. And that will be fine.'

So I met Jan as we had arranged. I was quite happy that Sheri was looking after Billy and Danny for a few shillings until Jock came home later that night. I told Sheri not to go home in case he was violent towards me and that she could stay overnight on the settee.

So I went out with Jan, who had lied to her husband that she was doing an evening shift at Bush Radio.

Jan picked me up outside Woolworths in her station wagon. With her were two young Greek men. As one of them had already taken the front passenger seat, I sat in the back with the other Greek man. Jan then drove half a mile to Turnham Green Terrace, where a third Greek man was waiting for us. He also got in the back beside me.

Jan then drove towards central London and to the restaurant near the Post Office Tower. As Jan had only passed her driving test two days before and had not previously driven in central London, she was nervous and hesitant. But after several near misses and a few wrong turnings we arrived at the restaurant.

Even though it was only eight thirty, the Greek party was already in full swing. For a couple of hours I was able to forget Jock and pretend I was single. When I next looked at my watch it was nearly ten o clock. I interrupted Jan, who was French kissing with a young Greek.

'Let's go home. Jock will kill me if I'm out.'

Jan ignored me. So I said it again. And again.

She laughed and said,

'No. No. He'll never kill you.'

After much pestering on my part, Jan prised herself away from the man and we said our goodbyes. The three Greeks who had accompanied us to the party also rejoined us, as did a fourth Greek, to whom Jan had promised a lift home. I was now crammed into the back seat of Jan's station wagon with three Greek men. I could smell from their breath that they had all had a few drinks, including Jan in the driving seat. And they still wanted to party. As the lone female in the back seat amongst the crush, I quickly became the object of their amorous attentions. An arm encircled my waist. A hand brushed against my thigh. And a whiskered chin nuzzled into my neck. It felt like sandpaper.

'I want you to come home with me tonight and be my girlfriend,' said the chin.

'I'm sorry but I'm already married.'

'Mmmm!' said the chin, nuzzling closer, its hand finding its way through my blouse and onto my breast. Another hand, belonging to somebody else, which had earlier brushed against my thigh, was now massaging it. But I was too tired and tightly hemmed in to push them away. Eventually we reached Chiswick and the Greeks got out – one-by-one – until there was only Jan and myself. She dropped me round the corner from our flat. I looked at my watch. It said quarter to one. Panic gripped me. Jock was usually home by half twelve.

'That was fun,' said Jan 'Let's do it again in a couple of weeks.'

'I'll think about it'.

I brushed down my clothes and walked nervously to the front door of our flat. I had not worked out what excuse I was going to give to Jock.

There was silence as I entered the flat. But Jock was already waiting for me on the stairs.

He had come home earlier and woke Sheri, who had fallen asleep in front of the television.

'Where is Free?'

Still half asleep, Sheri replied,

'Farida Aunty has just gone out with Jan.'

'Where has she gone?'

'I don't know. They just went to a party. Some Greek party. Jan and her went to a Greek family party'

I wished Sheri had never said that.

'Oh! A party. I'll sort her out. What did she wear?'

'Just ordinary clothes.'

The moment I walked in, Jock pulled my hair and pushed me right down on to the floor. He then wrenched the phone out of the socket and smashed the whole telephone on my head. I was screaming. And Sheri was screaming,

'Leave her alone.'

I tried to telephone for help and he kept hitting me like a ping pong. He was drunk and he beat me up. I had all these big lumps on my head. And I was crying. And all night I screamed.

The next day Freyni came round. She said,

'Men are not worth being married to. Why are you crying?'

And I just couldn't stop crying. I had something like a nervous breakdown that day. I kept on shaking and getting all the cries out of my heart.

At that time my parents weren't around because they were in India. They kept going to India because Papa had a bloody business: his glass factory and his Rembrandt and Vandyke Studio. Every time he buggered off there.

And every time Jock hit me I wouldn't talk to him for weeks

and weeks. I would just leave his food out for him but wouldn't let him touch me.

The next morning he went to Jan's house and said to her,

'If I ever catch you taking my wife out, I'm going to sort you out. I'm going to come round and tell your husband that you've been sleeping around with those Greek dirty scums and having their babies, whilst your simple simon bus driver is going long distances to keep a slut like you.'

Jan was stunned. All she could say was,

'How horrible. Who told you?'

'Well Free told me everything about you. And you've got a cheek to take my wife out.'

After that Jan wouldn't talk to me. I was so upset. I said,

'Jan. But that was only a conversation between me and my husband. And I didn't mean to say anything. Because your man is sixty. And you are only twenty five. You're like a granddaughter.'

After that I started working in the evening to get money whenever I could get Sheri to babysit for me.

I now had a three month a temporary job at Bush Radio as a canteen waitress. The staff liked me a lot and the job became permanent.

27 Death of a Ruler

'Farida.Farida! You must come straightaway to St George's Hospital. Papa's been taken ill'

I put down the telephone receiver.

It was Gustad. And it was October 1967.

I phoned Adil, as he was the brother who lived nearest to me and he said that he would pick me up in his car. But before Adil arrived, Jock came home drunk.

I was crying and said,

'Papa has become very ill and I have to leave the boys with you to visit him in the hospital.'

With me in Adil's car was Keki's wife Homai. She was heavily pregnant with her soon-to-be born first child Natasha. Homai held my arm as we walked into the hospital. She said to me,

'Don't cry. Papa is all right. They've put an oxygen mask on him.'

Papa wasn't all right. He lay flat on the bed with his face covered by an orange mask. He was having trouble breathing and his stomach was going up and down. I cried and knelt by his bed.,

'Papa I love you so much. You've given me everything. I'm

sorry that I ever married Jock. You must forgive me for what I've done by marrying him. I didn't mean to make you unhappy.'

And I had made Papa unhappy. He didn't want me to leave his property at Argyle Road, where I had been his right hand.

His doctor had put him on Warfarin to thin his blood. But it didn't agree with him. It made him faint and dizzy. At Mama's suggestion he stopped taking it. Then two days later he had a heart attack and was rushed to St George's Hospital, which was then situated at Hyde Park. It was the day after I saw him in hospital that he passed away and was buried at Brookwood next to Dara. On his gravestone the words,

'He was our ruler.'

28 Dropping Frankie

1969 saw the release of the film Carry On Up the Jungle. Dilnawaz and I were amongst the tribe of female amazons led by actress Valerie Leon, who captured Sid James and the rest of his team. Like Raquel Welch in One Million Years BC we were dressed in furry bras and bikinis. The Producer called us 'Roses.'

Prancing along with us, in a similar costume, was Chrissie. Other members of my family were there in other roles. During our month at Pinewood Studios I also made friends amongst some of the other Roses including Tanya. She was half-Turkish and very beautiful.

One of our jobs as Roses was to carry the leading actors on stretchers. One of us held each of the four corners. Groups of Roses took in turn to carry different actors.

One day Tanya and I were selected to carry the larger-than-life Frankie Howerd, who was playing the Professor. Tanya was standing next to me at the back of the stretcher. It was a struggle.

'I can't hold on. He's like a buffalo.' said the slightly built Tanya. 'I'm going to have to drop him.'

'Well if you do that,' I replied, 'It'll dislocate my shoulder. So perhaps it's best that we drop him together. Signal to me when you're about to drop him.'

Tanya signalled. We both let go of the stretcher and Howerd's bottom hit the ground. Tanya giggled. But comedian Howerd couldn't see the joke.

'Fuck! Fuck! Fuck! You girls want the money. But you don't want to do the work.'

One of the film crew then stepped in and supported Howerd's weight, whilst Tanya and I walked behind pretending to carry the stretcher

Tanya and I stayed friends after filming had finished. But contact was lost several years later when she moved to Italy to work as a professional model, whilst in the meantime I had moved house.

'It was also during shooting that we met and became friends with the lovely Charles Hawtree.

It was in the canteen that Chrissie saw Charles sitting at a table surrounded by a crowd of extras. He'd put his jacket on the back of the empty chair next to him to reserve it for a friend. But that didn't stop my Chrissie: the four foot eleven inch 'Rocker' who dressed in leathers and travelled everywhere on the back of motorbikes. Picking up Hawtree's jacket, she said to Hawtree,

'If you don't let me sit here I'm going to take your jacket and throw it on the floor. Then I'm going to climb on your back like a monkey.'

Hawtree laughed and invited us to sit down. After that we joined him at every meal during the rest of the filming. Hawtree then kept in touch with Chrissie and sent us invitations to various events.

It was three years after filming that that Mama decided to sell the Chiswick High Road Property in which we had our basement flat. She gave us £3,250 towards a down payment on a house of our own. But because she knew about the problems in our marriage, she didn't want to give the money to us outright. Instead the money was dressed up as a loan from Shirin to us.

To put the matter on record, Mama handed over the cash to Shirin, who then provided a cheque as our deposit for a three bedroom, house at St Albans Avenue, Chiswick, to which we then moved.

At that time I was waitressing at different places in between school holidays. I couldn't work permanently full time because the boys were still young. In winter they would catch colds and flu. Jock would then tell me,

'Pack the job up and look after them.'

And every time I went for a new job the prospective employer would ask me for the last job's reference. But I couldn't very well give them that as all my jobs seemed to end with the employer giving me my cards. They would always say,

'You've taken so much time off work because of your two children. You're a good worker but we can't keep having you keep taking time off from work. So we'll have to give you one week's money and say Goodbye.'

29 The Christmas Present

Christmas Eve 1971 has special memories for me. That is the date Jock broke my ribs.

At that time I was still working at Bush Radio.

Billy had wanted a Lego set for Christmas and Danny wanted a Batman car. I had previously asked Jock to give me the money to buy these presents but he'd said,

'No. I'm only going to give you the Christmas Shopping money.'

It was half past three in the afternoon on Christmas Eve and I was alone with the two boys. I knew Jock would be out drinking but expected him to arrive home at about half past four to give me the shopping money. But Jock had decided instead to stay at the pub a little bit longer and spend his shopping money getting drunk. I had needed that money to buy the Christmas turkey. I had already spent my own money getting the children's presents.

When Jock didn't arrive with the shopping money, I began to panic.

What was I going to do? I wished that I hadn't got the Lego and the Batman car and instead bought a chicken. There was no food in the house.

Jock finally arrived at six-thirty, crawling drunk. His first words were,

'Did you buy the turkey?'

'No. You didn't give me the money.'

'You bloody bitch. What did you do with your wages?'

'I only had £11. I went out and bought Billy's Lego and also I got Danny a new duffle coat because it was freezing. I also got myself a new pair of shoes. And then I'd only got a couple of pounds left. So I bought you a pair of shoes.'

I handed Jock a new pair of moccasins. He threw them aside.

'Pair of shoes? I didn't want a pair of shoes.'

'There were moccasins in the sale. So I bought them for you from the last two pounds I had left.'

I didn't mention that I had also bought myself a little pair of plimsolls to walk in the street when I needed to run to catch a bus. Because I couldn't walk with high heels with Danny running around my legs. It was then that I had seen some moccasins in the sale and I bought them for Jock. All my £11 had gone in shopping for children's clothes, children's toys and my shoes and his shoes.

'So you think that's a big deal? You get me shoes. I didn't want shoes.'

'Well I've bought them. You can throw them away if you don't want them.'

'I won't throw them away. But I'll deal with you.'

'Why Jock? I thought that you were going to give me the money and we'd go shopping and buy the turkey. Because I've been here since three o'clock.'

'Oh! So you waited for me?'

'Well you shouldn't be getting drunk. '

The boys were upstairs sleeping. It was now seven thirty. I

was not holding back. I told him how I felt.

'You are drunk. And I am sick of it. It's Christmas Eve: and look at us. We should be getting dressed and going out. Instead you come home absolutely drunk. Now all I want to do is to go to sleep.'

'Go to sleep? You won't be going to sleep. Not after I've finished with you.'

In the dining room Jock had built a breakfast bar against the wall. Now he pushed me against that bar and kept hitting me. He said that he was teaching me a lesson not to waste money. He pushed and beat me so hard that he broke my ribs against the bar. I screamed and collapsed onto the floor. My screams awoke Billy, who came running downstairs.

'Daddy – what did you do? What did you do?'

'It's all acting. She just collapsed.'

Billy tugged at me, crying.

'Mummy! Mummy! Get up.'

I couldn't get up. I just lay there. At four o clock the next morning even Jock realised that there was something seriously wrong. He picked me up and took me to Charing Cross Hospital. The casualty doctor shook his head.

'You've got some very bad injuries Mrs MacDonald. You are all blood shot across the whole of your body. What did you do?'

I started to cry. I looked the doctor in the eye and lied to him.

'I was cleaning the ceiling and I fell down.'

The doctor shook his head.

'Someone has beat you up.'

'No. I actually fell down when I was cleaning the ceiling.'

'You were cleaning the ceiling on Christmas Eve? You weren't cleaning the ceiling.'

There was nothing else to say. After some x rays, there was more head shaking.

'I'm sorry. The x rays don't show anything because there is so much bruising around your body, It means that we can't do anything at the moment except give you painkillers. We can't fit you with a bandage because you'll get pneumonia. Can you come back after one week when the bruises have cleared up? Then we'll take another x ray.'

'Doctor. I can't breathe. I'm in pain.'

The doctor took my left hand and pushed it against my chest.

'When you breathe, you have to push your ribs in like that.'

He gave my hand a gentle push against my chest.

'Then breathe slowly like this.'

He gave a demonstration.

That was how I was for the next three months. It was Jock's Christmas present to me. I had to give up my job. At home I couldn't do any housework. Gus did the shopping and made us food, which he brought round to us.

I told the same lie to my brothers about having fallen down from the ceiling. But like the doctor, they didn't believe me. Rusi was the first to find out the truth.

Late one afternoon he and Soli came round to my house whilst Jock was still at work. Billy and Danny were with me as the schools had closed for the Christmas holiday.

Rusi and Soli looked at me in shock. Then Soli called Billy over.

'Hi Billy. I see that your Mum has fallen down.'

Billy shook his head.

'Mummy didn't fall down. Daddy beat her up.'

I rounded on Billy.

'You liar!'

Rusi said to me,

'Why didn't you call us – or the police?'

I stuck to my story.

'No. Jock didn't beat me up. Billy is a liar.'

I turned to Billy,

'Billy I'll kill you. Why lie to my brothers?'

Poor Billy looked at me in disbelief. He was only nine.

'Daddy did beat you up because you didn't buy the turkey for us. And you were fighting that day. And all we had was my Lego and Danny's batman car. We were happy to get those toys for Christmas day.'

After one week I left Billy and Danny with Mama. She gave me the money to go alone by taxi to Charing Cross Hospital. Bless her heart. As the taxi driver was taking me there he said,

'You are not very well. Shall I stop the taxi?'

'It's the pain. The pain.'

'What happened?'

'I had just fallen down.'

'That's terrible.'

I never told the truth to anyone because I was ashamed. I was ashamed that Jock had beat me up.

At the hospital the doctor examined me and gave me another x ray. After an hour when the results arrived, the doctor spoke to me,

'We can just about see the bruise lifting up from the ribs. I'm afraid that you have two very bad cracked ribs – from one end to the other. You must have had a tremendous fall.'

He paused. Then said,

'Do you want to talk to me? I promise that we will keep quiet. We just want to know. How did it happen?'

'I told you doctor. I was cleaning the ceiling when I got a slight dizziness.'

'What kind of floor have you got?'

'Carpet.'

'So there was a bar and you were cleaning and you overbalanced onto it?'

I nodded.

'Try to demonstrate to me how it happened.'

I tried. Then the doctor said.

'It is very hard to believe Mrs MacDonald. All I can say is that you cannot go to work. We will give you some pain killing injections and a very strong pain killer to take when you get home.'

Over the next four months the pain slowly eased. I hardly spoke to Jock during the whole of those four months. I didn't want to know him. All I said to him was,

'I'm going to get a divorce. I made the biggest mistake in my life in marrying you. I did it to get out of the house. I married you on your looks. You are a very violent person. I'd do anything for you, Jock. But I can't stand your beatings.'

After four months, as my ribs were getting better, I went back to work at Bush Radio but my life remained bleak. Jock never gave me any money or bought me flowers.

On 19th June 1972 I met Rusi. I had said to him,

'Today is my wedding anniversary. We've been married ten years.'

Rusi said, 'What can I get you?'

'I want some net curtains for a new room which Jock has made for Billy and Danny. I'd love to have some new net curtains.'

I was so poor. If Papa was still alive he would have known the poverty in which Jock kept me. He would have got me a divorce years ago. Rusi replied, 'Haven't you got a net curtain?'

'No. I can't afford it.'

It was true. I couldn't afford it. My wages as a waitress were just going. So Rusi gave me £5 to buy a net curtain. That and another grubby bunch of flowers from Jock represented my 1972 wedding anniversary. Oh yes. And there was something else to mark that anniversary: another argument and another slap.

Jock had not offered to take me out and I was expecting to spend the evening indoors. Then the phone rang.

'Hi Free. It's Bill. We're just phoning up to wish you a happy wedding anniversary.'

'Thank you Bill. What are you doing with Rose tonight?'

'Nothing.'

Jock rushed over and snatched the receiver from my hand.

'Hello Bill. It's a bit short notice, but would you like to come over? Free's been cooking tonight.'

In fact I hadn't been cooking at all. There was hardly any food in the house and I had no money to buy any. I told Jock as much. He said,

'Haven't you got any money?'

'No. Rusi gave me £5 to buy some net curtains.'

I showed them to Jock.

'Don't you like my new net curtains?'

He was not impressed.

'Net curtains. That's all you think. Clean the house up you dirty bitch. I've invited Bill and Rose.'

Bill was Jock's horrible brother. Rose was Bill's lovely Irish wife. I said to Jock,

'I've got no money. You should be buying the stuff for them and giving me the money so I can cook.'

Jock slapped my face and I cried.

'I'm sorry that I haven't done any cooking. All I've got is a mince pie from Marks and Spencer which I was going to warm up and give to you because it's our anniversary.'

Rose noticed that something was wrong when she and Bill arrived an hour later. She said to me,

'Why are you crying?'

'Because we had an argument.'

I never even told her that Jock had slapped my face because my brother had given me £5 to buy curtains. Years later it was Rose who told Shirin that I was getting beaten up. And that's how my divorce eventually started. But in the meantime there was another disaster which I would have to face.

30 Bootsie

I had a dog called Bootsie. It was medium sized spiky haired mongrel. We got him as a puppy in 1967 when Danny was just over a year old.

Billy had become jealous of the attention we were giving his younger brother and had started hitting him in the eye. Billy would stand on a little stool to open his own bedroom door. He then went out and hit Danny in the eye before quietly returning to his room.

I was always in the kitchen and Jock was always in the pub – so it took us a while to discover what was happening. But for several months I had noticed that every time Billy came near Danny, he would blink. Even when Danny was only nine months old, he knew all about the slaps which his elder brother was giving him. It was Keki who had first said to me,

'I'll get a puppy. Then Billy will stop hitting Danny with jealousy.'

And as soon as the puppy arrived, Billy stopped being jealous towards Danny.

I loved Bootsie very much. But it meant that we couldn't go on holiday, as there was no-one to take him for a walk.

I was then working in the night in the administration

department at Radio Rentals' office at Power Road, Chiswick. I worked in the record section.

Jock would take Bootsie with him when he came to pick me up from work, But he would never hold Bootsie on a chain. Perhaps it was because he hoped that Bootsie would escape and get run over. He knew how much I loved Bootsie.

When we first moved from our basement flat in Chiswick High Road to our new house in St Albans Avenue, Jock had left Bootsie locked up alone all night in the basement flat. I cried but all Jock could say was,

'I don't want him here tonight.'

Next morning we fought. I took some food and picked Bootsie up and took him with me to our new house. Jock didn't like it. He was always saying that he wanted Bootsie to be put to sleep because he thought that Bootsie was vicious.

Each time the dustmen came they banged the dustbin against our back fence in Chiswick High Road, because they also thought Bootsie was vicious. But those dustmen were young and they just wanted to tease him.

Jock would sometimes take him for a walk and people would try to touch him. Bootsie would just jump up at them like mad and Jock would pull the chain and choke him. He was still only one year old and did not need teaching in that way. But Jock never gave him any love or attention. And – yes - it is true that Bootsie became vicious towards Jock at the end. He was my dog and I was the only one who could look after him and control him. One evening Jock said,

'My mother is coming over.'

I sighed.

'Jock. I don't want your mother. I'm sick of having your mother here. We go to Brighton. We go to Bognor. We go to Blackpool. I don't have any holiday with you and our children.

Now I'm working at Radio Rentals in the night.

'I want a holiday with you and the boys. You can have your own holiday with your mother.'

'No way.'

As I put my foot down he said,

'Why don't you want my mother.'

'Because things are not getting on between us.'

'You seem to love the dog more than my mother.'

'The truth is Jock, I have never loved your mother. I respect her. I look after her. But I don't want your mother here.'

Our marriage was already cracking up – and Jock's mother coming here would not make it any better. So Jock told me,

'I'm going to get rid of your dog.'

'You haven't got the guts.'

It was the worst thing I ever said.

'I'll show you whether I've got the guts, Nobody challenges me. If you don't want my mother, I don't want the dog'

'The dog is mine. You bought him for Billy six years ago. I don't want that dog put to sleep.'

Jock turned round. He put the chain on Bootsie.

'I'm taking the dog round the corner for a walk.'

He smiled. I relaxed. I went back to my cooking. As he walked out of the door, I said,

'Don't do anything silly. Because he's like a child. Where are you taking him'

What he said next chilled me,

'I'm taking him to Cronian.'

Mr Cronian was our local Vet. Though to be truthful I didn't know whether to believe Jock. Had he just said it to upset me? For the past few weeks Jock had been telling me he had been taking my dog to Battersea Dogs Home to ask about having him put down. He had also told me that he had been to other vets to ask about having him destroyed. I could only answer,

'Why?'

Jock said nothing and walked out with the dog trotting alongside him.

It took me a minute to think about what he had just said. And the way he had said it. Then I panicked. There had been a coolness in the way he said it, which convinced me that he meant it. My worst fears were proved right. It was the last time I would see Bootsie alive. I tried ringing my brothers. The first one I reached was Soli. I screamed at him down the phone.

'Jock's taken my dog to have it put to sleep!'

Jock took Bootsie to Mr Cronian and was seen straight away. The vet looked at Bootsie and said,

'He's a very healthy dog.'

'He belongs to my wife.'

'Are you sure your wife wants it put down?'

'Yes. She couldn't bear to do it herself. So she asked me to bring him along. Let me know what I have to sign.'

Jock signed the letter. And the vet carried on.

'All right I'll put him down. But why? He looks a lovely dog.'

The vet called a nurse and both of them put Bootie on the table. As the vet put the needle in Bootsie's arm, blood squirted upwards and splashed on to the ceiling.

'My God! Look at the blood,' said the vet.

Bootsie fought for his life, lunging, snapping and trying to kill the nurse who was trying to hold him.

'I'll have to put a muzzle on him. I don't want the nurse getting bitten. Are you really sure you want to do this?'

A phone rang at the reception desk. The phone was answered. Then the receptionist opened the door and said,

'Mr Cronian. Can you come here? There's an urgent call

from Mrs MacDonald's family.'

'Who?'

'Mr Soli Manekshah.'

Jock interrupted.

'Don't take any notice of him. I'm the owner.'

'Look Mr MacDonald. I don't want any trouble.'

The receptionist passed the receiver across to Mr Cronian.

'I'm Soli Manekshah, Mrs MacDonald's brother. The dog belongs to Mrs MacDonald. The marriage is cracking up at the moment. If you touch that dog you will come into serious trouble. If Jock doesn't want it, I'll look after the dog myself. I'm coming over now from Kensington by taxi to pick the dog up.'

'All right I'll go and tell Mr MacDonald.'

So Cronian went back and told Jock that my brother would be taking over the dog to solve the problem. He said,

'You don't like the dog. And she won't have your mother. So now she doesn't want the dog and will give it to her brother.'

Jock was unmoved.

'I'm the dog's owner. I've signed the form. Mrs MacDonald has taken him over but I'm the original owner. I want you to put the dog down.'

And the cunt put my dog down.

An hour and a half after Jock had left our house with Bootsie, he returned alone. He held Bootsie's chain, which he threw at me.

'Don't ever challenge me. I've put your dog to sleep.'

I cried. Billy was crying and holding me. Danny was crying. All I could say was,

'Bootsie is dead. Bootsie is dead. Daddy has killed him.'

And that was it. I vomited all night. I couldn't bear to be in the house. For the next six months I wandered the streets like a zombie. I spent all day every day just staring into shop windows or sitting in the park. Every morning I just washed and got out of the house. And I didn't want to know Jock at all.

One morning Mama telephoned me from India. Soli had told her what had happened and she was very upset. All I could say was,

'He killed my dog.'

Mama said, 'That's terrible.' She wrote Jock a letter telling him what a terrible thing he had done. It made Jock realise what an evil thing he had done and he was broken up with guilt.

The morning after the vet killed my dog, Shirin took me to his surgery.

Ignoring the other people waiting in the surgery with their cats, Shirin approached Cronian as soon as he stepped into the waiting room to call the next customer. As soon as he saw me he knew immediately what it was about. Pointing at me, Shirin shouted at Cronian,

'You murderer! You killed my sister's dog. Look at her face. You can see how much she's been crying. The puppy was like a baby.'

'I didn't mean to. He said that the dog was his.'

At that point all the other ladies picked up their cats and walked out of the surgery. They didn't want to see Mr Cronian when they heard what had happened. They shared my sorrow.

The truth was that Bootsie had never bitten anyone. Jock had lied that he bit the dustmen. He was only barking to attract their attention. He was a lovely dog and Jock had killed him.

I was on tranquilizers for the next six months. The doctors told me to get another dog. But I didn't. How could I? I had enough heartbreak with the loss of Bootie. I didn't want Jock killing any more dogs. After a year had passed I went out and got a kitten.

To take my mind off the disaster which had happened, I

had started doing voluntary work for the RSPCA. I saw a black and white cat which had five kittens. I started petting it. Mrs Pauline Blackburn, another volunteer who had made her home into a rescue centre, said to me,

'It's no use crying over Bootsie. Would you like to take one of these kittens?'

Instinctively I replied,

'I'd love to. Shall I take it home to show to my boys?'

So I put the kitten I had chosen in my little Mini and I brought him home. He was so cute that as soon as they saw him, Billy and Danny said,

'Mummy. Can't we keep him here with us? We will keep him hidden in our room so that when Daddy comes home drunk he won't put him down.'

So I said,

'I think so.'

The next day I went back to Mrs Blackburn and said,

'I'll give you fifty pence donation and I'll sign the form. And today is Monday.'

So Mrs Blackburn said, 'You will call him 'Monday."'

I had that cat for sixteen years.

31 A Double Win

1973 started badly. I was still grieving for the loss of Bootsie.

But later that year that something happened which brought some happiness back into our marriage. I won the pools.

I didn't just win a valuable second dividend. I won it twice over. And it could so easily have been a first dividend if I had really followed Papa's advice. It was lovely Gillian who had suggested that I pray to my father.

With her bleached blond hair she looked like singer Dolly Parton, only better looking. She was a hairdresser who also became my best friend. I had been going to see her every week to get my hair done where she worked in Chiswick High Road.

When the owners of the salon were not in, Gill would give me lessons in how to cut mans' hair. She was married to Francisco, a fat Italian businessman who was a lot older than her and who had no culture but lots of money. He was out a lot and, like Steptoe, would come home with bits of china, second hand electrical appliances and other junk which he kept stored in their double garage. One afternoon Gillian suggested that we both go out to Oxford Street to buy designer clothes.

'We are both good looking,' she said. 'So let's treat ourselves. Then we can go out and meet some nice men.'

It was true. Whenever we walked down the street together, men's eyes would follow us everywhere. We got wolf whistles. And we loved it. My problem was that I had no money to buy designer clothes. My existence with Jock was hand-to-mouth. One day Gillian took me to her country cottage at Colnbrook. It was beautiful. It made me think back to when I lived in Pakistan.

Then I had everything. When we moved to London I still had everything. But all that changed when I married a drunk. Now I had nothing, just a drunk husband and our two boys. So at Gill's suggestion I asked my father for help.

When he was alive he had looked after me, his favourite daughter. So maybe he could still help me now. In my thoughts and prayers I began asking my father for help,

'Papa I want to be a millionaire just like you were. I want you to help me.'

I kept repeating my prayer. One night Papa came into my dream wearing his black Parsee cap. He said to me,

'I'll give you million dollar advice. Pick any team beginning with A and any team beginning with E.'

He was talking about the football pools. Every week I'd do the football pools. I'd do two separate lines on two separate coupons and hand them with my money to the pools collector who called every week. As the British football season had finished, I was doing the Australian pools. On Papa's advice I only picked teams whose names began with the letter A or E.

For the first five weeks nothing happened. So perhaps it was all in my imagination. Then in August 1974 I got a letter from Littlewoods Pools, It said,

'Dear Mrs MacDonald,

You have hit one of the lines. You have won £10,000 on your first coupon. But we see that you have also sent in a second winning coupon and we are still calculating how much you have won on that second coupon. Yours sincerely, '

When I first opening the letter and saw it was from Littlewoods Pools I had thought that I'd perhaps won £25 or £50. When I read the letter I still couldn't quite believe what it was saying. I rang Shirin and read the letter out to her. It was Shirin who said to me, 'That's £10,000. But don't spend it all.'

I was jumping for joy, shouting, 'Oh my God!'

Of course £10,000 in 1973 was worth about £150,000 in today's money. And there was still another cheque to come,

Jock was at work so I phoned the company head office and left a message for him to ring me. At lunchtime he rang home, thinking that perhaps there was a toilet blocked. I told him all about the pools win.

'We are in the money!' he shouted.

'No. I am in money.'

On Shirin's advice I said nothing to Jock about the second win. When the second cheque came I quietly gave it to Shirin, who banked it and put the money aside for me.

'If I don't, Jock will spend it all,' she warned.

At that time Billy was nine years old and Danny was six. Two weeks later the second cheque came through, this time for £11,200. I handed it to Shirin to put away for me. The funny thing was that I could have won two cheques for £50,000 if I had followed Papa's advice to the letter. But instead of choosing a team beginning with A or E, I'd chosen one team beginning with the letter J, to honour his name, Jehangir. So although I'd won, I'd missed a first dividend and lost out on tens of thousands more. We wasted no time spending the money.

I bought myself a pleated skirt from Oxford Street. I also bought 'his and her' cars for me and Jock.

I bought a brand new white mini cooper for myself. For Jock

I paid £750 for a chocolate colour Vauxhall Viva. But it didn't take long for him to write it off. And with tragic consequences.

Jock was driving down Sutton Court Road towards the junction with the Great West Road. I was in the passenger seat. We were on our way to see Shirin. As usual he was a little bit tipsy. When we were still some way from the junction, Jock saw that the traffic lights were still green and he speeded up to get across the junction before they changed up to red.

As we were speeding across the junction, the lights changed up. From the Great West Road a car pulled away in front of us. We smashed into it.

The impact pushed the stem of the ignition key into my knee. I screamed as it bit into me. I was taken to West Middlesex Hospital, where it took a doctor and a morphine injection to get it out.

In the other car were a young foreign couple. They'd only been in London for a few days and the woman who was driving had been nervous and hesitant. She was knocked unconscious and sadly died. But the police said that Jock was not to blame for the accident.

'They were too quick to pull away' said the officer on the scene.

One of the things which frightened Jock was the speed at which I was giving money away.

I gave £1,000 to Keki. £500 to Jock's mother. £1,000 to Gustad; £1,000 to Aspi. £1,000 to Dilnawaz. And I gave £1,000 to Gill.

'We'll have nothing left,' said Jock.

In fact we did have enough left to enjoy several good holidays over the next six years. In 1978 we went to an Elvis memorial concert on the Isle of White, where we stayed in a caravan. The following year we went for a week's spending spree in Toronto, where we stayed in a four star hotel. Then the money ran out. But not all of it. As there was still several thousand left from the second cheque which I had handed over to Shirin.

That money later came to my rescue in helping to pay the mortgage after our marriage broke up.

32 Sexual Problems

When we first got married, our sex life was good. Though I wouldn't call it excellent.

Ten years into our marriage Jock began to have problems maintaining erections. It was because he was always drinking,

Jock would only want sex with me twice a week. Even then it was difficult.

He would work hard to obtain an erection. But as soon as he tried to put it in, his hardness collapsed like a burst balloon. So I sent him to the doctor. Though at first I was not particularly worried as we had been through it several times before.

On our wedding night we had so much sex. Yet after three months he could not perform at all and wondered what was happening to him. Doctor Guerken gave him tablets to build up his energy. She told him to sleep alone for six weeks on the sofa and not to touch me at all. Alcohol was banned.

The treatment worked. Our sex life resumed. But Jock started having lapses in 1972. We were trying it twice a week for a few months during 1972. Sometimes he could do it. Sometimes couldn't.

He spent even more time in the pub and did not give me any money. Instead he started buying me orange bikini pants and pale green bikini pants with holes in them. I said to him, 'Why are you buying me these horrible underpants?'

He explained, 'Because when me and my mate came out of the station at Bethnal Green, we saw a woman who had fallen down and hurt herself. There were staff standing around trying to help her up. She was lying on the ground with her skirt hitched up around her thighs. She was showing everything. So my mate said 'Look at that!' And I did. She was wearing orange and green bikini pants. They looked as though they had holes in them. But it was the way they were made. I could see everything. With her brown body she reminded me of you. So I thought that they would look sexy on you. So I bought you a pair just like them'

I was most distressed. It turned out he was picking woman's underwear and holding it up against his own body and visioning that he could bring it for me. He started going to ladies' boutiques just before Christmas and birthday times to bring me sexy lingerie for me to wear to turn him on. But I didn't like it. One day I said to him, 'What's the point of you buying me this underwear, because you don't do anything? Why don't you give up the drink and go to the doctor?'

Jock replied, 'I can't do it anymore. No use of me going to the Doctor. Cos I can't give up my drink. I like my drink.'

'Well then, I think we are going to get divorced.'

'Divorced? You've been talking about divorce every year and you haven't done it. You're stuck with me.'

So for the time being I decided to live with it. Sometimes in bed I would cuddle in to him. There was also something with Jock about magazines and Bethnal Green, where he was then working.

On returning from work one afternoon, Jock mentioned to me that he had been into a sex shop and had got hold of a magazine to see if there was something for the lady's pleasure. He pulled out of his hold-all something which looked like a little torch with a rubber on it. He showed it to me and said,

'This is a vibrator.'

I'd never seen a vibrator before and didn't know what it was.

'It will give you a little tickling sensation,' he said.

We used the vibrator every two to three nights, whenever I needed it. He also kept a store of batteries, as each set of batteries barely lasted five minutes. One night I got upset and said to him,

'I'm going to tell my friends what you are doing with this dirty vibrator. You're not a real man. You're just a pervert.'

He felt bad. He stopped coming upstairs to sleep with me. It didn't worry me because I knew that our marriage was already on the rocks. But sometimes I missed his company and called down to him,

'Are you coming upstairs? I don't mind you using the vibrator. Just come upstairs. We can try again.'

He said,

'No use. I don't want to use the vibrator anymore. I'm not going to bother about it. I'm not your dog and I can't do it. You'll just have to forget about sex until the boys are big. If you don't like it then perhaps you should start a divorce.'

Then in March 1974 Mama died.

Because she had difficulty breathing she was taken to St Mary Abbots Hospital. She never came out. The official cause of death was septicaemia.

But Shirin didn't believe it and wanted to sue the Hospital. She wanted a post mortem to discover the true cause of death and whether it could have been prevented. Rusi said, 'No. We don't do that in our religion.'

33 New Home – New Start

Jock made a mistake when he hit me once in 1977 in front of Rose, my Irish sister in law. She was a nurse. I had previously told her that I was not happy.

In front of the two brothers she said to me,

'Each time you come here to see me and Bill, I keep on asking you, 'Why are you living with him? You could get someone better, while you are young and you've got young children. Why don't you leave?'

Jock was the first to respond,

'Shut your gob. Don't encourage her at all. She's all right.'

Rose replied,

'No. You're not very good to her. She's making lovely dinner for us. And you treat her like dirt. I don't know what she sees in you.'

I tried to calm the conversation down,

'Maybe I do love him Rose. You know – one day I might lose my temper and divorce him.'

The truth was that things were getting very bad between us. There was no love left anymore. And no conversation. I used to leave his food out, like a dog. And, without a word, he used to get up, get ready, and go to work. Then he'd go to the pub and get drunk. I had no life.

I would work and watch television with the boys. My life was going out with my friends during the daytime whilst the boys were at school.

As they were still only eleven and fourteen I couldn't really leave them alone at night. So I decided to sell our house at St Albans Avenue in the hope that I could have a fresh start with Jock in a new home.

Maybe the house was not good. All the neighbours knew that Jock was getting drunk. I was also ashamed of him beating me up. So I told Rusi that I wanted to move. He said,

'I've already got a lovely buyer for your house if you ever want to move. I'll also get you a good price because you've got an extra room in the loft.'

I nodded. Rusi went on,

'They are a very nice Japanese family. The mother is English and the father is Japanese and he's a businessman. And he's got two lovely sons. They are living in my friend's flat.

'Now the mother told me the other day that she's looking for a lovely house which doesn't need anything doing to it.

'I told her to come and look at my sister's house. She said that she had already spoken to her husband in Japan, who had said that she'd better have a look and put down a deposit straightaway.'

Rusi could see that my house was immaculate. Jock had recently done the kitchen.

To me it was just a stone in the dark. But at that time houses were going up in price. And within two weeks the family had looked at it and made a substantial offer. At the same time I had put the house on the market with a local estate agent, who had suggested an asking price of £22,500.

It was worth every penny. I had a new cooker and other fitments. There was also a very nice open plan dining room and sitting room – and of course the warm room in the loft. Overall it was a pretty house. But my face dropped when Rusi said to me,

'Of course you will have to ask Jock. Because although it's not really his house, it is still in your joint names. So we'd better ask.'

'I'm not happy. Things are not going well with me now.'

'I could see that.' He added,

'Well. Maybe a change might do him good.'

'The bastard,' I said,

So that night after Jock had come home from work, Rusi popped in and said to him,

'Before you go out, Farida has got something to tell you.

'She wants to sell the house and I've got a nice Japanese family who want to buy it.'

Jock frowned and said, 'No. No.'

He thought for a moment and then said,

'How much is it?'

'£22,000,' said Rusi.

Jock smiled,

'£22,000? I think that's good.'

What Jock didn't know was that the buyers were giving £5,000 extra, making a total of £27,000. I had agreed with Rusi that he would take that £5,000 and put it away for me He knew the marriage was bad. So Rusi said to Jock.

'All right. We've got the £22,000 which the agent put it up for'

In fact we had had three offers through the estate agent, in addition to the family's offer. So Rusi said to the buyers,

'I've spoken to my sister and she wants £27,000 for the property, because it's got an extra room in the loft.'

The wife said, 'We'll agree £27,000.'

Rusi then added, 'But I want £5,000 of it in cash because of the fixtures and fittings. Like the new kitchen, the bathroom, all the wooden panelling and all the shelves. And the whole house has been recently carpeted and includes fitted cupboards. So that is the £5,000. We'll only put £22,000 on the contract. But the £5,000 I must have in cash.'

The woman spoke to her husband and deal was done.

I then had to rush to the estate agent to find a property to buy. I found a beautiful house called Ridgeway off Gunnersbury Avenue. I fell in love with it.

It had a beautiful kitchen. Beautiful through-lounge. A marble fire-place. And a full size snooker table. But there was one thing wrong.

It was off the North Circular Road where my two cats could have been killed if they wandered on to it. I refused that house and started looking again. Then I found another house, just round the corner, in Princes Avenue. We bought that house. And in June 1979 we moved into our new house thinking that our marriage would get better.

The Princes Avenue house was on the market at £29,000. When Jock saw the property he also liked it. He said to the sellers, '£29,000 is a lot for us. Will you take an offer?'

Their response was, 'Sorry. We've got a 146' garden with fruit trees and strawberries. We haven't got a new bathroom nor a new kitchen. But we've got a through-lounge. And we're not going to let it go for less than £29,000 because it's semi-detached and with its own garage.'

So Rusi told Jock, 'Put the £22,000 down and take a £7,000 mortgage. I'm sure you could afford it. It's her money and her house. You just need to pay the mortgage. Put it in your joint names.

'No. No. No. I can't afford a £29,000 house.'

'Come off it Jock. You want everything on a platter. If you split up we'll take the house over and then you can get a divorce from her.'

Jock didn't like the idea. But the bastard signed the contract. He also signed a letter to Rusi.

Rusi had said to Jock, 'To make it easier for you I'll give you an extra £5,000 to put in a new kitchen and bathroom. But I want an I.O.U from you to repay that money to me if anything happens between you and Farida and if the house is sold. I will make an affidavit saying that you have promised to give me the £5,000 back.'

And that was the deal between Jock and Rusi.

So Jock took on a £7,000 mortgage and we put in a new kitchen and bathroom. After that I rarely saw Jock.

He would come home very late at night and very drunk. He became very violent and aggressive and screamed at me. I always knew when he was coming home because I heard his car going round and round the block looking for our house because he was so drunk. What was worse was that all my new neighbours quickly discovered that I was married to a drunkard. I was so ashamed.

They complained to me that he was beeping his horn and waking them at 2am as he drove round. He would then get out of his car with a loud 'poooof' – as he blew the alcohol out of his system. I started putting a chain across the door because I didn't want him coming in and screaming at me. But one night he broke open the door and beat me up. I phoned Rose up and said, 'I'm not happy. He's beat me up very badly. I don't know what to do. Can you suggest something?'

She replied, 'The only thing I could tell you is that he's a house jackal and a street angel. I'm going to phone your sister up right now.'

She phoned Shirin up and put her in the picture.

She said, 'Do you know your sister is very unhappy since her mum and dad died? I want to tell you that Jock is beating her up all the time and Free has told me just now that she's getting a breakdown.'

Shirin phoned me up and she came straightaway and confronted Jock, saying,

'What have you been doing?'

I told everything to my sister: how he'd been drinking and beating me up. Plus the fact that for ten years he hadn't slept with me. My sister was so shocked. She said to me,

'Why didn't you phone me up and tell me the truth about this?'

'I couldn't. I was too ashamed to tell you that my marriage was on the rocks.'

Shirin turned to Jock and stabbed her finger at him saying, 'All right. I'll take her to South America and she'll get a divorce in twenty four hours. I've got the money.

'Either that or you stop drinking and treat her nicely. Because she's not going to sit at home knitting and getting your beatings.'

34 Locked Out

Jock was coming home very drunk every night and one evening I put the chain on the front door because it was so late.

Jock banged on the door. He shouted and swore at me. It awoke Billy, who ran down the stairs and opened the door. Jock pushed his way through the door in a fuming rage. I was sitting halfway up the stairs wearing only a flimsy nightdress. I said,

'You're drunk again.'

'Come here you bitch.'

'You're drunk again.'

Jock lunged towards me. He grabbed hold of me and dragged me down the stairs. He then pushed me along the hallway towards the front door. In doing so he rammed me against the legs of a large planter situated behind the front door. I could not go any further, so he hit me in the ribs, and I cried. Billy said,

'I'm going to ring Aunty Shirin up if you don't stop hitting her.'

'No. I'm not going to stop hitting her. I'm going to push her out of the house in her nightdress.'

He pushed me out of the front door and locked it shut. It was 2am. I shivered with cold. Now it was me who banged on the door.

'Let me in.'

'I'd like to see you getting locked out. You bitch.'

Then I heard Billy say,

'I'm going to ring Aunty. I'm going to take her in.'

Jock pushed Billy back saying,

'I'm going to teach her by keeping her locked out without any clothes.

So I went next door to Min and Tommy and kept knocking on their door to get them out of bed. Eventually they came down and were surprised to see me standing half clothed. I explained that Jock had got drunk and that he had locked me out of the house. Both of them came with me and knocked on my door. Min said,

'Jock. Please open the door. It's two o'clock. Don't be silly.'

They knocked and knocked. It was several minutes before they got any reply.

Jock had fallen asleep in the lounge and it was Billy who eventually came round and took me in.

Min and Tommy went away. I ran inside and up to bathroom and was shocked when I looked at myself in the mirror. My hands were bruised and torn where I had banged on the door.

So the next morning I phoned Shirin. She said,

'Don't go to work.'

At that time I was working in the Institute of Advanced Motorists, having left Multiple Sound in 1977.

So after Jock had gone to work, Shirin came round and took me to a solicitor called Whittington of Ramsey Murray Solicitors. I sobbed into a handkerchief as we sat in the waiting room. Then Whittington called us in. As he led us through to his office, he touched my arm, saying,

'No need to cry.'

'But I don't really want a divorce. My sister is forcing me to get a divorce.'

Shirin gave me an angry look. Whittington ignored it and said, 'Look at your arms Mrs MacDonald. How long has this been going on?'

'Nearly thirteen years. He's become very violent. And I've got no relationship with him. He doesn't do anything except drink. He can't do anything.'

'Mmm. We'll come to that later. But now I'm going to ask you to sign this green legal aid form.'

Shirin chipped in.

'It was our house. But he wanted it put on his name. He's got a violent streak and he's been throwing her about. He's even broken her ribs.'

Over the next weeks we put together a divorce petition. In the petition I said how he had cracked my ribs in 1971 and how he had killed my dog. And there was another thing.

On one occasion he had come home late from the pub and told me to go into the kitchen and cook him something. I replied. 'I'm not going to bother about the kitchen. There's no food.'

'Well make me something.'

'No. You're drunk. If you have time to get drunk, you have time to come home and have a proper supper with your wife and your sons. If you don't want to do that, I'm not doing any cooking.'

'Come along. Come along,' replied Jock as he pulled my arm towards him. Then he burned it with a cigarette. I could only scream.

I put everything in that petition. And a copy of that signed petition was posted to Jock. He was terrified. His friend told him at work,

'That divorce petition is very bad. And if you don't answer it they're liable to get a summons against you. So you need to get a quick solicitor and answer it.'

So he went to a woman solicitor called Keane. But it was something else which brought those particular divorce proceedings to a halt.

35 The Heart Attack

One morning at the beginning of 1980 I was cooking the boys' breakfast. Jock had gone out the previous night and had not returned home: which at that time was not unusual. In fact we barely spoke to each other. But as he was leaving for work the previous day I had said to him,

'I want to talk to you. I'm going to go through with this divorce.'

'I don't want to talk to you. You bitch.'

He walked out.

Around half past eleven the following morning, I got a phone call from a nurse at Charing Cross Hospital,

'Is that Mrs MacDonald? I'm sorry to tell you that your husband has collapsed.'

'Is that so? The old bastard.'

The nurse paused and carried on.

'He's in intensive care. We don't know what happened last night. Can you come over?'

I started to cry and finished giving the boys their breakfast. I then grabbed the boys and packed them in my Mini and raced over to the hospital.

Jock lay quietly on a bed attached to a heart monitor. He'd

had a mild heart attack Over the weeks he lay there he thought a lot of me and regretted his violence. During those weeks and during his convalescence afterwards he depended on me. When he came out of the hospital he followed the specialist's advice and gave up drinking. Even Shirin felt sorry for him. She said to me,

'Everything was on him. He's not such a bad chap.'

He was a bastard. And during the coming weeks and months he got better and regained his strength.

I had given him all the dishes which the Hospital had told me. I gave him chicken without skin and all the lovely vegetables but there were no potatoes and no sugar. Only semi-skimmed milk. Slowly I nursed him back to health. I was coming home with all the shopping whilst he lay ill in the house. Every time he smoked I screamed at him. And he stubbed the cigarette out. Just to keep me happy.

It made Danny very distressed. Because it seemed that we were fighting all the time. Each time he ate or touched anything he shouldn't, I screamed at him. And he won his health back. Thanks to me. Perhaps things were going to work out for us after all. But as that happy thought was going through my head, a plane was landing at Heathrow Airport.

A Scotsman got out of the plane. He was tall and well-tanned and in his mid-thirties. He went through passport control and to baggage reclaim. There he collected two suitcases and cleared customs. He then parked his trolley alongside a telephone booth and dialled a number. It was me who answered the phone.

'Hello. Is that Free?

'Yes.'

'It's Alli. I've just flown back from Saudi Arabia and I'm at the airport.'

'Alli. What do you want?'

'What do you mean – what do I want? I want my friend Jock.'

'I'm sorry. Jock hasn't been very well and he's just getting better. I don't want you to take him anywhere for drinks. Because it's against the doctor's rules.'

The old bastard was lying down on a green couch looking at the ceiling. I could just sense that he was dying for a drink. He looked at me with one eye and said,

'Who is it?'

I ignored him and said to Alli,

'I'm sorry Alli. He's not coming out.'

I slammed the phone down and said to Jock,

'It was your drunk friend.'

'Which drunk friend?'

'Alli.'

'What did you tell him?'

'Your doctor's orders are that you're not supposed to drink.'

Jock got off the sofa, came over and slapped me hard across the face.

'You tell my friend that I've got doctor's orders?'

'You bastard. Three months ago you were dying and I brought you back to health. And you are not drinking because the doctor told you that if you have another heart attack it will kill you. And I'm in charge.'

'You will never be in charge. You told my friend that I'm not coming out. Where is he now? I'm going to the airport.'

An unshaven Jock went to the bathroom and slammed the door. He ran the bath. Forty five minutes later a clean shaven and sweet smelling man reappeared and went into the bedroom to get dressed. He then went to the kitchen to get himself something to eat. His mood had changed. He was singing. As he was preparing to leave the house that there was a 'ding dong' at the door. Jock opened it.

'Alli!'

'Jock!'

Alli stepped inside. And like long lost lovers, both men cuddled in to each other. I stood back thinking, 'Oh my God!'

Alli was first to break away. He said to Jock,

'Don't listen to that bitch. You're coming out for a booze up.'

Both men looked at me. Then Jock said,

'Bloody bitch. Just because she got me right she thinks she owns me. Bloody bitch. I'm going to come round and have a real good booze up with you. Come on. We'll walk to Acton Town Station and get a mini cab.'

Both men walked out. And that was the last I heard of Jock until next day. I saw nothing more of Alli as he went straight back to Saudi Arabia,

At six thirty the following morning, the phone rang. It was the police.

'Are you Mrs MacDonald?'

'Yes.'

'I have to tell you that we found your husband absolutely drunk and sitting in his car on the hard shoulder of the Great West Road. He had suitcases with him.'

'I'm surprised you didn't find him dead.'

'What do you mean?'

'I thought you were going to give me some good news. He beat me up last night. And three months ago he had a heart attack.'

'We don't want to know about your domestic problems. You need to go to your solicitor to sort out that problem. But I'm here to tell you that he's not dead but that he's very drunk. We've told him that we're going to charge him. He said to us that he didn't drive and gave us the address of the mini cab. And we're going to find out from the mini cab company whether he was picked up.'

Apparently a passer-by had come across a dead body in a car on the hard shoulder of the Great West Road. That man then went to the police station and reported his discovery.

So four policemen rushed round in a squad car. One of them opened the car door and shook the dead body awake. Around half past three that afternoon a tramp arrived at my door. I opened it and turned my face away.

'You bitch. Have you got any grub for me?' said the tramp.

'Jock. I don't want to talk to you.'

He hit me.

'I'm going back to Mr Whittington and I'm going to restart my divorce proceedings now. I'm going to start a new petition.'

So I went back to Mr Whittington.

36 A Bad Dream

I first went to Mr Whittington during 1980 to start divorce proceedings. Because I was hesitant, Whittington had said,

'You've got three weeks from service of the petition to think it over and see how he gets on.'

Later I'd phoned him up and said,

'I don't want to go on with the divorce. He's promised he'll give up the drink.'

'Then we'll keep the file open for you for six months. If in the meantime he beats you up, you can come back to me.'

Of course he did beat me up. It was after the episode with Alli. I went back to Whittington with my mind made up. I told him everything.

I told him that Jock hadn't touched me for years and that he was impotent. Whittington put it all down in letter to Mrs Keane. And she copied the letter to Jock, saying,

'Your wife says that you've become impotent. That you haven't bothered about sex. And by the way: don't drink. Because she's trying to get you out of the house. Don't give her a chance to get rid of you.'

'I'm not impotent. I'll show her that I'm not impotent.'

That is why he raped me.

Each night, after he had staggered home drunk, it was the same ritual. From my bedroom I would hear Jock coming upstairs to the toilet. I would hear the cistern flush and Jock's footsteps as he went downstairs to the green couch to go to sleep. But this night it was different.

Jock pushed his way into my bedroom. He put a cushion on my mouth and then he raped me.

Danny's bedroom was off the main bedroom like an ensuite and he could hear what was going on. He came in and saw Jock on top of me.

'What are you doing to her?'

'She had a bad dream son.'

'You're not even in your pyjamas Daddy.'

'I'm never in pyjamas. I sleep in my jeans.'

He was so horrible that at the end he never had pyjamas.

I said, 'He's done a horrible thing to me.'

'What are you doing? You're choking her.'

'I'm letting her go to sleep. Because she had a bad dream.'

Jock raped me. Even though he couldn't get a horn. He went into me and shot his stuff inside me so he could make me pregnant. He wanted to give me another baby so that I didn't have to leave him. He was an animal.

At that time I had started trying to rebuild my life. I had been going out with my Yugoslavian friend Mara and her circle of friends. I was coming home to give the boys their dinner and going out Friday nights with Mara. When Jock was coming home he would ask Danny,

'What are you doing?'

'I'm waiting for Mummy. She's gone out.'

'You should go to bed.'

'No. Tomorrow's Saturday Daddy.'

Danny, the poor chap, was so nervous each time Jock and

I were fighting. He left his school work. That's why he became ill. He had been going to school all right. But our marriage destroyed his schooling. He couldn't concentrate. Every time the school report came it said that Danny was falling behind very badly. His teacher wrote, 'Is there a problem at home?'

My son had never been like that. It was because of my marriage which affected him very badly.

Following the rape, I became pregnant. So I told Dr Guerken that I hadn't got my period and that I was very upset.

'I think Jock's done that.'

She said,

'Don't worry. We'll have your urine tested. Take time off from Institute of Advanced Motorists. Before 10am, drive all the way to Kensington and go to St Mary Abbots Hospital'

At that time I was working as a clerical assistant at the Institute of Advanced Motorists at Chiswick High Road. So after the urine test I went back to Dr Guerken. She said,

'You're positive. What do you want to do?'

'I'll have to tell Shirin.'

Shirin came round and said,

'When did it happen? You said that he hadn't touched you for so many years?'

'That's right.'

'How?'

'It was that letter Keane sent it to him.

'As he was raping me he kept saying,

'I'm impotent? I'll show you. Bitch.

'I'll show you. Bitch. I'm impotent all right. I'll really sort you out.'

So one morning I broke the news to him,

'You bastard. I'm pregnant now.'

Jock laughed,

'I don't know who made you pregnant. You're fucking around with your Yugoslavian friend. It must be one of her mates who made you pregnant. Not me.'

'Then I'll tell you that if you don't pay for the abortion, I'll have that child.'

'I'll give you fuck all. That's what I'll give you.'

'If you don't pay for the abortion, I'll do one thing. I'll see Doctor Guerken. Then I'll divorce you and have the baby. Then you'll be paying me for the next sixteen years.'

Jock went away.

He returned at five thirty in the afternoon. Earlier that day Shirin had said that she would pay for the abortion. But she asked me not to tell that to Jock.

'I want to talk to you – you bitch.'

'You call me bitch? I've never been out with any man in my life. All I go out with is Mara. And that's just for a drink. I swear on Mama that I've never had any boyfriend.'

And at that was the truth. I had Chris and Malcolm afterwards.

'How much is it for the abortion?'

'No – you don't have to worry about that. I've decided to have the baby.'

'Get rid of that fucking thing. The marriage is over.'

'No. No. I think I'll have the baby. And you pay for it.'

Billy then interrupted. He ran in to the room crying with embarrassment,

'I heard your conversation. I'm sixteen and you're having a baby?'

'So what. That bastard raped me.'

Then Danny came in.

'Ask Danny what happened that night.'

We all looked at Danny.

'Daddy said that Mummy had a bad dream.'

'No. He had a cushion on my face and he was raping me. When you came round it was 2am. It was not a dream. Your father was raping me. Do you understand what is rape? It's a horrible thing. He was forcing me to have sex with him. Most disgusting.'

Jock then confessed all.

'Oh God! I'm sorry Danny, I got carried away. She wrote a horrible letter to me... Her divorce petition said that I was impotent. And I lost my temper. And I was going to give her a lesson... Yes I did rape her.'

Billy turned towards me, his eyes filled up with tears.

'I'm so upset. You're going to have a baby? I don't want you to have a baby.'

I was crying in the kitchen. And Danny was getting all upset in his bedroom. It was so bad for the children. I hoped Jock would die. I just hated him. I was destroyed by this horrible monster. I was married to a bastard. A monster. And I hated him.

When he came home from work the next day, Jock threw £250 in cash at me.

'Get the abortion done.'

After he had left for work I phoned Doctor Guerken. She sent me to Margaret Street. There I went to an abortion clinic and waited in the sitting room. Abortions were now legal in the UK.

It was packed with middle aged women; young girls; unmarried girls; everybody. A nurse handed me a piece of paper,

'Can you fill this form up?'

I had taken Danny in the train with me. He was on holiday. He was so good. He had wanted to come, saying, 'I'll come on the train and sit with you. And I'll get the train back.'

I was so grateful for his company. Because I had no-one else to go with me. When we arrived at the clinic, Danny said,

'I'll come in and sit with you Mummy.'

'No. No. You go straight back to Chiswick and go home. I don't know how long I'm going to stay. Don't worry.'

So Danny took the train back. I had told him that I didn't want to go alone. Shirin had arranged the abortion. She had said,

'First go to the clinic and sign all the necessary forms.'

So I sat in the waiting room holding the blank form. My hands were shaking so much that I didn't know where to start. A nurse came over and helped me to fill up the form. She was very nice. As we were doing so she talked to me saying,

'Why don't you have the baby? And then we'll give you extra family planning.'

'No. The marriage is broken down and I'm going through a divorce.'

Still she tried to talk me out of it. Because psychologically that is what they had to do. At the end of the conversation she said to me,

'All right now. You've made up your mind. I want you to go and see a doctor. Go up to the first floor.'

The doctor was very nice. He looked at me and said,

'What is the problem? I've read your notes. I'm sorry the child was not really expected. I see that your marriage is broken up. We'll give you an abortion. It'll be £250. And you have to take these notes to the Rosalind Clinic at Twickenham. Take the money with you. Don't leave anything behind.'

He handed me a small bottle containing a single tablet.

'Break this in half and take it one night before to relax you. You must have nothing to eat after 11pm that night.'

I went home and cried. Then Shirin phoned me up to say that she would be picking me up in the morning. The bastard then said to Shirin, as if he was doing us a favour,

'Don't worry. I'll drop her because I'm going to work.'

'No. No. We don't want you Jock. You've done a lot of damage.'

'No. I've got the money. I'm going to take her. You could come with me if you want.'

Shirin said,

'All right. But I'll come later on.'

Jock took me from our home at Princes Avenue, Chiswick at eight o clock the following morning. I had told Danny to feed the cats. Billy went off to school. After I had arrived at the Rosalind Clinic, the nurse said to me,

'If anybody rings about you – shall we give them the news that you are all right?'

'Yes. I'm going to be all right.'

The nurse carried on,

'Yes. You're two months into your pregnancy. But don't worry. We do abortions up to three and a half months. You've had an abortion before – haven't you?'

'This time it's a new system. We just put a hose underneath and suck it out. It won't hurt at all.'

I was crying.

'Take all your jewellery off. Everything. And clean the nail varnish off your nails.'

'What for?'

'We want everything cleaned up.'

After I had undressed and taken everything off the nurse said to me,

'Now we'll give you a little tablet to relax you. But without water. You're supposed to swallow it.'

I put the dry tablet in my mouth and tried to swallow it. I nearly choked on it.

'You have to try. You have to put it on your tongue.'

I tried again and managed to swallow it.'

Then Shirin phone up,

'What time shall I come and pick her up?'

'Ring up at three to see if she is up. We're giving her a very mild anaesthetic and she'll be out.'

So as I was going upstairs from the bedroom, a doctor came round. He was a Doctor Sherif, who was going to do the abortion. He said to me,

'Farida. You're Zoroastrian. I found out about them when I was in Israel. Why don't you stop crying?'

'I'm feeling depressed and frightened here.'

'Rubbish! We do it everyday. But you are a very depressed person at the moment.'

'I'm going through a divorce.'

'Listen. I don't want you to cry. I want you to be happy here. You're having an abortion. No man is worth your tear. I want you to smile. I'm not going to give you anaesthetic unless you smile. Because I don't want you to feel upset'

So nice doctor. God bless him. I was crying but to please him I said, 'All right'. And I forced a smile.

'You will be in and out. I'm going to do the abortion. My colleague is going to give you a little prick here. Next thing you'll get up in the ward.'

'How long will it take?'

'Ten minutes to half an hour.'

He did the abortion. Next thing I was in the ward. I got up and there was a girl in the bed next to me. She smiled and she said, 'How are you feeling?'

'I'm all right. What are you doing?'

'I've had the same thing. I was a bunny girl and I had an affair with a client. He paid for it. I didn't want the baby.'

Three o clock came round. I was lying and relaxed. The nurses gave me lovely soup with some bread and butter. A nurse said to me,

'How are you feeling?'

'Much better. I'm not feeling sick from the anaesthetic. It's a lovely clinic.'

'I'm going to bring your clothes. And your sister is waiting to take you home.'

Shirin took me home. She had got all the lovely food from Marks and Spencer. Gus had made it up. The boys came home from school and Shirin sat with us in the sitting room. The bastard came home after a few drinks. He said to Shirin,

'How is she?'

'Fine. We don't want to talk to you Jock. Are you going to leave us or are you going to come home drunk tonight? Because I could take her home to my house if you're going to come home drunk. The doctor in the hospital told us to keep her very quiet. She's become very nervous. And we're going to go ahead with the divorce.'

He said,

'Yes – that's the best thing to do. Because I'm not going to give up the drink.'

Shirin said to him,

'She's very distressed. I want you to leave now.'

'Yes. I'm going to Eddie's. I won't come home drunk. And if I am drunk I will stay at Eddie's.'

Jock didn't come drunk that night. He came home quietly and slept downstairs. I stayed in my room. And Danny kept coming in and out of my room to see how I was.

I had an abortion – and that was it. I got a certificate from the Rosalind Clinic to say that I had gone there to have my womb scraped. A D and C they called it. I couldn't tell the women at the office that I was raped and that I had an abortion. After a week I returned to work.

It was later that I confided in my colleague Moira that I had an abortion. She couldn't believe it. She said,

'Why didn't you tell us?

'I didn't want to tell you. Because he was like an animal.'

37 Malcolm and Chris

After I had fully recovered from the abortion – both physically and mentally – I started to go out again Friday nights with Mara. She was a divorcee and we started to go out socially together in the evenings – although I always tried to make sure that I was home before Jock arrived staggering drunk after the pubs had closed.

Mara wanted me to keep her company because she was too shy to go out alone. I was with Mara when I met Malcolm.

He was an attractive English divorced man who had been living in Australia before his marriage broke up and who now owned a flat in Northolt. I met him at a party on a boat. It was a singles party and that evening we boarded the boat off the Westminster Embankment. After a buffet meal the disco started. As I was sitting with Mara I noticed a man sitting opposite who was looking at me. He was tall and handsome, I would say in his mid-thirties, and with salt and pepper hair. I caught his eye and he turned his head away. Then he was looking at me again.

'I think he likes you,' whispered Mara.

Then he came over. My face went red like a beetroot.

'Hello. I'm Malcolm. I'm on my own. Can I join you?'

He did. As the evening ended, we exchanged telephone

numbers and agreed to meet up. A month later we were lovers.

For thirteen years I had had no real sex life and I hungered to make up for lost time. But I had to keep it secret from Jock.

In the beginning I met Malcolm once a week. Then it was twice a week: Tuesdays and Fridays. Then it was on Saturdays as well. And when Jock returned home before me and I was not at home, he went berserk.

He would go out and get very drunk and then come round and turn the house upside down. He was jealous and would shout at Danny,

'Where is your mother?'

A shaken Danny would try to cover up for me.

'She's just gone out.'

'Just gone out? I've just come in.'

'Well now she's going out because the divorce has started.'

'Oh I know. Well I'll sort her out. Just wait till she comes home.'

One savage night it all caught up with me.

That Saturday night Malcolm had invited me out to celebrate the fact that he had won a prize because he had designed the interior lighting for a shopping mall. That man was a genius. He was the managing director of his own company. And we went to a lovely steakhouse in Sunbury. But the evening was slow.

Because of its popularity we could not be served immediately but had to go for a drink in the bar until a table came free. It was not until half past eleven that we finished eating. It put paid to my plan to be home by midnight before Jock got in.

After we had left the restaurant and I had got in his Jaguar, Malcolm turned round and said to me,

'I want to take you back to my flat.'

I snapped back, 'Look here. My husband still comes home and I'm very frightened. He's a violent person. Can't you be without sex till Tuesday? I'll see you on Tuesday because he comes home very late on Tuesday.'

Tuesday was the day the bastard always went out to take measurements and look at all the jobs on the building sites. On the back of all those new jobs, he would afterwards go the pub, get drunk and come home late. So I repeated,

'I'll see you on Tuesday. It's only three days away.'

Malcolm would have none of it,

'No you won't see me on Tuesday. I want to sleep with you tonight.'

'No I'm not going to sleep with you Malcolm. By the time I get home he's going to be waiting for me. And he'll beat me up. So you can drop me at the back of Ealing Common Station.'

Malcolm looked at me in frustration.

'I said 'No'. We are now in Sunbury. By the time I go to Northolt with you and sleep with you for an hour and you then get ready to take me back to Ealing, it'll be two o' clock in the morning. He's very violent.'

'No. No. Farida'

'Malcolm. You're very selfish.'

'No. No. No. You're coming to sleep with me. And that's it.'

I realised then that Malcolm cared more about his own pleasure than my safety. But I stood my ground. Eventually he said,

'Forget about it. Because you're crying I'll take you straight back to Ealing.'

He pushed the car into gear and roared away, swerving round other parked cars as he made his way towards Ealing. He was driving like mad. After several near misses I said,

'All right we will go to your place.'

Malcolm reduced his speed and rerouted towards Northolt. Back in his flat, Malcolm wasted no time in taking me to his bedroom. When he had finished, a relaxed Malcolm dropped me back at Ealing Common Station, where I picked up my own car and went home. Jock was already waiting for me in the sitting room. As I walked through the door I was greeted by the words,

'Look at the tart just walking in. Had a good time?'

Because Jock couldn't sleep with me he had become very aggressive.

'Where have you been?'

'I've been with Mara.'

'But you haven't got your lipstick on.'

I realised then that my lipstick had smudged off during my twenty minutes of lust with Malcolm. I thought quickly.

'Well. Yes. We went for a drink and something to eat. I smudged my lipstick as I was having my meal.'

'Meal? Who paid for it?'

'Mara.'

'You and your tart Mara? You liar. You haven't been to Mara. I can see it on your face. You've been out with a man.'

I was never a good liar.

'No I haven't.'

'Come in. I want to show you.'

With that, Jock snatched my handbag and emptied its contents onto the carpet. He began sorting through.

His eyes lit up when he came across a small business card with Malcolm's name on it. He held it aloft.

'Who's that?'

'Mara must have given it to me. I told her that I wanted an architect's job done. He's an architect.'

Jock came towards me.

'He's an architect? So you have met him? You fucking bitch'

I put my hands up as if to push him away.

'Look here. I'm getting a divorce. Don't you touch me.'

There was a rumble as Billy and Danny came running down the stairs. Billy looked at me accusingly,

'Mummy. You have caused trouble. You know he gets violent when you're out.'

And he was violent. Jock beat me up very badly that night. I was crying and Billy was crying.

'Mummy. You started the trouble by being late. No wonder he hit you.'

I said to him, 'Don't interfere!'

'You came home late. You shouldn't be going out. He's coming home early looking for you.'

'He's coming home early? At eleven o' clock or eleven thirty? And still being drunk?'

Next morning after Jock had gone to work, the phone rang. It was Malcolm.

'How are you?'

'I don't ever want to see you.'

There was silence at the other end of the phone and then.

'I'm so sorry Farida. I didn't realise it would be so bad. How can I make it up to you?'

I slammed the phone down. After a minute the phone rang again. I ignored it. After the ringing had stopped, I took the receiver off the hook. Afterwards Malcolm kept ringing me up and apologising. But I wanted nothing more to do with him. And that was the way I finished with Malcolm. Then in 1982 I met Chris.

I met him one evening when I was out with Mara and another friend Nina at the Overseas Club in the West End. Mara had been working at a pub in Holland Park and it was one of her pub customers who had invited her to that exclusive venue. She had said to me, 'Would you like to go to the Overseas

Club?'

So that evening I had parked my car at Notting Hill Gate and we arrived at the Club by taxi.

It was a dinner-dance and there was a five piece band playing on stage. Whilst they were playing, a handsome blond guitarist kept catching my eye. During the interval he came over to where we were sitting. He pointed to an empty seat and said,

'Can I sit here? Or is that somebody's seat?'

'It's nobody's seat.'

He sat down and joined us and started to talk to me.

He told me that he was polish but had been born in England. His father was polish and his mother English. And he said that he would like to see me. I told him that I was Zoroastrian and that my divorce was going through.

At thirty one, he was five years younger than me. He was tall and skinny and dressed up in a nice blue uniform with a tie and long hair. I said to myself,

'Oh God!'

'Mara said,

'Farida. You seem to meet nice young men.

Chris said,

'Can I meet you?'

'No really.'

'Please'

'Well I'll let you know. '

'Give me your number.'

'All right. I'll give you my number. But you need to be careful. Don't say anything when you ring up. If you ring up and I talk to you, then you could answer me. But if I say it's a wrong number, then you know that I've got my son or my husband in the house.'

'I understand.'

So one afternoon at about six o'clock, while Billy and Danny were watching TV, the phone rang. I picked it up.

'It's Chris. Hello Farida. How are you? Did you have a nice evening? Do you like shows?'

I said, 'Yeah!'

'I want to take you to a lovely show.'

'I don't know Chris. Because I don't think I can see you. Because I am still married.'

There was a pause.

'Then will you come to the Overseas Club.'

'Only to listen to the music.'

'Oh please. You're going to get a divorce.'

'But I don't know when. I don't really want anything at the moment.'

'Oh please. I must see you.'

'All right. Do you know Kensington High Street?'

'I'll find my way.'

Chris laughed.

'Of course I know Kensington High Street. Because I'm doing The Knowledge. Because my brother is a taxi driver. And if I don't become a policeman perhaps instead I'd like to become a taxi driver.'

So he said to me,

'I do the knowledge. I do the gigs. And I am also in the army, as you know. So I want to see you.'

'Then I'll see you outside the Old Town Hall in Kensington High Street. I'll park my car in Argyle Road where my father's old house was. And I'll meet you at eight o'clock tonight.'

I quickly fed the boys, dressed up and slipped out of the house. It felt just like the classic Japanese film Onibaba, where a young married woman frightened and deceived her mother in law by wearing a warrior mask as she stole out to meet her lover, whilst her husband was away fighting for his country. One day it rained and the mask stuck permanently to her face. It was with that same shabby feeling that I went to meet Chris outside the Old Town Hall.

There I saw him sitting in his old junk Triumph two-seater, looking at me through his little front mirror. He was waiving at me. Then he got out of his car and closed the door. He said,

'What shall we do? Shall we go to the show? Or shall I take you out for a meal?'

'Well I haven't eaten anything.'

'Then I'll take you to this nice Greek Italian restaurant.'

He was already holding my hand. I was wearing a nice dark dress and he was over the moon with me. He was absolutely in love with me. We enjoyed the meal and I was able to get home before my drunken husband came rolling in. So there was no trouble.

We arranged to meet again – and again. But it soon became apparent that he was trying to possess me. Sometimes I would see him waiting in his car outside my house. Then he would go to the nearest phone box and phone me up. It was driving me crazy.

After I had been seeing Chris for about two months I started a relationship with him. But I didn't want to be going out with him all the time. Sometimes the old bastard was in because he was not going out until later to meet his friends. Then Chris would ring and I would answer the phone saying,

'Hello. Yes. What?'

Chris would say,

'Please come out. I'm so desperate.'

And I would reply,

''Wrong number. What number do you want?' Before

slamming the receiver down.

Chris would wait hours and hours in his car outside my house and as soon as he saw me near the window he would flash his lights like a lunatic. He had bought himself a new Chrysler especially for me.

It was all because I'd said that I didn't like his junk Triumph. Before long I was seeing Chris every Friday.

I was going to Chris's house. His mother was coming home late. So whilst she was out, I was going to his house in Tottenham. We would go inside and Chris would lock the door and I would sleep with him in his bedroom. He was a terrific lover. Which I loved. And once I liked the sex, I didn't want to give it up.

So one day Shirin told me that some Americans were coming to look at her four bedroom town house in Clive Road, Bedfont, which they were looking to rent for a month. She said,

'Can you open the door for them and keep the spare key?'

I agreed. Then she told me that if I was feeling lonely, depressed and desperate I could use the house myself. She said

'Now you are already going through a divorce, having a relationship might make you feel better.'

She didn't know about my earlier affair with Malcolm.

So I would meet Chris in Chiswick: then park my car and go and sit in Chris's car. We then drove to my sister's letting house in Clive Road.

There we would show the Americans round to look at the house. And after they had gone, it was just me and Chris. We made use of every part of the house. I just loved it.

I went out with Chris for three years. But it finished when he wanted me to spend Christmas with him. I said, 'No'. I wanted to spend it with my family. I would only spend Boxing Day with him.

In the end his obsession with me made it impossible for me to continue with him. He seemed to be following me everywhere. My friends in the office soon began to notice. As one of them commented,

'He buzzes around you like a blue arsed fly. He's everywhere.'

On Saturdays he would go round to the Mara's house and say,

'Where is Farida?'

When I came to see him in the evening, Chris would say to me,

'Where have you been? You've been out all day.'

It was making him miserable. In the end I said to Chris,

'I don't think that it's working out between us.'

'Why not?'

I told him that I could not take the pressure. To which he replied,

'You used me.'

'We used each other Chris.'

But he had a point. Shirin had suggested that I used Chris to get information about my husband which I needed for my divorce. One day I'd said to him,

'Chris. If you really love me there's something I need you to do for me.'

'Anything Farida. Just tell me.'

'I need some information for my divorce. But I haven't got the money for a private detective. Can you follow my husband? Because I want to know where are his business contracts.'

So Chris agreed to follow all of Jock's movements. He would come at six o'clock in the morning and wait outside on his motorbike. And as soon as the old bastard left the house and took off in his car, Chris would follow him. Half an hour later the phone would ring,

'I lost him. He was too fast.'

Shirin said to him,

'Never mind. You can try again tomorrow.'

So Chris would again be waiting near my house at six o'clock in the morning. Again the morning after that. Until one day his mother said to him,

'Where are you going at five o'clock every morning?'

'To deliver somebody's parcel.'

He was able to tell his mother that because he was working a minicab whilst training to be a taxi driver. Later Chris would come back and wait on the opposite side of the road outside my house. I opened the curtain and he would waive at me. Eventually Chris's efforts bore fruit. He phoned Shirin up,

'This morning I followed him to Covent Garden. He's got a job on there.'

Then Chris followed Jock to Kentish Town, where he had another job. He would do anything for me. At the end he said that he wanted to marry me. But the truth was that I couldn't really marry him because his possessiveness was making my life a misery.

38 Put Out

After one particularly bad beating I went to back to Whittington's office with Shirin. I showed him the bruises on my arms.

'Good grief! Did the police come round?'

'Yes they did.'

On Whittington's advice I had started calling the police each time he beat me. And they always came round. But eventually a police officer told me,

'Even if you call us round, there's nothing really we can do unless you get us a power of arrest.'

So I went back to the solicitor. And we went to Brentford County Court and got a power of arrest.

I kept on copy in the house, hidden away in the filing cabinet. Another copy was kept at the police station filed under, 'Violent Husbands.' That way the police arrested Jock and got him out of the house. It was in June 1982. Danny was crying his eyes out.

Two police officers came round to the house and said to Jock, 'Come along'

He said, 'Could you wait a moment whilst I put my slippers on?'

'I'm sorry. Quickly go up to the bedroom and take what

you need.'

It happened late one evening after Jock had beaten me up because I had refused to make him a coffee. I'd said to him,

'You've got a habit of getting drunk. So you make the coffee yourself.'

So he punched me on my head. He punched me on my face. He kept hitting me. So I took a whole loaf of bread and flung it at him.

'Are you throwing bread at me? Nobody could beat me up.'

Bread. All I could do was to throw bread at him. I daren't throw a chair because he would have killed me. Because I was so much in fear.

'I'm going to hit you.'

'You keep hitting me anyway.'

Jock laughed as he threw the bread back at me. Then he broke the bread into pieces and stuffed them in my mouth, trying to choke me. That was why the police came. My lips were blue. As soon as I could break away I phoned Shirin. And she called the police from her home.

Shirin knew that I had to go immediately to the hospital. The police asked Shirin and me to come to the hospital because they wanted to take a statement.

So Jock was arrested and locked up in a cell. Shirin and I were there in the police station until thirty minutes past midnight. Afterwards Shirin dropped me back home..

What's going to happen about the mortgage?' I cried.

'You are lucky he didn't kill you.'

That same night, Shirin drove to Doctor Guerken and got me a prescription for some tranquilisers. Then she and George drove to the twenty four hour chemist at Piccadilly to get it dispensed. But getting Jock put out didn't make me feel any better.

It didn't help that I started receiving abusive phone calls. The phone would ring. I'd pick it up. And a man with a thick Scottish accent would say,

'Hey bitch. Are you getting well fucked?'

Sometimes the voice would be a woman's. But the message was the same. I always gave as good as I got.

'Who you calling bitch? You bastard. You get fucked. Or get yourself a blow up dolly.'

Eventually it got to me. I dreaded picking up the phone. In 1983 I had a nervous breakdown, which lasted a year.

After I recovered from my breakdown, Chris moved in to my house at Princes Avenue to pay my mortgage. But Billy hated him terribly.

I told Billy that Chris was a lodger. He was not fooled.

'Billy had tears in his eyes. Later he said to Chris,

'My Mum needs a psychiatrist – because she didn't get on with Dad.'

I said to Billy,

'Why did you say that?'

'Because I hate that bastard being with you. So if I say that you are mental, then he will leave you.'

39 It's Over

Six months after Jock was put out, I got my divorce absolute. It was not a day for celebration. I was just depressed when I opened up the brown envelope.

The previous September when I had gone to Brentford County Court, the judge had asked me if I had sex with my husband. I said, 'No.'

The judge then said, 'Did you ever have sex during the time after he was put out?'

'No.'

'I grant you the decree absolute. It will be coming by post.'

It was 7th December 1982 when the envelope arrived. I was crying and very upset. But I would have been even more upset if I had known that it would be another five years before the ancillary matters were resolved and I was able to move on with my life. From the date Jock was put out, Shirin had been paying the mortgage on our home.

Although our home had originally been bought out of Mama's money, it was Jock who had been paying the mortgage. And for that, the house needed to be on our joint names. He claimed half of its value. It was not until 1987 that a judge finally said,

'The house should go to the Petitioner. And the Respondent will be paid £5,000.'

So after seven years of taking me through the courts, Jock was only going to get a measly five thousand pounds. Served him right.

Before the final hearing my sister had offered him £12,000 to sign the house over. He refused, saying that his solicitor had advised him to reject it.

Even when the game was up, Jock still refused to sign the papers transferring his share over to me. Instead he disappeared off to Ireland and it was a judge who finally signed the papers on his behalf.

As we were outside in the foyer waiting for the case to come on, I noticed that Jock seemed especially close to his young lady barrister. It annoyed me that they behaved more like a couple of lovers than a lawyer with her client.

'Jock. Could you come over here a minute?' she cooed.

Jock ran over like a puppy dog. I interrupted.

'Why are you calling him Jock – and not Mr MacDonald? Are you his tart? Are you going to open your legs and let him fuck you? He can't fuck me. So how is he going to fuck you?'

Shirin rushed over and pulled me away. The young lady complained to my barrister, Harwood Stevenson: a distinguished gentleman who was known as The Silver Fox. Stevenson took me to one side,

'What was it you said to the respondent's barrister?'

'Nothing. I was just passing by to go to the Ladies.

The girls at the Institute of Advanced Motorist would laugh at the length of time it was taking to finish my divorce. The 'Case of the Century' was what they said. It was a moment of light relief. Now it was over and I could move on with my life.

40 Pictures

'When I marry I shall make my son's name Beheram. My sweetest brother Beheram. Many years may pass but I will never in my whole life forget you till I shall die. You were my darling brother and when I get married to an Englishman I shall keep your name.'

I was fourteen when I penned those words on the back of a 3' x 3' black and white photograph of my darling brother. In his grey suit and tie and with his immaculately brushed hair, Beheram looks older than his 18 years. It was taken at the end of the school year as he was about to graduate to a higher class. His ambition was to work as a radio operator on board ship.

With his handsome mature looks, it is small wonder that young ladies loved to ride side-saddle on the back of his motorbike as he circled round. That photograph is my only memento to Beheram. I keep it safe in a bedside cabinet. A larger framed print of the same photograph sits on the wall unit in my lounge. Sometimes I will put a tea light in front of it. The steadiness of the flame tells me that his soul is at rest.

Over the years other framed photographs have joined Beheram's. There is a large tinted portrait of Papa standing tall and proud, wearing his Freemason apron. He hated me marrying Jock.

There is Mama. Dara, Keki and Soli. All of them have passed on. Amongst them is a smiling photograph.

It is me, wearing my white silk wedding sari and cuddling up to Jock, my handsome new husband. But I'm sure I wouldn't have been smiling if I'd known the high price I would be paying for my freedom over the next nineteen years. It was a price which included being burned with cigarettes, getting broken ribs and the killing of my beloved dog Bootsie.

Each time a close family member dies, it is for me a tragedy. But Beheram's death was different.

It was not only because he was so young. It was not just that it was my first experience of death. It was not just because of the sudden and horrific way he died. It was the feeling that, with Beheram's death, my childhood had been snatched away. We were so close.

Sometimes I wonder how my life would have might have been different if it hadn't rained on the day Beheram went hunting with Douglas and Conchita.

Perhaps a cheerful Beheram would have been sitting with us as we ate our meal, instead of drifting lifeless in the waters off Hawkesbay. Suppose he had remembered the sadhu's warning and came straight home instead of going swimming? Suppose? Suppose? But perhaps it couldn't have been any different. As Mama had once said,

'When death comes, the whole world becomes blind.'

There is one part of Beheram which he will always share with me: his love of animals. A memory I will always carry with me is Beheram walking back to our holiday-home in the hills of Shimla.

Walking alongside him and holding his hands were two

monkeys which he had picked up along the way. On another occasion he brought back one of the many wild horses which roamed around Shimla. Somehow it didn't seem so wild when it was with Beheram

When the rest of my world was falling apart, it has always been my own love of animals which has sustained me. It is my escape. Though it is a mistake to call it a 'love'. It is more of an obsession.

In Pakistan I had my four geese. My Madajee as I called them. They were a male/female pair and their offspring. They followed me everywhere. Any stranger they would chase away. And it was with broken heart that I left them at Karachi Zoo before my long and lonely flight to London.

As a child I nearly starved myself to death after our khansama slaughtered my pet chickens to make a meal. I also wanted to be a vet when I grew up. But I have always had a phobia of anything flying towards me. I flinch away.

'If you want to be a vet, you'll first need to see a psychiatrist,' said Papa.

Who knows? A trip to a psychiatrist at that early age might have been beneficial to me in more ways than one. I'm sure that a strong dose of sanity would have helped me avoid much of the later stupidity which had reduced me from being the rich heiress to being penniless. As someone whom men had always found attractive, I could have married anyone.

Perhaps a lawyer or a doctor. Perhaps even my lovely Janusz. Perhaps I could now be living as Mrs Zybielski in a luxury apartment in Geneva. But I didn't. I could never see past the looks of a man.

But it was in the dark months after the destruction of my dog Bootsie that I found escape by becoming an RSPCA volunteer.

Since that time I have always had cats: often three or four at a time. Some are rescued cats which I have taken over. Others, such as my Taboo, are strays living nearby which have come to my door and which I have adopted. But it is not just cats.

It as if I can't pass an animal in the street without feeling in some way responsible for it, particularly if it appears to be wandering. And - yes - I know people say it's bad to feed foxes and pigeons. But somehow I can't help myself. And there are also squirrels and hedgehogs.

For others, a perfect holiday is about relaxing by the pool or sight-seeing. For me it is about trying to make a better life for the many stray cats and dogs I always encounter in Spain and Tenerife. It is why I don't go to holiday to Greece or back to India because I've heard about the large numbers of stray cats and dogs which are everywhere.

It began fifteen years ago when I came across an undernourished stray tabby munching its way through the dried remains of a sparrow on a street in Old Benidorm. There was nothing I could do for that cat, which quickly disappeared into the crowd. But it made me determined to find help for these poor animals.

During hotel meal times I began taking scraps off my plate and going out in the night to feed stray cats. It was during one evening walk along Avenida Mediterrano that I came across Olga, an elderly German ex-pat who was living in Benidorm and doing exactly the same as I was. It was through Olga and a young Spanish lady, Maria, that I met other Benidorm residents who were doing exactly the same thing. It made me realize that everywhere in the world – even in the most unlikely places – there are people as mad as I am.

When my dear brother Keki passed away in May 2003 I used £5,000 of my modest inheritance to set up the Benidorm

Cat Trust to help fund the neutering of its feral cat population.

Under the supervision of my friend Valerie Sinclaire, teams of young volunteer vets and trappers go to Spain and the Canary Islands to neuter and restore to health hundreds of feral cats and kittens.

Whilst I continue to breath. Whilst I can get up in the morning. Whilst I have money in my pocket. I will always do what I can to help the animals. I also kept my promise to Beheram in the naming of my first child Billy.

Oh! And there's something else.

At the top of my landing there is a large colour photograph. It is a picture of Meher Baba, the silent master. A garland of flowers hangs around his neck. As I climb the stairs, he smiles down at me.

Meher Baba was born a Zoroastrian like myself but during his life he came to embrace all religion. His message to the World is that Everything is One and that there is a little piece of God in all of us.

Printed in Great Britain
by Amazon

72582509R00160